BLOSSOM

A NOVEL

BLOSSOM

A NOVEL

#1 *NEW YORK TIMES* BESTSELLING AUTHOR

HELEN HARDT

Entangled Publishing, LLC
644 Shrewsbury Commons Ave., STE 181
Shrewsbury, PA 17361
rights@entangledpublishing.com

Amara is an imprint of Entangled Publishing, LLC.

Visit our website at www.entangledpublishing.com.

Edited by Lydia Sharp
Cover art and design by Elizabeth Turner Stokes
Stock art by Natalia van D and Smiltena/Shutterstock
Interior design by Britt Marczak

ISBN 978-1-64937-303-8
Ebook ISBN 978-1-64937-575-9

Manufactured in the United States of America

First Edition January 2024

10 9 8 7 6 5 4 3 2 1

AMARA
an imprint of Entangled Publishing LLC

To everyone searching for that one special someone.

At Entangled, we want our readers to be well-informed. If you would like to know if this book contains any elements that might be of concern for you, please check the back of the book for details.

PROLOGUE

Mary

He meets me outside the club, gives me a temporary collar for the evening, and then leads me to his reserved suite. After he closes the door, I shed my black trench coat and display my candy-apple-red panties…and nothing else. I wait a split second for his reaction to my nudity, but it doesn't come.

I walk to the bed in the corner and lie down on my side—my seductive pose that all the Doms seem to love. My hair tickles my shoulders.

"Hello, my dark prince," I say.

He doesn't reply.

He doesn't want to talk, and that's fine. I understand.

I'm here for him, to do what he wants. I'm a good sub.

But I'm not his sub.

I don't belong to anyone, and that's how I like it.

He will keep me safe while we share a scene together. Once we're outside the club, we'll go our separate ways. Perhaps we'll play again.

Perhaps we won't.

I watch him. I always watch my Dom, especially when it's

clear he doesn't want to talk. He gathers some leather rope, glides his fingers over it. This particular Dom likes leather rope, which is good. Leather is safer than silk or cotton. It can be untied more quickly in case any problems—which are rare— arise.

He removes his jacket. He's wearing only black jeans.

He's gorgeous, with tanned skin, muscled abs and arms, thick sandy-blond hair, and beautiful hazel eyes.

"Kneel before me," he says gruffly.

He doesn't ask for a kiss.

Good thing. I won't give him one. I don't kiss my Doms. It's not a hard limit for me, but it's something I prefer to avoid.

Kissing is too personal, and that's not why either of us is here.

We're here for a scene. To play together. To dominate and submit for each of our pleasures.

I amble off the bed—not too quickly—and drop to my knees before him, my head bowed.

"Thank you," he says, his voice low and husky. "Thank you for trusting me this evening. Thank you for agreeing to do a scene with me."

I nod, my gaze still on the floor. I won't look into his eyes until he commands me to do so. It's a sign of respect to my Dominant during a scene.

My flesh ignites. Submitting is empowering to me. I learned long ago that giving up my control in a sexual setting frees me, allows me to let go of my ego and put someone else's desires before my own. It also allows me to explore my own limits with Doms I trust to see to my needs and safety. Since becoming a member of Black Rose Underground, I've learned to trust— something I never learned growing up or in the one BDSM relationship I've had outside of the club.

I've played with this Dom several times in the past. He's powerful yet calming, and he's damned good at pleasing a woman. We have mutual respect for each other. He doesn't let emotion get involved. I try not to, but how can I not? I like some Doms better than others. I enjoy some scenes more than others.

This Dom, though... He's here for one thing. A scene. Sexual gratification.

"Rise," he says.

I obey and hold out my arms. He binds my wrists with the leather, and then he leads me to the pole in the center of the room and fastens my wrists to the top so I'm standing, arms elevated, tied to the pole.

He turns away from me then, and because I'm bound, I know better than to look over my shoulder to see what he's doing. No doubt he's choosing a toy for my flogging.

I love being spanked, flogged, and whipped. Something about the warmth of a riding crop coming down on my ass, sizzling through my body and arrowing straight between my legs... It never fails to get me going.

Snap—

I hold back a gasp. He's using a whip this time. Odd. This Dom has only used a whip one other time in a scene with me— the night I experienced one of the most intense orgasms ever.

So I'm down.

Snap. *Again.* Snap. *Again.*

The pain. The beautiful, tingling pain. It surges through me, around me, arousing me not just in my pussy but in my tingling nipples, my burning flesh.

Snap! Snap! Snap!

He's being harsher than usual tonight, but I can handle it. I crave the pain, for it morphs into pleasure as the release I desire surges through me like lightning. I close my eyes, succumb to the pain, the transcendence, the freedom—

    Until I gasp.

    My skin. It's broken. I'm bleeding, and—

    "Tesla!" *I shout.*

    My safe word. The car I love that I'll probably never be able to afford.

    The first time I've had to use it.

    But he doesn't stop.

    Snap! Snap! Snap! Snap!

    Tesla! Tesla! Tesla!

    But my lips don't move. My larynx makes no sound. I'm falling, falling, falling...

    Bleeding, bleeding, bleeding...

    Snap! Snap! Snap!

    And—

    I jerk upward in bed, my heart thundering against my chest.

    The nightmare is always the same. It begins with my last scene at the club—the scene where the Dom went too far. He drew blood, which is a hard limit for me.

    But he stopped after my safe word.

    Blossom, forgive me.

    The words pulse in my mind. He uttered them, and then he took care of me. Cleaned the wound, applied antiseptic, apologized again and again.

    I told him it was okay.

    And I thought it was.

    But then the nightmares began. The nightmares where he keeps going, where he ignores my safe word, and where my lips become glued shut.

    I'm helpless.

    He keeps whipping me and whipping me and whipping me, and just when I think I'm going to lose consciousness forever—

I wake up.

I've tried going back to the club several times since the incident, but I haven't been able to participate in a scene.

I feel so lost, as if part of me is gone forever.

I breathe in, hold it as long as I can, and then exhale. A few more times, and my heartbeat finally slows.

I take a drink of water from the cup at my bedside, and then I lie down.

But sleep doesn't come.

CHAPTER ONE

Mary

"Thank you," I say, handing the black bag to the customer. "Hope to see you again soon."

She smiles, turns, walks out the door. The fur-lined handcuffs in her small black bag could be anything. We don't put our logo on the bags, nothing that could help identify the contents, for the sake of the customer's privacy.

I head back out on the floor and approach a young woman looking at corsets.

"May I help you with anything?" I ask her.

She meets my gaze as her cheeks redden. "I'm just looking. Thank you, though."

"Absolutely. My name is Mary if you need anything."

"Sure. Thanks." She turns away from me.

I'm used to customers who are embarrassed to be here. We sell lingerie, bras, panties, bustiers, and corsets. We also sell eveningwear and clubwear.

And leatherwear.

And toys.

All types of BDSM paraphernalia.

We do a good business, and I've been the top salesperson every year since I began, assistant manager for a year now. Still, though, selling leather gear won't get me a Tesla anytime soon.

Brenda thinks I'm crazy for even wanting a car in New York City. She's probably right.

My phone buzzes, and I check the caller ID. Speak of the devil.

"Hey, Bren," I say into the phone.

Brenda Loring is my best friend and also a fellow submissive. She and I met back in college at Mellville University. We've been in the scene for a while…until Brenda did something that we both swore never to do.

She fell in love with her Dominant.

They're engaged now, and they go to Black Rose Underground together.

"Drinks tonight?" she asks.

"Sure. Nothing else to do on a Friday night, is there?"

"Dalton is out of town," Brenda says, "I was thinking…"

I take one more look at my customer to make sure she doesn't need me, and then I walk toward the back of the store and lower my voice. "I've tried, Brenda. It's not happening."

"You've got to get back in the saddle, Mary. Jack went a little too far on you, but it was only because he was fighting his own demons. He never meant—"

"I know that. I know how sorry he is. I see it for what it is, but I don't know that I'm ready."

"You'll never be ready if you don't get back in the game."

"Maybe I'm tired of the scene. Maybe I want to be a little… vanilla from now on." I gaze at the shelves of BDSM toys in the back—whips, floggers, bindings, cuffs. Trying to be vanilla while still working here would be difficult. Maybe it's time to move on.

"I suppose you could try that," Brenda says. "Have you gotten on Tinder or Lustr or any of those sites?"

"No."

"What are you waiting for?"

"I don't know that I'm waiting for anything, really. I just know that nothing seems to feel right these days. Not the club. Not a relationship. Nothing." I sigh. "Maybe I'm meant to be alone."

"Someone as hot as you was never meant to be alone, Mary."

"Maybe," I say again. "But I'm thinking about getting a different job."

Brenda's gasp hits my ear through the phone. "You're going to leave Treasure's Chest? They love you there. Plus you teach those classes for them."

"I'm not sure I should be teaching classes anymore, either," I say. "What if being a submissive just isn't...*me* anymore?"

"Drinks tonight," Brenda says again firmly. "Like I said, Dalton is out of town, so meet me at the bar."

"Which bar?"

She scoffs. "You damned well *know* which bar. You meet me there, Blossom, and be ready."

Brenda ends the call before I can object.

I suppose there's no better way to find out if my submissive days are truly behind me than to try once more. Brenda and I haven't gone to the club together since she and Dalton professed their love to each other a year ago. We used to have the most fun, going to the club together as single women, submissives looking for scenes. Meeting potential Dominants, sharing a drink, and then, if we felt comfortable, playing.

She and I never played together. We both like to be alone with our Dominant, and Black Rose Underground gives us a safe place to do that.

Another customer enters, and I head toward her.

It'll be nice to go to the club with Brenda again, like we used to, even if nothing happens. Until then, time to get to work.

"Welcome to Treasure's Chest." I flash a big smile. "May I help you with anything?"

• • •

"Hey, Al," Brenda says as she and I take a seat at the bar.

I gaze at the mirrored shelves behind the bar, the expensive liquor, the neon lighting. The bar is shiny dark wood. To the untrained eye, this is simply a Manhattan bar, but Alfred isn't just any bartender. He works for the underground leather club here in the building. Black Rose Underground is owned by blue-collar billionaire Braden Black, who also owns this residential building.

"Brenda, Mary," he says. "The usual?"

"You bet," Brenda says.

I give him a nod.

Alfred smiles as he fixes our drinks, shaking first my lemon drop, and then Brenda's cosmo. He's tall, blond, and gorgeous, and he and I have been crushing on each other forever, but even though he works for the club, I have no idea if he's actually in the lifestyle.

And I wonder...

Is it time to give him a chance?

No, not yet. I came here tonight at Brenda's request, and I won't let my best friend down. I'll go to the club with her, and I'll see how things go.

Maybe tonight is the night.

Maybe tonight is the night that I'll get over this hump and play in a scene with someone.

There are several Dominants I play with who frequent this club.

Two of them, including the one who accidentally broke my skin, are now hooked up with their own submissives in committed, monogamous relationships.

But there are still a few others I like and who like me.

Perhaps one of them will be at the club. Someone I feel safe with.

Of course, I felt safe with Jack, too, until...

But anyone can have a glitch, and to his credit, he stopped as soon as I said my safe word. He took great care of me afterward, too.

I take a sip of my lemon drop. The tartness of the lemon, the sweetness of the simple syrup, and the alcoholic bite of the vodka all tickle my tongue. A lemon drop is the perfect drink for me. Not too sweet, not too tart, not too alcoholic. I like to taste the alcohol in a drink, but I don't like to taste only alcohol. One of the Doms I used to play with before he got serious with his permanent submissive always drinks martinis. Martinis taste like ammonia to me.

I take another sip and look around. A trained eye can tell who's here for a drink and who's here for something more. Those here for something more are usually wearing coats to cover their garments—or lack thereof—underneath.

I'm wearing my black trench coat because it covers my clubwear—and I have a lot of clubwear thanks to my fifty-percent employee discount at the store.

In the past, on nights when I was feeling especially frisky, I'd be wearing nothing at all under the trench coat.

Tonight, though, I'm wearing a little black dress—a basic that can be worn at any club, not just a leather club. I want to feel safe tonight, which means I need to be fully dressed under my coat.

Brenda's trench coat is dark red, like the rich hue of merlot, with undertones of warm mahogany.

Red is Brenda's color. She has dark brown hair and eyes, so it's perfect on her. With my auburn hair, I rarely wear red, except for undergarments.

I have no idea what Brenda's wearing underneath. It can't be anything too risqué, though, because she's not going to play tonight. She's coming to the club for me, to help me feel comfortable. Help me get back up on the horse.

No pun intended.

She takes a sip of her cosmo. "See anyone you like around here?"

I scan the patrons in the bar. "Not everyone who comes here is a member of the club," I remind her.

"I know that. You can probably pick out the ones who are."

"That's not the route I want to go tonight," I say, "if I go that route at all. It's going to have to be someone I've played with before."

"Okay. I get that." Brenda picks up her stemmed glass and swirls her pink cosmo. "But you know the Phantom is taken now."

I nod. "Yeah, I know. By the sister of Jack's fiancée, no less."

Brenda shakes her head. "Crazy, huh? The Thomas sisters take two of the best Doms."

"Let's not forget you took one out yourself."

She smiles and looks down at the two-carat sparkler on her left ring finger. "What can I say? I guess a relationship was in the cards for me after all. It could be for you, as well."

I take a sip of my lemon drop. "I don't think so, Bren. I'm not sure anything is in the cards for me at this point. Maybe I'll just be celibate the rest of my life."

Brenda nearly spits out her drink. She takes a hard swallow. "Come on now, Mary. You are sex on a stick. Even I was turned on the first time I saw you at that corridor meeting freshman year."

I can't help a chuckle. I did my share of experimenting in college—with men *and* women—which is how I found out I'm a natural submissive. But Brenda? She never strayed from men. The woman is as straight as an arrow.

"You're full of it," I tell her.

"Hey, I can still appreciate beauty." She winks. "I'm just thankful I got to Dalton before you could get your hooks in him."

"He's not my type," I say with a shrug.

That's a lie, of course. Dalton is tall, with dark brown skin and abs that won't quit. He was a new member of the club when he and Brenda met and he asked her to play a scene with him.

Neither one of them has played with anyone else since.

"Bullshit," she says. "He's totally your type."

"Okay, you got me." I put my glass down and spin on my bar stool so I'm facing Brenda. "What if Dalton and I *had* played together? Would that have messed up our friendship?"

"Besties forever." She takes another sip.

I finish my lemon drop.

"You want another?" Alfred asks.

When I look up at him, his eyes are sparkling.

If I'm going to the club, I want to keep my wits about me. They serve alcohol down there, but the bartenders are very careful. Anyone who appears to be the least bit inebriated isn't allowed to go back into any of the playrooms.

"No, but thank you." I give Alfred a smile.

He returns my smile with a nod and then moves down the bar to help another customer.

Brenda finishes her cosmopolitan, sets the glass down, and then turns to me. "You ready?"

I sigh. "Not even slightly."

She hops off her barstool, grabs my hand, and pulls me off mine. "Look. You don't have to do anything. Let's just go down there. You know I'm not going to play tonight. We can sit at the bar the whole time if you want. Or at a table. Or we can dance. Just have fun. Girls' night."

I roll my eyes. "Right. Girls' night. At a leather club."

"Why not?"

"I've tried going down there before, Brenda. It just hasn't worked."

"Mary, you paid all that money for a membership."

"It's not that much. You know that. Single women's memberships are pretty cheap."

"Still, you want to get your money's worth, don't you?"

I breathe in. "What if I told you I'm thinking about not renewing?"

Brenda drops her mouth open but quickly closes it. "Well... that's up to you, Mare. But while you're still a member, take advantage of it. We won't do anything you're uncomfortable with. We'll have another drink. Do some dancing. Maybe chat a little. Nothing serious. And we'll leave as soon as you want to leave." She grins wide.

I eye my empty glass that Alfred hasn't picked up yet, tempted to order another. Not because I really want one. Because I'm stalling.

She's right, though. I can go to the club and do whatever I want. This doesn't have to be anything I don't want it to be. And the minute I'm ready to leave, I will. I should at least try...

I draw in another breath. "All right, Brenda. Let's go."

The two of us check in with Alfred and then take the stairs behind the bar down to the club.

Claude, head of security and the bouncer, doesn't hide

his surprise—or his delight—to see me again. I can count on one hand the number of times I've seen him smile, including tonight. He's usually stoic, almost cold, but looking at him now gives me a warm jolt of something familiar. Maybe this wasn't such a bad idea after all. So far, so good.

He steps aside to let us in after we surrender our cell phones. Photography isn't allowed at Black Rose Underground.

It's early yet, so the club isn't hopping too much. Things don't get exciting until around ten. The dance floor is nearly empty. Only a few move to the light jazz music, the soft red lights casting a sultry glow over their bodies.

Brenda and I find a table and take a seat.

Jennifer, one of the topless waitresses, walks to our table. "Hi, Blossom. Lotus," she addresses Brenda. "Where's Dalton tonight?"

"He's out of town," Brenda says.

Jennifer nods. "What would you ladies like to drink?"

"I'll have my usual, a cosmo."

"I think just water to start," I say.

"Good enough. I'll be right back." Jennifer turns, her boobs wiggling.

I sigh and look down at my fingernails. I'm in desperate need of a manicure.

"Who the hell is that?" Brenda says, snagging my attention. She widens her eyes, watching someone at the entrance.

I turn to follow Brenda's gaze.

And I literally have to clamp down my jaw to keep it from dropping.

CHAPTER TWO

Mary

The most magnificent man I've ever seen just walked into the club.

He's a newcomer. He's never been here before, at least not when I've been here. Granted, I haven't been here much lately.

He has a mane of hair redder than mine, and he's wearing a kilt. A fucking *kilt*.

It's plaid.

Green-and-blue plaid.

A tartan.

Complete with the buckles, clasps, and a freaking sporran—the traditional Scottish pouch worn as part of traditional Highland dress. His is black leather with some type of white fur trim, and it hangs from a chain around his waist, just below the belt line—and right in front of the goods. The look is completed with knee socks and black shoes.

But from the waist above?

He wears nothing.

And my God, he's a sight to behold.

He's tall, first of all. Way over six feet. Probably around six five.

Broad shoulders, fair skin, and just a smattering of auburn hair over his chest.

His pecs... And my God, those abs. That's not a six-pack.

It's a fucking eight-pack.

His nipples are large and coppery.

His arms, muscular and corded.

And even from here, the bright blue of his eyes is visible in the dim light.

"Have you seen him here before?" Brenda asks.

I can't put my lips together to form words, so I simply shake my head.

"Damn." Brenda scratches her chin. "If I weren't so in love with Dalton..."

I continue to stare.

"You going to say something this century?" she asks.

I blink. "Sorry."

"Don't be. He's hard not to look at."

"To answer you, no, I've never seen him in here before."

Brenda giggles. "You already answered that question."

"Did I?"

Jennifer returns with our drinks, sets them down, and leaves.

Brenda takes a sip of her cosmo. "You shook your head," she says. "I figured that meant you had never seen him."

"Yeah, yeah. Right."

Brenda laughs again.

My mind has gone to mush.

And then it goes from mush to completely liquefied when the Highlander himself walks right past us—turning to make eye contact with me—and collides with Jennifer, who is bringing drinks to another table.

Jennifer drops the tray and then slips on the slick wooden floor and ends up on her ass, her face right at the front of the hottie's kilt. He reaches down to help her up, but I can't hear what he's saying. Probably apologizing.

But she doesn't take his hand. Instead, she cocks her neck back and—

Oh my God... She's peeking under his kilt.

I should look away. But I can't. Jen's eyes are wide as dinner plates, and she licks her lips.

My heart thumps.

Brenda's eyes are also glued to the scene. Jennifer finally takes the man's hand, and another staff member hurries over to wipe the drinks off the floor. The kilted man leads Jennifer— who's smiling at him longingly, which for some reason I don't like; I mean, I really *hate* it—back to the bar and takes a seat.

And again, my heart thumps, faster this time.

He looked at me.

At *me*.

And because he was looking at me, he ran smack into Jen, who now is looking at *him*. And she saw what's underneath that kilt, and whatever she saw had to be impressive.

I feel his presence in every part of my body, especially between my legs. My nipples harden against the stretchy fabric of my dress. It's suddenly too hot, and I grab my glass of water.

"You should go over there," Brenda says. "Talk to him."

I nearly spit out the sip of water I just took. "Are you out of your fucking mind?"

"Hell, no. He's obviously new here. He didn't stop to talk to anyone—other than Jen when he rammed right into her."

Because he was looking at *me*. Those sparkling blue eyes met my own.

"You're clearly interested," Brenda continues. "Just talk to him. You don't have to *do* anything. Besides, you look hot tonight, Mary."

I glance down at myself. "This is just a basic black dress from the shop."

"Yeah, and it looks amazing on you. Sometimes less is more." She flicks her gaze to the man sitting at the bar. "Go talk to him."

"Yeah. Okay. Just let me finish my drink first." I take the tiniest sip of water and then set the glass back down. "Very refreshing. I want to savor it."

Brenda rolls her eyes. "Fine. If you're not going to talk to him, *I* will."

I point to the diamond on her left hand. "That rock may be a little bit of a turnoff, *Lotus*."

She shrugs. "Why would it be? For all he knows, Dalton and I have an open relationship."

"But you don't."

"We might," she counters. "All I have to do is get my phone from Claude, text Dalton, and describe this dude. He'll probably give me a free pass."

A spear of jealousy lances through my gut.

I don't know why. I don't know this man from Adam. But damn...there's something about him. He's giving off an energy that has my whole body taking notice.

I have a mix of Irish and Scottish ancestry myself. Hence my reddish hair. But what I'd give for those baby-blue eyes. I've always thought my brown eyes were plain and kind of dull.

What would it feel like to have those searing blue eyes staring down at me? Smoldering...

Brenda grabs her cosmo by the stem and advances toward the bar with purposeful strides.

Damn it. This was supposed to be a girls' night for us.

My legs act on their own. They push me to rise, and they follow her.

Then midway to the bar, they turn back, head to our table, and sink me back down onto my seat. *Chicken shit.*

Brenda sits next to the Scottish God and begins her Lotus flirting.

My stomach sinks.

Brenda is a master at flirtation. She always has been. We always said we never wanted to settle down. We would just enjoy being submissive for the evening and then live our own lives. I honestly thought if one of us went back on those words and settled down, it would be me, not her.

But she and Dalton are so beautiful and perfect for each other.

They fit together like Yin and Yang.

Either she's making a move just to get *me* to make a move... or she really is interested and she knows Dalton will be okay with it.

She's so good at what she does, I honestly can't tell the difference.

I gulp down the rest of my water, and then I wave to Jennifer.

"What can I get for you, Blossom?" she says as she approaches.

"Nothing. Are *you* okay?" I ask.

"Oh, yeah. I'm fine. I mean, I might have a bruise on my bottom, but who cares? Getting knocked over by *him* was worth it."

Black Rose has a strict "no fraternizing with the members" policy, but from the sound of Jen's voice, I'm pretty sure she'd willingly get herself axed for another look under that kilt.

The green-eyed monster roars through me—but why? He's

gorgeous, no doubt, but he could be a complete asshole for all I know. Except he's not. Not the way he looked absolutely horrified when he ran into Jennifer and then helped her up and escorted her back to the bar.

"Did you need anything else, Blossom?" Jen asks.

"Yes…I'm going to have a lemon drop, I think."

"You got it." She starts to move, but I stop her.

"And Jen?"

"Yeah?"

"Just one more thing. Who *is* he?"

CHAPTER THREE

Ronan

"You're a pretty thing," I say to the brunette who just sat down next to me at the bar.

She's wearing a red halter top and a denim miniskirt.

And she *is* pretty. Long dark hair, warm brown eyes, full thick lashes.

But she isn't the one I noticed when I walked by her table a few minutes ago.

I noticed her auburn-haired friend.

Her friend wearing a simple black dress, nothing special.

It was something about her eyes, though…a lighter brown, like well-aged, single-malt scotch.

"Thank you." She smiles. "My name is Lotus."

"That's a beautiful name."

"It's my submissive name. The name I'm known as here."

"Ronan," I say, holding out my hand.

She takes it, returns my handshake. "So are we just going to not acknowledge your little faux pas when you passed my table?"

I chuckle. "First time that's ever happened to me." And it

happened because I glanced at her gorgeous friend and then couldn't look away. "I'm just glad the server is all right."

"Jen's tougher than she looks," Lotus says. "I haven't seen you here before."

"It's my first time. I just moved here from Glasgow."

She tilts her head slightly. "You do have a little bit of a brogue, but it's light."

I get that all the time, especially when I'm in my plaid. But I have no brogue. Not even slightly. "I lived most of my childhood here in the States. My mother's American."

"I see."

"Who's your friend?" I glance over at the beautiful redhead again—the reason for my faux pas, as Lotus so eloquently put it—who's staring at her hands. She has "submissive" written all over her, and that only intrigues me more.

"That's Blossom. She and I are besties."

I steal another glance at the young woman who is nervously sipping from a glass of what looks to be water. Curiosity spikes in me. Why is she agitated? More importantly, why is she alone? "Tell me about her."

"You mean you don't want to know about me?" she asks coyly.

"You're gorgeous, and I like talking to you, but I don't touch what's not mine." I nod toward the giant "no trespassing" sign sparkling on her left hand. "Plus, you're clearly collared."

She grins. "My fiancé and I have an open relationship."

"I'd have to hear that from his lips, not yours. No offense. I learned that lesson the hard way."

"Fair enough," she says, keeping her grin in place.

Besides, even as pretty as she is, she's not really my type. I have a thing for redheads.

But it's not just the hair that drew me to her friend.

It's her eyes…and something else I can't put my finger on.

My gut is telling me to pay attention, and I never ignore my gut.

"Are you a Dom?" Lotus asks.

"Guilty."

"Blossom is a submissive."

I nod. I already knew that. A good Dom can tell a submissive from one look.

It's not the fact that she's focusing on her hands, and it's not the fact that she's acting oddly timid. Submissives aren't shy or hesitant. They're obedient. They can be bold as fuck when given a command, making sure to carry it out exactly as they've been told because that's what pleases them *and* their Dom.

I can tell she's a submissive simply by the way she's sitting. Legs crossed, shoulders back.

She waits to be approached.

But the rest of her body language means something else. The way she keeps fiddling with her hands…

Something is bothering her.

And I can't just sit here and watch it from a distance anymore.

I finish my glass of water and stand. "It was nice to meet you, Lotus."

"The pleasure was all mine," she says.

Then I walk toward the table where her friend sits. I stand above her. "Good evening."

She looks up at me with those whisky-colored eyes. "Good evening." She clears her throat. "Are you…okay?"

"Only slightly embarrassed," I say. "But I've been through worse. I'm Ronan O'Connor."

"Blossom."

"May I sit down?"

She nods slowly. "Sure."

More details of her strike me now that I'm up close. The way the fabric of her black dress complements every curve, making everything about her appear soft and touchable. The way her hair catches the light and shines in several different shades of terracotta. And that mouth—those glossy lips on that pert little mouth.

"I met your friend," I say once I'm seated. "Lotus."

"She's engaged."

Why would that be her first response? I can guess. Blossom doesn't want me near her friend. *Good*.

"I know, I saw her ring. But I'm more interested in *your* relationship status." I move toward her left hand, and at her nod, I take it. It's cold. Is she still nervous? "I don't see a ring."

"That's because I'm not wearing one." She lets out an uneasy chuckle. "Not on my left hand anyway. This ruby on my right hand is my birthstone. A gift from my father."

I sense there's a story there, but I don't know her well enough to pry, even though, for some reason, I want to. My curiosity is roaring.

"Are you involved with anyone?"

She pauses a moment. Then, "No."

I can't help it. I let a slow smile spread across my face. I don't usually allow my feelings to be known to a submissive. I don't usually even *have* feelings for a submissive, other than fondness and genuine regard for her wellbeing and pleasure. Blossom is different.

I'm not sure why, but I want to find out.

"I'm not involved with anyone, either," I tell her.

She stares at me as if she can see inside my brain. "I don't recall asking."

"No, you didn't." I lean closer to her, still holding her left hand. It doesn't feel quite so cold anymore. "But I'm not the kind of man who waits to be asked, and I think you know that."

Her cheeks blush, and in the dim lighting of the club, she looks even more beautiful.

"This is my first night here," I offer. "I only moved to New York a couple of months ago, and I researched all of the underground leather clubs in the city before choosing this one."

"Oh? What attracted you to Black Rose?"

"I know the owner. He and I have done business together."

"I see."

"But that's not the reason I chose this club. That's just how I heard about it. I chose it for its privacy. Its security. They take a lot of safety measures here, make sure everyone who comes in here feels at ease. It feels similar to the club I attended in Glasgow."

"So you're truly Scottish?"

I glance down at my tartan. "Guilty, I'm afraid."

Her eyes spark with interest. "How come you don't sound like Jamie Fraser, then?"

"Jamie who?"

Her gaze falls on my chest...and then lower. "From the Outlander series."

"Never read it. Or watched it."

Her cheeks redden further. "I suppose you're not one for romance. But anyway, I meant you don't sound Scottish."

Right. "I grew up here in the States. My mother's American. I did all my schooling here."

"I grew up here, too," she says. "On Long Island, I mean."

"But you live *here* now?"

"In the city? Yeah. I've been here for years. I love it."

Interesting.

"You know, in most other circumstances, I'd ask if you're

willing to participate in a mild scene with me. See if we click."

She opens her mouth, but I gesture for her to stay quiet.

"I'm not going to do that tonight, Blossom. I want to get to know you *outside* of the club."

"You do?"

"Yes."

If I ask her to do a scene with me tonight, she would refuse. Not because she's not attracted to me. I feel the chemistry between us—it's hot, thick, and palpable. I see how she's been checking me out.

Something is bothering her, though. She's a seasoned submissive. Of that I'm sure. But she's clearly not looking for a scene tonight.

Neither am I.

I was before. That's what I came here for. But now that I've met Blossom, I'm not.

A scene takes my mind elsewhere—to that place where I wield instruments to bring pleasure to myself and my partner.

But...

The timing isn't right.

Not for me.

And not for Blossom.

I *will* be a Dominant again. It's how I'm wired, and I won't give that up.

I was forced to end things with my submissive recently, and when this business opportunity to merge one of my enterprises with one of Braden Black's landed in my lap, I jumped at the chance to leave Glasgow. To come back to America, which I also consider my home.

I needed a break.

New scenery.

And the scenery I'm looking at now? The beauty of Blossom

before me?

Perhaps I've found what I'm looking for.

She has a past I know nothing about, just as I have one *she* knows nothing about.

I've been in this lifestyle long enough to know how to read a situation. I'm attracted to her. She's attracted to me.

But neither of us is ready for a scene right now. And neither of us wants to part ways, not yet.

We'll just have to see where else the night takes us.

CHAPTER FOUR

Mary

"Would you like to get out of here?" Ronan asks me. Is he serious?

I gape at him. And not just because he's the most gorgeous hunk of male flesh I've ever seen.

But because he's asking me to leave the club. I know nothing about him other than how my body is reacting, which both frightens and arouses me. After months of not wanting to play, not wanting to even be here at the club...now I'm actually considering leaving this safe space with a complete stranger.

"What does that face mean?" he asks.

I blink. "What face?"

His mouth morphs slowly into what I thought might turn out to be a smile but is more of a simper. "Your eyes are round as saucers, and your mouth is dropped open."

"It's just... No one has asked me that before." I glance around the club—at the few couples dancing, the few talking at tables, Brenda still at the bar. "I mean, not *here*, anyway."

"Why?"

"Well. Usually someone asks me if I want to play. Then

maybe we do and maybe we don't, but no one's ever asked me to leave the club with him."

"So I suppose you're wondering why I'm asking."

I let out a nervous laugh. "Yes, the question has crossed my mind."

"Because you don't want to play tonight." His tone is direct, and his assumption is spot-on.

I gape at him once more.

His blue eyes smolder. "There you go again."

"I... I mean, I came here to... How did you know?" I glance again at Brenda at the bar. "Did Lotus tell you?"

"No. All she told me was that you were her friend—her best friend—and that you're a submissive."

My cheeks and the top of my chest warm. "All of that is accurate."

"You're not acting like you're looking for a scene, Blossom. In fact, you're acting like you'd rather be anywhere but here."

"That's not..." I blow out a breath. "Okay, you're right." We just met, and he's already reading me like a book. No sense in denying it. "I'm not interested in playing with anyone tonight, and that's not anything against you personally. I mean... You're..."

Fuck, it's hot in here. I reach for my water glass but realize it's empty.

"If you don't want to be here," Ronan says, "why did you come?"

Myriad phrases barrel into my mind.

Because Lotus asked me to.

Because I need to get back in the game.

Because I can't let one bad scene rule my life.

But I don't utter any of it. I smile, and different words emerge before I have a chance to think about them. "To meet you?"

He narrows his gaze, and his blue eyes burn. My God, if he doesn't look away soon, I may erupt into flames just from his stare.

"I think maybe *I* came to meet *you*," he says.

"That's not true." I let out a nervous laugh that sounds more like a croak. "I saw you saunter in here. You came for a scene."

"Originally, yes. You're right. But then I saw you." He rakes his gaze over me, and if I didn't know better, I'd think he burned my dress right off me. "And because I saw you and couldn't look away, I ended up making a complete fool of myself." He chuckles. "Do I want to play with you? Absolutely. But not tonight."

"So you're not ruling it out," I say.

"Oh, no, Blossom. I'm not ruling out playing with you. The two of us *will* do a scene together. I will bind you, spank that sweet ass, sink my cock deep into you, all while you're begging me for more."

My legs are crossed, but even so, I squirm. His words...in that deep voice...the images and sensations he's conjuring in my mind... I'm not ready to play, but...

"You like that idea," he says.

He's not asking me. He's making a statement—a statement based on his observation of me.

As Dominants and submissives, we know body language, even something as small as the change in another's eyes or the subtle movement of muscles tightening. And he sure as hell can read mine right now.

A good Dominant has to be able to read me in case my mouth is bound and I can't speak for myself.

Clearly he's a good Dominant, so there's no reason to deny what is completely obvious. My nipples are pressing against the stretchy fabric of my dress, my cheeks are on fire, and the party going on between my legs is in high gear.

"Yes," I say simply.

"But not tonight," he says.

I nod. "Not tonight."

"I understand, and let me state up front that you'll be perfectly safe with me if you choose to leave with me. So, I'll ask again, would you like to get out of here?"

Black Rose has a top-notch vetting process. The club wouldn't have accepted Ronan as a member if he had even the smallest blemish on his record or reputation. I don't doubt I'd be safe with him. I'm more concerned, because of my intense attraction to him, that I'll end up doing something I'm not ready for.

I swallow. "And do what?"

"Have a drink. Or"—he glances at my empty water glass—"a soda or coffee. A light meal. Anything. Whatever you'd like."

The urge to leave with him is so great I have to wonder if he's got some kind of hypnotic pull over me. But that's ridiculous, of course.

What's something we could do that's safe? And public?

"You said you've been in New York only a couple of months?"

He nods.

"Have you had a slice of genuine New York pizza yet?"

He pauses a moment, and then it seems he's going to smile, but he doesn't. He hasn't smiled yet. Not truly.

"I'm afraid not," he says. "Pizza's not really my thing."

I rise. "It will be after I show you the best slice in the city. Let me just tell my friend I'm leaving."

He stands as well. "All right."

I walk over to the bar, where Brenda is still sitting.

"I knew you'd get back on that horse," she says, grinning.

"My God, and with *him*." She twirls the ring on her left hand. "If I weren't taken…"

"You still wouldn't because you're in love with Dalton," I say with a laugh.

She smiles. "True that. Is he going to take you into a room?"

"Actually, no, we're getting out of here. Are you okay staying by yourself?"

Brenda jerks, eyes wide, and nearly slides off her stool. "Say *what*?"

"I know. It's not like me, but I feel okay about this. About him."

"You're sure?"

I smile. "Yes. But are you good if I go?"

She nods. "Yeah, of course. I love it here. I can have Alfred get me a cab later."

That wasn't convincing. "I won't leave you if—"

She waves off my concerns. "Mary, go. If you're not ready, you're not ready. But what do you know about this guy?"

"Enough to feel okay about this," I say. "We're just going to go for a slice or something. I won't go anywhere private with him."

"Okay." Brenda gestures to her cosmo that's still half full. "I won't be long. I'm almost done. If you need anything, text me. If I don't answer right away, it means I'm still here, so call Claude."

"I will. Thanks, Bren."

I'm really doing this. My stomach flutters—actually fucking flutters.

I haven't been this attracted to a man in a long time. I'm not sure if that's good or bad. I'm physically attracted to all the Doms I play with, of course. I have to be for the scene to be enjoyable. But Ronan… I've never seen anyone as gorgeous as he is. I've never hung on a man's every word like I do with him.

I walk back to where he's standing beside the table, waiting for me, his chest on display for everyone to ogle.

And boy, are they ogling.

Jennifer stands next to him, laughing flirtatiously and wiggling her bare tits.

"Oh," she says when I return. "Hi, Blossom. Ronan here was apologizing to me again. I've been telling him not to worry."

"I'm glad you're okay," Ronan says, stepping away from her and toward me.

"Looks like we're leaving, Jen," I say. "Brenda's still at the bar. She's staying."

Jennifer moves her gaze to Ronan. "You're leaving?"

"Don't worry, lassie," he says, this time in a practiced brogue. "We'll be returnin' as soon as the sun sets."

I open my mouth to tell him that the sun has already set, but then I close it.

He's clearly giving Jen some bizarre Scottish flirting. Or something.

Jennifer gives him a dazzling smile, her cheeks red, her breasts blushing, her nipples sticking out hard.

My own nipples are just as hard, and they're protruding against the stretchy velvet of my little black dress.

But Ronan's gaze isn't on Jennifer's bare breasts.

His gaze is on my face. Not my hard nipples, not my long bare legs.

On my face.

And God...that makes me want him all the more.

"Blossom," he says, his tone warm but firm, "let's go get that pizza."

We walk to the exit, and I retrieve my black trench coat and my phone. Ronan grabs a hunter-green shirt and pulls it over his head. It looks like it's made of cotton or linen, and its V-neck is closed with a leather tie. It has a billowy design and long sleeves that gather at the wrists. He doesn't tuck it into his kilt, letting it hang loose. It looks sexy but comfortable.

"Do you have some pants to change into?" I ask.

"No."

"I mean... You really want to go in your kilt?"

This is New York City. People dress all kinds of odd ways. But still, it isn't every day you see a big, brawny man in a kilt and knee socks walking about at night.

"Why not?" he says. "I like my kilt. This is the O'Connor tartan, and I also have two utility kilts in black and khaki. I wear them often."

My mind hurtles back to Jennifer's gaze of awe as she looked up Ronan's kilt. "What exactly *do* you wear underneath your kilt?" I ask.

This time he grins. Not a huge grin, but it's a grin. "Lipstick, if I'm lucky."

Oh God...

He really is naked under there.

I have no idea how to respond to that, so I move my focus up his body. "That's an interesting shirt."

"It's called a Jacobite shirt." He pauses, eyeing me. "Don't tell me you're embarrassed to be seen with me like this."

"Are you kidding? No. Of course not. But people are going to stare at you on the street. Gawk even. And not just because you're dressed strangely. Because you're so..." I sigh.

"I'm what, Blossom? Say it."

I can't *not* say it now. "Because you're so fucking hot."

He burns an ice-blue stare into me.

"If that bothered me, I wouldn't dress like this. Besides, *mo leannan*"—he piles on the brogue again—"no one's going to be looking at *me* if you're by my side."

My cheeks warm, my legs threatening to turn to jelly. "What did you call me?"

"Mo leannan. It means"—he leans toward me, his mouth close to my ear—"my *lover*."

This time my legs do give out, but Ronan steadies me, and in a moment, our bodies are touching. He's so warm, and even with his shirt on, I can feel the cords of his muscles through all of our layers of clothes.

"Mo leannan," he whispers into my ear. "How about we have that pizza now?"

I breathe in and let it out slowly, gathering my bearings. Then I move back a few steps. "Absolutely." I lead him toward the stairwell, which takes us up behind the bar in the building.

"Leaving so soon?" Alfred asks as we come to the bar.

"Ronan here wants a slice of mouthwatering New York pizza."

"Gianni's?" Alfred suggests.

"You got it."

"What's Gianni's?" Ronan asks.

"Only the best New York–style pizza in the city. It's not far from here, only a few blocks."

"Sounds perfect," Ronan says. "See you, Alfred."

"Ro," Alfred says, smiling.

"Ro?" I ask as we leave the bar.

"Not my favorite, but Alfred's a good guy."

"What *do* you like to be called?" I ask.

"Ronan, mostly. But for you? I'll settle for...*sir*."

God...

There go my legs again.

I'm not sure I'll make it to Gianni's if he keeps this up.

Gianni's is a few blocks away, and it's after ten o'clock. The night is warm, though. I don't really need my trench coat, but I certainly won't be taking it off to walk down the streets of New York in my little black dress.

As I expected, Ronan gets a lot of stares as we walk by. He takes my hand and places it in the crook of his arm. Very gentlemanly.

And it feels good—my hand touching the soft fabric of his Jacobite, feeling the corded knots of his beautifully muscular arms underneath.

"Should we hail a cab?" he asks.

"If you'd rather. Or we can walk the few blocks."

"Walking sounds perfect. It's a gorgeous night."

I look upward. Because of the bright lights of the big city, you can't usually see too many stars at night, but it's clearer than usual tonight. I see the North Star, and I can make out the Big Dipper.

"Tell me everything about yourself, Blossom," Ronan says.

With his command, I want to spill my guts. But I say only, "My real name is Mariah. Mary for short."

"Mary?" He looks down at me, his eyes smoldering once more. "You don't look much like a Mary."

I stifle a giggle. "You're not the first person to say that, but I've been called Mary ever since I was a kid. No one calls me Mariah. And at the club, everyone calls me Blossom."

"How did you come up with Blossom?"

"One of my first Doms at Black Rose gave me the name. He said I blossomed under his touch. From then on he called me Blossom, and it stuck."

"And did you?"

"Did I what?"

"Did you *blossom* under his touch?"

I hedge a bit. "We had fun together. He's no longer a member of the club. This was when I first started going, years ago."

"I see." Ronan brings his other arm over and covers my hand with his. "Perhaps you budded, bloomed, and blossomed with him. But for me, Mary, you're going to *effloresce*."

Effloresce?

It's not a word I've heard or seen before, but I don't need a dictionary to know what he means by the context.

"You think so?" I say coyly.

"I know so," he confirms. "I knew it the moment I laid eyes on you. You're not ready for a scene with me yet, Mary, but you will be. And when you are? I'm going to make you forget every other Dominant who ever touched you."

CHAPTER FIVE

Ronan

I feel the shudder that flows through her body.

I'm going to have her.

I'm going to have her in ways she never dreamed of.

But I need to take it slow. Something has her rattled, and for me to be a good Dominant, I need to know what happened.

She's clearly an experienced submissive, but she's spooked. She's not ready to play yet. Some subs like to get to know their Doms outside of a club atmosphere before they play. Blossom isn't normally one of them—she said as much when she admitted no one ever asked her to leave the club with them before—but at this moment, she is.

Moreover? *I* have the desire to get to know her.

Odd.

I didn't think it would happen so soon.

Not after...

I shake my head to clear it. I can't go back to the past. I can't dwell on what I've lost. I must move forward. That's why I came back to the States. It's why I got involved with Braden Black and his company, Black, Inc.

I plan to stay here. Because right now? Glasgow—all of Scotland—doesn't seem like home anymore. Not with Keira wanting more from me than I can give and my parents—who I love—doing the same thing they've always done. Putting business and themselves over me, their only child.

Mary stops at a brick building with a neon sign flashing "Gianni's." Underneath it is another sign: *The best pizza in the city!* Actually, it says, *The best zza in the city!* as the P and the I are burned out. This place has been around for a while, and that instantly warms me to it. I've always been drawn to things with a history behind them.

I open the door for Mary, and as she walks in, I follow. The robust scent of roasted tomato and cheese wafts toward me, and I inhale deeply.

"Smells amazing in here," I say.

"Told you, didn't I?" Mary walks toward the counter, but no one's standing there. "Mikey? Are you here?"

A young, gangly-looking man walks out from the back. He stares at my getup for a split second. "Hi, Mary. Mikey's off tonight."

"Hey, Greg," she says and smiles. "My new friend here wants to try the best pizza in the city."

"Not a problem." He gestures to the massive pizzas on display. "No vegetarian tonight, though. We're out of onions and peppers. Delivery comes in the morning."

"Is that a problem for you, Ronan?" she asks.

"Hell, no. The more meat, the better."

"Two slices of pepperoni, then," Mary says. "And two... What do you want to drink?"

"Water's fine." I noticed Mary had only water at the club earlier, and I don't want to risk making her feel uncomfortable by drinking alcohol in front of her.

Greg grabs our slices, warms them in the oven, and Mary pulls her wallet out of her purse.

"My treat. It was my idea to leave the club." I take a credit card out of my sporran.

"Next time," she says. "It's cash-only here."

I raise my eyebrows. Not that cash-only is a problem for me. I have plenty of cash on me. I'm just surprised. "Seriously?"

"You *are* new here." She gives me a smile. "You'll get the hang of things. This one's on me."

If she wants to pay, it's not my place to say she can't. I tuck away my credit card.

The tiny restaurant is cramped, but it does have three small tables, two of which are vacant. I assume because it's hours past the dinner rush.

"Here you go." Greg sets our slices on the counter.

Mary pays him, and then she gestures to a small display of condiments.

"On pizza?" I ask.

"Only if you want to. I like to add a little parm and red pepper flakes. There's also garlic and oregano."

She shakes her cheese and pepper onto the slice. I take a little parmesan cheese, like she did, but stay away from the pepper and garlic. Adding more cheese to pizza can't hurt, I suppose. This is just new to me. We don't eat pizza like this in Glasgow, and I don't recall ever doing this as a kid, either. But when it comes to food, I'll try anything once.

When it comes to some other things, too.

I follow Mary to the table near the window, set down my paper plate, and then hold out her chair for her.

She murmurs, "Thank you," and sits.

I sit across from her. "This pizza must be something pretty special."

She nods. "It is. But sometimes it takes some getting used to for people who don't live here."

"I grew up in the States. I told you."

"But did you grow up *here*? In the city that never sleeps? Because things are different here."

"No," I tell her. "In New Orleans. My mother was a Southern gal."

Mary picks up her slice and glances at the napkin holder on the table. "Greg," she says, raising her voice and waving her hand a little to get his attention, "we're going to need more napkins."

Greg walks out from behind the counter and grabs the chrome napkin holder. "Yeah, right away. You'll definitely need them."

"Are you going to make me wait for napkins?" I ask. "Or can I dig in? I wasn't hungry before, but now that I'm smelling this, I'm starving."

"Oh, we can dig in," she says, "but you'll have grease dribbling down your chin."

"Normally I wouldn't mind that, but my kilt is dry clean only."

She smiles. "Then we'll wait for the napkins."

With luck, we don't have to wait long. Greg comes back with the now-filled napkin holder. Mary grabs at least ten of them and then looks at me.

I take a fistful of napkins, as well, placing several in my lap and the rest next to my plate.

She taps her fingers lightly on her pizza. "I think it's cool enough that we can eat it now. Here's what you do." She picks up her slice. "Obviously, it's too big to eat like this without making a mess of everything, so you fold it over." She literally folds the pizza slice in two so that only the crust is visible, and then she takes a bite from the tip of it. "See?" she says, her mouth full. She chews and swallows. "Delicious."

I mimic her movements, folding my pizza over into a smaller and narrower triangle. It's still huge, though, and a drop of grease dribbles onto my plate.

I take a bite off the tip, like Mary did. It's still hot, but not hot enough to scorch the roof of my mouth. I let the flavors scatter over my tongue—the yeasty zest of the dough, the robust acidic tartness of the tomato sauce, and the creamy umami of the mozzarella cheese.

Damn. This might just change my mind about pizza.

Mary raises her eyebrows after I swallow. "Well?"

"You were right, it's delicious. I'm not sure I've tasted anything quite like it, and I've had my share of pizza."

"But this is New York pizza," she says. "A lot of places try to copy it, but they're never successful. Even a lot of places here in the city say they have traditional New York pizza, but it's not like this. Here, at Gianni's, it's always warm, and it's always perfect."

I take another bite, and true to Mary's word, this time a drop of grease slides down my chin. I grab one of the napkins and wipe it up.

"Told you." She grins, wiping her napkin across her chin. "So...I've never been to New Orleans. What's it like?"

"In a word, amazing. You may love the Big Apple, but you haven't lived until you've experienced the Big Easy. Talk about a city that never sleeps."

She widens her eyes. "Oh?"

"Yeah. New Orleans is something that's indescribable. You can read about it, watch movies set there. But you don't really know it until you go there. Live it."

"Do you still have family there?"

I nod. "My grandmother. She runs a Creole restaurant."

"Really?"

"I know what you're thinking. She'd be too old to still be working, right? But she's young for a grandmother. She had my mom when she was only fifteen years old."

Mary's eyebrows nearly shoot off her forehead. "Wow."

"She's an amazing woman. She kept her baby and lived at home for a few years, learning to cook family recipes from her mother. Then she started her own business."

"And your grandfather?"

"Not in the picture," I say. "I know who he was, somewhat."

"Who was he?"

I hesitate. But I've told her this much already, no reason to stop now. "He was a thirty-year-old businessman traveling through the city."

Her jaw drops.

"It wasn't rape. Well, legally it was, but my grandmother was okay with it. She told him she was nineteen."

"Did he know he had a daughter from her?"

"Nope. He was in and out of her life pretty quickly, and she had no way to find him. Not even a last name."

Mary shakes her head. "My God, what a story."

It is. Though I haven't thought about it in a while. Anyone who meets my grandmother would never think she had such a difficult past.

"And your parents?" Mary asks.

"They're still in Glasgow. I doubt my father will ever leave Scotland again. He agreed to move over to the States when my mother got pregnant with me. She wanted to raise me here. Then, when I decided to go to school in Scotland after I graduated high school, the entire family moved back."

"So you're an only child?"

"Guilty."

Her face falls into something akin to pity. "Was it lonely growing up?"

I swallow the bite of pizza I'm chewing. "Not at all. When your grandmother runs a Creole restaurant—one of the most popular in the city—there's always someone around to talk to."

"So you spent a lot of time with her there?" Mary takes a drink.

"I practically lived there. My father was always off on business, doing something or another, and my mother accompanied him a lot, which left me in Mémé's care."

"May may?"

I wipe my lips with my napkin. "Creole French. It's like calling your grandmother Nana."

"You speak French, then?"

"Somewhat. Do you?"

She blushes. "I'm afraid not. I remember a little bit of high school Spanish, but that's about it."

"That's a shame. French is a beautiful language. The language of love, mo leannan."

Her cheeks redden further.

I'm not sure why I keep calling her that. I've never called anyone mo leannan. I've never looked for love, not in the way most people do. Keira and I were together for five years in Glasgow. We were in the lifestyle there, at an exclusive club, but then she decided she wanted more than I could give her.

She wanted marriage, family, children.

I'm not cut out for that.

Not even slightly.

I swallow another bite of pizza and bring my thoughts back to the beautiful woman sitting across from me. She's what I need to focus on. Not the past or even the future. Just right now, in this moment, with her.

And all the possibilities arising between us.

CHAPTER SIX

Mary

Is this a date? I'm trying to think about the last time I was on a date with someone. Not since Lucas, who introduced me to this lifestyle.

I've been rethinking the lifestyle after the episode with Jack. It affected me more than I thought it would.

He wasn't the first man to draw blood during a scene without meaning to, but there was something about his lack of emotion during the scene that hit me hard. It got me thinking that maybe—just maybe—I need more than what I've been content with for so long.

Maybe I don't want to submit anymore. Maybe I want a more equal relationship in the bedroom.

Which doesn't explain why I'm sitting across from this gorgeous Scotsman. He exudes dominance.

He would've taken me back to a room in the club tonight if I'd allowed it. He said as much.

And boy... A couple months ago, I would've jumped at the chance.

I haven't been this attracted to—or this aroused by—

someone in a long time.

Brenda must think I've completely lost it.

God, Brenda…

I know she said she was okay, but I feel terrible about leaving her there in the club alone. She's well known there, and everyone knows she's Dalton's sub—she's been wearing his collar forever—so no one will harm her. The club is about as safe a place as she can be.

Still, I feel bad.

"Would you excuse me a minute?" I say to Ronan.

"Sure." He wipes his chin.

I rise and quickly walk to the tiny restroom behind the counter. Then I grab my phone to text Brenda but remember she won't have her phone if she's still at the club.

She must have left already, though, because there's a text from her.

Brenda: *How's it going with the Highlander?* (Lots of hearts)

Me: *We're having pizza at Gianni's.*

Brenda: *Are you going to take him home with you?*

Me: *Absolutely not. You know I don't do things like that.*

Brenda: *Yeah, I know. You can always take him back to the club if you change your mind.*

Me: *When did you leave?*

Brenda: *About a half hour after you did. I'm in a cab on the way home now.*

Me: *When does Dalton get back?*

Brenda: *A few days.*

Me: *Okay. See you at the gym tomorrow.*

She texts back a thumbs-up.

Brenda and I have a standing date at ten o'clock every

Saturday morning for the gym. We exercise for a few minutes and then spend the rest of the time chatting over smoothies in the small cafeteria.

I head back to the table, where Ronan has polished off his slice. "Everything okay?"

"Yeah, I was checking on Brenda."

He raises his eyebrows.

"Sorry, I mean Lotus."

"Ah," he says. "Does anyone at the club know your real names?"

"The owner and the head of security, Claude. They have to approve all the applications. Then it's up to Brenda and me whether we tell anyone else our names, so you can't let on that I told you hers."

"My lips are sealed."

I've finished my slice, and one slice is a lot. I think about ordering another, just to make my hands look busy, but then I don't.

For some reason, I don't feel the need to make small talk with Ronan or to pretend like I'm busy eating. I feel comfortable with him, which makes no sense at all, since I've been out of the dating scene for so long.

"Are you going to get another?" I ask.

"No, I'm done. I actually ate a pretty good dinner before I came to the club tonight."

I can't help a chuckle. "Then why on earth did you just eat a huge slice of pizza?"

"I'm a growing boy," he teases. His eyes twinkle. "I have a huge appetite. Always have."

"From what I saw tonight, there's not an ounce of fat on that body."

"I work hard, lassie," he says, imitating a brogue again.

"Throwing blocks, Scottish games."

I shake my head, still laughing. "I have to say, Ronan O'Connor, I've never met anyone quite like you."

"Nor I you, lassie."

I take the last sip from my bottle of water. We're done eating, and we could go. But I want to keep talking to him, learning more about him, and he doesn't seem eager to go, either. "So you said you've partnered with Braden Black's company. What is it that you do?"

"I took over my father's company last year," he says. "O'Connor Enterprises. We're real estate developers, and we build high-end resorts all over Europe. When I was growing up, my father traveled overseas a lot. He was making a killing, and he wasn't interested in breaking into the American market at that time, despite the fact that we lived here. But Black, Inc. has decided to build a new resort and casino in Las Vegas."

I lift an eyebrow. "Don't they manufacture work goggles?"

"That's their key product," Ronan says. "What put Braden Black on the map all those years ago. But they've diversified since then. You don't become a billionaire by producing construction goggles."

"I suppose not. I'm surprised they haven't gotten into the hotel game before now."

"Their company has many other branches. Once this came across my desk, I couldn't say no. Besides...it was a good time for me to leave Glasgow. To leave the UK altogether."

"Why is that?"

He doesn't speak at first, and I wonder if I've overstepped my bounds.

Then he says, "My relationship, if you can call it that, ended."

"Do you feel like elaborating?"

"Not really."

Definitely a story there, but he just met me. I can't blame him for not wanting to spill his guts. Still…I'm curious. I want to know his story. I want to know what makes him *him*.

He rises. "You ready to go?"

Yeah, I must have overstepped. "Sure," I say.

He reaches into his sporran and pulls out a money clip. So he does have cash, after all.

And the clip is full of hundred-dollar bills. *Damn.* I resist the urge to let my eyes go wide. There's having cash, and then there's having *cash*.

He pulls out a crisp hundred, places it on the table.

"You don't have to tip here," I say.

"We ate here, didn't we?"

"Yeah, but it's not—"

He holds up his hand. "I believe in being generous."

"That's beyond generous—"

He holds up his hand again. "I do it because I can. Because I know it means a lot to the people who work in service positions. One day, if I can no longer do it, I won't. But while I can, I will."

I cock my head, look up into those gorgeous blue eyes. He's genuine. This isn't a flex. It's simple generosity. He can, so he does.

He's a good man.

A good man who's affecting me in ways I can't quite understand. And even though he's ready to leave this place now, I'm still not ready to say good night yet. I'm pretty sure I offended him before by getting too personal, and I don't want to end our night on that sour note.

"Ronan," I say, my mind turning over an idea, "would you like to see something amazing?"

His eyes sparkle as he meets my gaze, but his lips don't

curve into a smile. "I'm looking at something amazing now."

My cheeks go hot...again. "I mean...you just got here. I'm wondering... Have you been to the Top of the Rock?"

"What rock?"

I let out a short laugh. "The observation deck at Rockefeller Center."

"Is it higher than the Empire State Building?"

"Lower, actually, but I like it better. First, you can see the Empire State Building from the Rock, and you get a way better view of Central Park. Plus...I guess it's just that...well, *everyone* goes to the Empire State Building. I like to be unique."

"You, Mary, are the *definition* of unique."

Simple words, yet the way he looks at me... I can't hold back a shudder.

I glance at my phone, check the time. "If we hurry, we can catch the last elevator."

. . .

Ronan gets more than a few glances from both women and men as we ascend to the seventieth floor of the Rockefeller Center.

When the elevator door opens, he gasps, visibly in awe at the 360-degree panoramic view of New York City. The entire seventieth floor of the building is dedicated to the observation deck, which is designed with expansive floor-to-ceiling glass panels. Ronan walks forward, out of the elevator, so quickly that for a moment I think he's going to walk right through the glass.

Next to him, I take in the view of the gorgeous Manhattan skyline. In the dark, the top of the Empire State Building shines with its iconic blue lighting.

"This isn't Glasgow," Ronan says softly.

"I'm sure Glasgow is beautiful too," I reply.

"It is, but this is something else. It's so vast, and the feats of architecture..." He turns to me. "It's so very...American. I grew up down South, and I've spent most of my adulthood in the UK. What I appreciate about this view is its newness."

"New York City isn't new. It's nearly four hundred years old."

"You probably don't realize, having never lived anywhere else, but America is a young country, Mary. Four hundred years is new compared to a city like Glasgow that's been around for over *fifteen hundred* years. And there is beauty in newness."

"I suppose there is. I just don't know anything else. Too bad we couldn't see the sunset. Or the lush green of Central Park. You should come back here during the day sometime."

He continues to stare at the skyline. He really is mesmerized.

"Do you want to go to the outdoor observation deck?" I ask.

He grabs my hand. "Lead the way."

I'm tempted to snatch my hand away. Not because I fear him...but because I don't. The feel of his large hand around mine is warm and soothing as well as intriguing and arousing.

I suck in a breath as we walk outside and observe the view from different vantage points. We don't talk much, and it's okay. There's a comfort in the silence I've never had with anyone else.

When the last elevator descends for the last time today, Ronan and I are on it.

And he's still holding my hand.

"Will you allow me to see you home?" he asks once we're back on the street.

Everything I know about safety tells me not to.

But my body is throbbing for him, and my heart tells me it's okay to trust him.

I'm about to open my mouth and tell him yes when—

"I'm sorry. I shouldn't have asked you that. This is New York City, and I'm a complete stranger. I'll get you a cab."

I bite my lip. "That's probably best."

He calls for a cab, and while we're waiting, "We didn't get to talk about you much tonight. It was all about me. What do *you* do here in the city?"

"I work at a shop called Treasure's Chest. But I'm off on weekends."

He lifts his eyebrows. "What kind of a shop is that?"

My cheeks warm. Not because I'm embarrassed by where I work, but because he's putting me on the spot. I liked talking about him, learning about him. Talking about me? Not so much. But I answer him, anyway. "It's a lingerie shop that also sells clubwear and…toys and stuff for the leather community. I also teach classes there. For people new to the lifestyle."

For a moment, I think he may actually smile, but the smile in his eyes doesn't quite make it to his lips. I should know better by now than to think he would smile so easily. "Perhaps we'll see each other again tomorrow night," he says.

The cab pulls up at the curb. Time to say goodbye—for now.

"I'd like that," I tell him. "I'll be at the club tomorrow at eight o'clock."

"Then I'll see you there." He gives me a searing gaze. "Good night, *Blossom*."

I get into the cab, and Ronan closes the door for me before he walks off. I watch him for a moment, watch the way he moves in that kilt and his Jacobite shirt. Then I give the cabbie my address and close my eyes for the drive home, thinking about Ronan's long, thick, silky hair and what it might feel like between my fingers.

And a million other things I want to feel with him.

CHAPTER SEVEN

Ronan

I'm staying in the Countess Regalia hotel in Manhattan. I've got my realtor in the city, looking for an apartment for me. She'll be showing me some places tomorrow.

The cabbie drops me off, and I head to the elevators and up to my suite.

Since it's only a bit past eleven, I get my usual looks as I walk through the lobby. I enjoy wearing a kilt. I wasn't lying to Mary when I told her I have utility kilts. I also have a black leather kilt that I wear to the club sometimes. It's too thick for all the necessary pleating. But tomorrow, when looking at apartments, I'll be wearing jeans and a button-down, like the regular American guy that I am.

Because I was born here, I'm an American citizen. My father never became a naturalized citizen of the United States. He was able to live and work here because of his marriage to my mother, but he didn't ever want to give up his Scottish citizenship.

I get to the elevator, slide my key card through the reader, and head up to the top floor, where my suite is. I open the door, flick on the light switch. The lavish velvet sectional sofa comes into view, and floor-to-ceiling windows offer panoramic views of the city's skyline.

Adjacent to the living area is an elegant dining space, complete with a stylish dining table and designer chairs. A crystal chandelier hangs from the ceiling, but it's not currently illuminated, so my gaze is drawn to the sliver of light coming from the door to the bedroom.

That's odd. I know I turned off the light when I left, and housekeeping hasn't been here. They were here this morning.

I stride straight to the door, open it and—

"I thought you'd never get here."

Fuck.

I know the voice.

I know the naked body.

It's Keira. My submissive for the last five years.

The one who left me because she wanted more—more than I could give her.

She wants a husband and a family in addition to our current lifestyle.

I don't want any of that. I'm married to my job. Always have been. I watched my mother compete with work for my father's attention, and I won't do that to a woman or child.

Besides, I don't feel that way about Keira. I consider her a friend. She's a submissive, and I'm sexually attracted to her. That is the end of it. I don't feel the emotion necessary to go further. She deserves more, and so do I. If I want to focus on my career and not bring a wife and children into the picture, that's my business, and I deserve to have what I want.

So does she. If she wants a husband and children, I'm not the man for her.

Yet here she is, naked, lying on my king-size bed. This is

a hotel, so there are no rungs on the headboard to bind her to. But she holds her wrists together above her head, as if they're bound by invisible rope or silk.

"I don't need rope to bind me," she says. "I'm bound solely by your will."

"What are you doing here, Keira?"

"I couldn't leave things the way we left them." She wiggles slightly, as though she's truly bound. "I can be what you want, sir. I know I said I wanted more—a family—but I've given it all kinds of thought. I no longer need those things. All I need is to be yours in the bedroom. To submit to your desires."

I sigh. I need to approach this gently. I never wanted to hurt Keira, but she and I have different needs at this point in our lives, no matter what she's saying now.

"How did you get here?" I ask.

"I flew, of course."

"How did you find me?"

"There aren't too many Ronan O'Connors staying at posh hotels in Manhattan. It didn't take long."

I walk a few steps toward the bed. "Perhaps the better question is how you got into my suite."

"I convinced them I was your wife." Her eyes smolder. "It wasn't difficult."

"Whoever let you in should be fired," I say under my breath. And I'll make sure they are. They let her into my private space without any kind of proof of her claim. "All right. There's nothing else to do except get you your own room at this point."

She grins. "The hotel is booked, sir."

I sigh again. "Fine. You take the bed. I'll take the pullout in the living area."

Just what I need. A shitty night's sleep and a backache in the morning from sleeping on a pullout couch. Even in the

Countess Regalia, pullout couches suck. They're never long enough for me. My legs will be hanging off the end.

"It doesn't have to be this way, sir." She pulls her arms down, flips onto her stomach, and crawls toward the foot of the bed. So much for my commanding bindings. "I can change."

"Keira," I say as gently as I can, "don't try to change for any man. Never give up who you are and what you want. *You're* important. Don't forget that."

She rises onto her knees and touches my face. "If I'm so important, why don't you want me?"

I gently remove her hand. "I know what you want, and I can't give it to you. You deserve to be with someone who can."

"I don't want anyone else, sir."

"Yes," I say, again as gently as I can. "I understand that, but *I* do."

I don't realize the truth of my words until I say them. I know next to nothing about Mary. I don't even know her last name. But already, I feel something brewing inside me. Something foreign and far from unpleasant.

Mary's already a submissive, but something has her rattled. And for some reason I want to be the one to help her.

"I hope you brought something to sleep in," I say. "If not, grab one of the bathrobes from the bathroom. You're not going to sleep naked in my suite."

I close the bedroom door. All of my stuff is in the en suite bathroom. I strip off my shirt, kilt, and hose, gently folding the kilt to keep the pleats in place. My suitcase is also in the bedroom, and it contains my underwear and my pajamas. I don't wear anything under a kilt, so I'm naked.

Great.

I pull out the bed, make it up with the sheets and blankets provided, and slip between them.

Damn.

I have a naked woman in the next room—a woman who would let me do whatever I want to her right now.

And all I can think of is Mary. Sweet Mary who introduced me to New York pizza. Who showed me the spectacular skyline of Manhattan from her favorite viewing spot.

Sweet Mary, who's a little bit broken, but who trusted me enough to spend the evening with me.

She gave of herself when she didn't have to.

And I want to give something back to her.

CHAPTER EIGHT

Mary

I only make it about ten minutes on the elliptical the next morning at the gym before I tell Brenda I'm heading down to the small dinette on the first floor to have a smoothie. By the time I have my smoothie ordered—today's special is raspberry pineapple—Brenda has joined me to order her own.

"You're quiet today, Mare," she says.

"Am I?"

"Spill it. You haven't said more than three words about the Scottish hunk."

"We went to Gianni's for a slice," I say. "And then we viewed the city from the Top of the Rock. Other than that, there's nothing to tell."

"Do you trust him?"

"He seems trustworthy enough."

"Yes, he does. And the club vets everyone who applies for membership. You're going to be perfectly safe with him."

I sip my smoothie. "Yes, I know that."

"So...do you think it's time to get back on the horse?"

"You're beginning to sound like a broken record, Brenda."

"Yeah, I can hear myself. But the club has been such a huge part of your life the last several years. I can't believe you'd give it up."

"I never thought I would before, either." I set down my smoothie and rub the back of my neck. "I'm not even sure it was the scene. It's not like Jack hurt me that much. I healed up right away. There's no scarring."

"Right. And Jack honored your safe word as soon as you said it."

I slowly draw in a deep breath. "It's just that his head was somewhere else, you know? And I think that's what bothers me the most. How do you know when a Dominant has his head in the game? How many times have I been with someone who's thinking about something else while we're doing a scene?"

"Does it matter?"

I meet Brenda's gaze. "I never thought it did before. But now I wonder… What is it that I really want? I'm beginning to think maybe I want what you and Dalton have."

"Dalton and I weren't looking for it. It found *us*."

I take a sip of my raspberry-pineapple smoothie. The tanginess of the Greek yogurt punches through the sweetness of the strawberry and pineapple, giving the smoothie a full-bodied yet fruity flavor. It's delicious. "I know. That's what makes it so special, Brenda. You found something you weren't looking for, and now your lives are all the more complete for it. I always thought my life was complete just being a submissive. Meeting Dominants at the club, playing together, and then going about my day-to-day life. I was happy without a man in my life. Without a partner. I like living alone, and I like being responsible for my own needs. Except in the bedroom, when I give up the responsibility for my needs to someone else."

"A relationship doesn't mean giving up responsibility for

your own needs," Brenda says. "It means sharing responsibility for each other's needs. It means thinking about someone else as well as yourself."

"I know." I sigh. "That's always turned me off about it, to be honest. I suppose it sounds selfish, but I never wanted to bother worrying about anyone else. Not in my day-to-day life. It's difficult enough making a living, making ends meet in Manhattan. Yet I love living here, and I don't want to leave. It's my home."

Brenda's eyes gleam with mischief. "You could find yourself a billionaire, like Braden Black. Then you'll never have to worry about money for the rest of your life."

I chuckle. "Clearly I'm not making myself clear."

"Clearly you're not." She sips her smoothie.

I take a look around the small dining area, at the people in workout clothes chatting. Specifically at the couples. "I watched my parents' marriage fail, Brenda. He had a secret apartment and many lovers. You know all the stories. And then the fiasco with Lucas turned me the rest of the way off. It's not something I ever wanted."

"I know. It's not something I thought I wanted, either. When I met the right person, that changed."

"I haven't met the right person yet, and I don't see myself falling for any of the Doms I've been with. But I wonder if something more is in the cards for me. I'm not expecting it to happen like it did for you and Dalton. But what if I left the lifestyle?"

Brenda slurps the last of her smoothie through her straw. "Then you'd be leaving your hunky Scotsman."

She's right about that. Ronan O'Connor made quite an impression on me. Part of me wishes he had invited me to a private room last night, because in some strange way, even though we just met, I do trust him. I've met Dominants like that before.

But I didn't have it in me.

I like Ronan. I like him a lot. But he's a Dominant through and through. That won't change, and if I'm thinking about leaving...

He and I can't be together. Not in a scene or in any other way.

Except...

"I told him I'd be at the club tonight at eight o'clock," I say.

"Well then..." Brenda waggles her eyebrows. "Seems you *are* ready to get back in the saddle."

"I'm not sure." I sigh. "Let's just put it this way. I won't be wearing leather or lingerie. I'll be wearing another club dress like I did last night."

"You looked hot as hell last night."

"Maybe I'll try not to look so hot tonight," I say.

"Mary, you can do hot in your sleep."

My cheeks warm at the compliment. It's funny. I've never thought of myself as hot. My reddish-brown hair and brown eyes are far from special. I'm not like Brenda, who's drop-dead gorgeous with creamy skin, dark hair, and deep brown eyes with lashes to die for. And then her body... Yeah, swimsuit model material.

"If you say so."

"I say so, and so does everyone else who sees you at the club. You radiate there, Mary. Your submissiveness radiates. You know that. You've attracted some of the hottest Doms there."

She's not wrong. Something about my freckled girl-next-door look, I guess.

"Are you going to be at the club tonight?" I ask.

"I wasn't planning to," Brenda says. "It just feels weird to be there without Dalton. But if you need me there, I'll be there for you. You know that."

I mull it over for a minute and then shake my head. "You know? This is something I need to do for myself. I'll go. I'll sit at the bar. But did you notice that only Ronan approached me last night?"

Brenda cocks her head. "I guess you're right. I didn't think about it."

"Normally a couple Doms approach me."

"Don't forget about the fact that Ronan was sitting at the table with you for quite a large part of the night. He definitely has *hands-off* exuding from him."

"Maybe. Or maybe I'm the one who had a neon *hands-off* flashing on my forehead last night. None of my usual Doms came up to me."

"Maybe it's because you've been avoiding the club ever since the incident with Jack."

"Or maybe I've lost my mojo."

She gives a short laugh. "You haven't lost any mojo."

"No, really, I think I have. Before the incident, I would've rushed to get back into a scene with Ronan. We certainly conversed enough for me to feel comfortable with him and trust him in the secure environment of Black Rose. He's the best-looking guy to come through those doors in a long time—and that's saying a lot, because you know how good-looking most of those guys are."

"Don't I know it."

Indeed, Dalton is nearly as hot as Ronan, just in a completely different way.

I sigh. "I'll be honest, Brenda. I do want you there with me tonight, but I'm going to specifically ask you *not* to come. This is something I have to face myself. Perhaps tonight I'll figure out whether the scene is for me anymore."

"I just can't imagine you leaving. This is such a huge part of your life," she says. "You work at Treasure's Chest, and you teach those classes."

"I can still teach those. I can certainly still sell the stuff. I'm good at it. I'm an experienced submissive, whether I'm currently in the lifestyle or not. Nothing stops me from teaching it to others."

Brenda reaches across the table and squeezes my arm. "True. But are you sure you want to be alone? I can be there for you."

I'm far from sure, but if Brenda is there, holding my hand, I won't be able to figure out how the scene figures in my future. She's a submissive through and through. She and Dalton will never leave the scene, and that's okay.

But I need to find out what's right for *me*.

"I'm sure," I say, hoping my voice sounds as confident as the words. "This is something I need to do alone."

• • •

I wear a burgundy minidress and platform sandals to the club. This particular shade of burgundy has mostly blue undertones to it so it doesn't clash with my hair. I was amazed when I found it at the store. My platform sandals are basic black and strappy. At five seven, I'm already tall without the heels, but I love wearing them. Especially tonight. Ronan is so tall I'll still feel petite in his presence.

I say hi to Claude, surrender my phone, and enter the club. It's Saturday night, and Black Rose is always busy, even this early. But it doesn't ever get to full capacity until around ten.

I look around, but I don't see Ronan.

It's only a little past eight, so I wouldn't consider him late yet. But then a thought rushes into my head.

What if he *is* here? What if he found someone else already, and he's in a room doing a scene?

The thought saddens me, and jealousy sinks into my gut.

Ridiculous, I know. I only met the man twenty-four hours ago. So we shared a slice of pizza. I showed him one of my favorite places in New York. So what?

He's obviously a Dominant. He's not going to want to put up with my questioning attitude right now. Except he did last night.

He didn't just put up with it. He put me at ease about it.

Maybe I'm overthinking this.

There's one empty seat at the bar, and I grab it.

I order a lemon drop.

Then I wait.

CHAPTER NINE

Ronan

After putting Keira in a cab bound to the airport, I head to Black Rose. I'm already running late, and I hope Mary won't be upset.

The morning with Keira was not pleasant.

Her attempts at seduction were persuasive for sure, but I couldn't get Mary out of my head. Mary, who wouldn't play with me last night.

Mary, who introduced me to the most delicious pizza I've ever tasted. Who showed me the beautiful New York skyline.

"Please, sir," Keira begged, more than once. *"I can change. I don't need those things. I just... I was falling in love with you, sir, but I've got a handle on it now."*

Her words made my heart ache, but they didn't move me. Keira was never more than a submissive to me—a good submissive whose company I enjoyed and who I loved as a friend, but nothing more. I didn't fall in love with her romantically. I've never fallen in love with a submissive.

I've never fallen in love, period.

She cried, and I tried to comfort her. But despite her words, she clearly wanted more than comfort from me, and that I couldn't give her. So I booked her on the next flight back to Glasgow.

Then I changed into my leather kilt and a black Jacobite shirt.

As I walk into the club, I check the clock on the wall. It's eight forty-five.

Damn.

I'm late.

Mary will be upset, and understandably so.

I spy her, then. She's on the dance floor, wearing a wine-colored dress that somehow brings out the same hue in her hair under the disco lights.

She's dancing with a man. A nice-looking man who's smiling at her.

Before I realize it, my hands are clenched into fists.

Mary's not mine. I'll do well to remember that. She has the right to dance with whomever she pleases.

And I have the right to cut in.

Which I do, tapping the man on the back.

He turns. He isn't quite as tall as I am, but he's handsome, with dark hair and eyes.

"Yes?" he says.

"I'm cutting in," I say adamantly.

"All right." He gives Mary's hand to me. "If it's all right with you, Blossom."

Mary's cheeks redden. "Yeah, it's fine, Ben."

I take Mary in my arms as the slow jazz continues. "Who was that?" I ask.

"Ben Black."

Her words stun me. Ben Black is the brother of Braden Black, my new business partner. How did I not recognize him?

"Now that you mention it, he looks a lot like his brother."

"Yeah, only, his eyes are brown and Braden's are blue."

I'm done talking about Ben Black or any other man with Mary. "I'm sorry I'm late."

She shrugs against me. "That's okay. I passed the time."

"Dancing with Ben Black?"

"Part of the time."

"Did you do anything other than dance?"

"I had a drink."

"You know that's not what I'm asking."

Her cheeks flush in the disco lighting. "Ben and I don't play together."

"Why?"

"Ben is no longer in the lifestyle. He left it a while ago. He only comes to the club every now and then to see how things are going."

News to me. And I don't really care. It's not my business. I'm just glad she had no intention of playing with him.

"Drink?" I ask when the music gets a little faster.

"Sure."

I lead her to a small table in the corner that's unoccupied and pull out a chair for her. "I'll get it. What would you like?"

"Ronan, you don't have to. The service here is impeccable. Someone will be here before—"

"What can I get you to drink?" a topless server asks.

"Hi, Kaylee," Mary says. "I'll have a lemon drop."

"Macallan fifteen-year," I say.

"Absolutely." Kaylee walks away, her tits bouncing.

I sit across from Mary. "Is there any chance you'll go to a private room with me tonight?"

She looks down at the table, examines her fingernails, which are painted a burgundy that matches her dress. Very sexy.

"If you want to do a scene tonight, Ronan, you'll have to find another submissive."

"I suppose I could do that."

Her lips curve downward.

Interesting. She doesn't want me to find another submissive. But she knows I'm a Dominant. She knows I'm craving a scene, and she wants me to have what I want, even if it isn't with her.

"I can introduce you to a few if you'd like," she says.

I raise my eyebrows. Perhaps she feels nothing of what I'm feeling—intense attraction, intense desire.

An intense desire to dominate.

Almost more than that, though. I might be satisfied just to kiss those lips.

"I'll stick with my date tonight," I say.

"Date?"

"Yes. We had plans to meet here."

"And you were late."

"Yes, I was. It was unavoidable, and I'm sorry."

"You could have called Claude."

She's right. But I didn't because I was dealing with Keira. I'm the Dominant here, though, and I'm done explaining myself. "This is a date, Blossom."

"If you say so."

I grab her hand, meet her gaze. "I *say* so," I command in my best dominant voice.

Her lips tremble. Only slightly, but I notice.

Good. I'm having an effect on her. Perhaps not the effect I normally have on a submissive, but I'm happy to take what I can get.

So strange. I had Keira in my hotel room all day, and not the slightest desire to give her what she was asking for.

Tonight?

I'd play with Mary in a minute, but it's not what she wants.

And because she doesn't want it?

It's not what I want, either.

Slow and steady.

I never thought I'd be one for that, but I *can* convince Mary to be my submissive.

I can, and I will.

Determination sweeps through me as I look into her brown eyes.

"Have you been in the back yet?" she asks me.

"I took a tour of the place when I made my application. But not in the way you mean. Last night was my first night here while the club was open."

"Are you interested in seeing the rest of the club while people are playing?" she asks.

I take a sip of my scotch, let the smokiness trickle down my throat. "Are you?"

She looks down at her fingernails again. "I've been a member here for years, Ronan. I've seen it all."

"Are you a voyeur?" I ask.

"Sometimes."

"An exhibitionist?"

She shakes her head. "I've tried it, and it's not my jam. What I do with a partner is private, and I don't like other people watching."

"Even if you like watching other people?"

"Only sometimes," she says. "And yes. I prefer to play in private. But there are others who don't, which lets me be a voyeur sometimes when I feel the urge."

"Do you feel the urge now?"

She looks up from her fingernails. "Not really, but I will accompany you if you'd like to go to one of the exhibition rooms."

I pause a moment, thinking. What is the best move here? She's clearly not ready to play, and she doesn't really have the urge to go to an exhibition room. Yet she'll accompany me if I ask her to.

In a normal situation, as a Dominant, I'd say absolutely. Let's go. Let's be voyeurs for the evening together.

But this isn't a normal situation.

"If you're not into it, then no," I say. "I don't need to do anything you don't want to do."

"You're an interesting Dominant, Ronan."

She has no idea.

I'm looking for a true submissive. One who will bend her knee at any time. One like Keira, who was happy just to submit…until she wanted something more.

I ask a lot of my submissive, which is why I usually only play with one at a time. I don't call it a relationship. I think of it more as an understanding between us.

We're exclusive when we play together. Not only because it makes practical sense. Exclusivity means you don't have to worry about sexually transmitted diseases, which means condoms aren't required. Personally I hate them, though I always use them the first time with a new submissive.

But practical sense isn't the only reason I do it.

I prefer exclusivity because then we both know what to expect.

My submissives find out soon enough that I exert complete dominance over them. That understanding is crucial, because in all of the time that I've been in this lifestyle, I've never had a submissive use a safe word.

That's because she knows, before we even begin, that I will be in control. She understands, before we ever begin, that *I* am her master.

Which is why I should probably walk away from Mary. If she's this reluctant to play with me, she will never be one to let me have complete dominance over her.

But I *can't* walk away.

In some strange way, she's beguiled me. It's like she's a bird of prey and she's sunk her talons into my soul.

Funny. I never thought I had a soul.

I'm not in love with her. I hardly know her.

But I feel like fate has led me to her. As if I'm in some strange paranormal romance and I found my fated mate.

Because the one word that comes to my mind when I look at Mary is just that.

Mine.

CHAPTER TEN

Mary

When he looks at me with his blue eyes, I'm ready to follow him anywhere.

But I know better. I know I'm not ready, no matter how much Brenda tells me I need to get back in the saddle.

I'm just not ready to give myself over to a Dominant yet.

As attracted as I am to Ronan, and as much as I'm beginning to like him, I don't expect him to wait around forever.

Still, a concrete block dropped off my shoulders when he told me he didn't want me to introduce him to other subs.

That would've cracked my heart in two, which makes absolutely no sense.

I don't normally see Dominants outside the club. We don't date. Yet I took Ronan to get a slice of pizza last night, and it felt...right.

It felt normal. It felt so normal that I didn't want the evening to end, so I took him to the Top of the Rock, one of my favorite places in the world.

Maybe I *do* want to date.

But I can't date Ronan O'Connor. He's as forceful a

Dominant as I've met in a long time.

Power exudes from him, as if he's surrounded in a glowing gold halo of dominance.

Yet he thinks this is a date. He actually used the word *date*.

Maybe the best thing is to ask him.

"Ronan?"

"Yes?" He takes a sip of his drink.

I pause a moment, trying to gather the right words. "Why are you with me tonight? Why don't you want me to introduce you to another submissive?"

He leans into me. "I've met the submissive I want."

My cheeks warm, and my nipples harden against the stretchy fabric of my dress. I'm sure my whole chest must be scarlet, even in the dim lighting.

"You seem very sure of yourself," I say.

"A good Dominant is always sure."

He's not wrong.

"What if I'm not sure this is *me* anymore?" I ask.

"Then you wouldn't be here."

Again, he's not wrong.

This lifestyle will always be a part of who I am, whether I play or not. But if I'm never comfortable enough to play a scene again, what am I doing here? I paid my membership dues for the year, so I can say I don't want to waste the money.

That's not really the reason, though. Membership for single women is not all that expensive in a club like this. Single men, on the other hand, get hosed with the fees.

"What if I want to leave?" I ask.

"No one is stopping you."

But *he's* stopping me. He doesn't realize it, but he is. I feel bound to him in some strange way—as if he came all the way across the Atlantic to find me. Still, I'm not ready to play. Not even with this gorgeous Dominant who arouses me just by his presence. My flesh is sizzling, and I'm squirming against the heat between my thighs.

As if he's reading my mind, Ronan drops his gaze to my chest. "You sure you don't want to play?"

"I'm sure."

His brows draw downward. Have I upset him?

"I didn't say I wasn't attracted to you, Ronan. Look in the mirror. Any woman would be attracted to you. Any submissive."

"Yet the woman I want most right now doesn't seem to want me."

I shake my head, take a sip of my tangy drink. "It's not that simple."

"Do you want to level with me?"

"About what?"

"About what happened to make you this way. Something spooked you, Blossom," he says, taking care to use my submissive name at the club. "I can assure you, you have nothing to fear from me."

"I don't have anything to fear from anyone in here."

"Still...something has you changing your tune. What is it?"

I sigh. I want to tell him. I really want to open up to him.

"The last scene I participated in...went wrong, but that's not even the issue. Scenes have gone wrong before. Something about this one, though... I think maybe *I'm* changing. Maybe this is no longer the life I want."

He says nothing for a moment. Then, "You came back here tonight."

"I did."

"Did you come to see me?"

My cheeks are on fire. "I did."

"Yet you won't do a scene with me."

I finger the stem of my martini glass. "No. Not tonight, anyway. I'm not ready, Ronan."

"Are you uncomfortable here?"

"Not at all. You saw me dancing. This is a safe place for me."

"But it's not. Not if a scene went wrong."

"But it *is*." I drum my fingers on the table. "I know I'm not making any sense. If I understood it myself, I would gladly enlighten you."

He pauses again. "Do you want to leave?"

"No. That's not it, either. But if you're looking for a playmate tonight, Ronan, I'm afraid it's not going to be me."

He reaches across the table and grabs my hand, stopping my nervous finger drumming. "I *am* looking for a playmate, Blossom. And it *will* be you. Maybe not tonight, but eventually."

His deep voice mesmerizes me. He sounds so sure of himself, and he makes me feel sure as well.

Because I can see it. I can see myself in a scene with him, submitting to him.

But something holds me back.

"I'll tell you what," he says. "If you give me your number, I'd like to take you out. On a real date. Something that requires planning, making sure every moment is perfect."

I bite my lip. "I don't date."

"I don't, either."

I look into his smoldering blue eyes. "Then why do you want to date me?"

"That, Blossom, is the question of the century. I wish I had an answer for you."

I smile then. Something about him fills me with an emotion that's unfamiliar. It's not the elated feeling of endorphins after a scene. But it's a happy feeling nonetheless, like maybe I found a friend. Or more.

He rises, takes my hand. "Come on."

He leads me out of the club, and we retrieve our phones from Claude. Then we head upstairs to the bar. I put my black trench coat back on.

Ronan takes me to a vacant table near the middle of the room. "Will you give me your number?"

"All right." I recite the digits as he plugs them into his phone.

He sends me a quick text. "Now you have mine," he says.

June, one of the servers here at the upstairs bar, heads over to our table. "Can I get you two anything?"

"Fifteen-year Macallan," Ronan says. "Blossom?"

"Just some water, please." My stomach growls. "And an order of fries, maybe."

"That sounds good." Ronan nods. "Two orders of fries."

"Right away." June whisks away from the table.

"Tomorrow is Sunday," Ronan says. "When can I take you to dinner?"

I check the calendar on my phone. "I don't work weekends, so tomorrow will work fine."

"So you work Monday through Friday at the shop? What are your hours?"

"Ten a.m. to six p.m. Sometimes I stay late and help with inventory."

"Good to know."

"How about you? What are your hours?"

He gives me his now-famous almost-grin. "Whatever I want them to be. I'm the boss. Though this new contract with Black, Inc. is taking up a lot of time. Lots of meetings, lots of teleconferences. I've been working ten- to twelve-hour days since I got back to the States."

"Can't anyone fill in for you?"

"I'm a hands-on kind of guy." He narrows his gaze, and his blue eyes burn.

His words in tandem with his eyes make me squirm.

"Though I do have a great staff here," he continues. "They can fill in for me when necessary. I just prefer to tackle as much of the business as I can by myself."

"I understand."

"Do you?"

"Yeah. I mean, you're a Dominant. You like control."

"Not all Dominants are controlling in real life," he says.

"I know that," I say. "I've met all kinds of Dominants. I've also met submissives who love control in their real lives, which is why they enjoy submitting in the bedroom. But something about you, Ronan O'Connor... You like control in every aspect. I can tell."

His blue gaze smolders as he stares at me. "How exactly can you tell, my beautiful Blossom?"

CHAPTER ELEVEN

Ronan

Her gorgeous face splits into a grin. "I've been around the block a few times, Ronan. I've been in this lifestyle for years. Trust me. I know."

She's more correct than she knows.

It's always been my fantasy to have my submissive on her knees for me in all aspects of my life.

I never had that with Keira because we didn't have a relationship outside of our lifestyle. She and I wanted completely different things.

Another reason why I'm not sure I'm cut out for a relationship. I don't know of any woman—any submissive—who would kneel to me twenty-four seven.

"We shall see, Blossom."

Her cheeks redden. "I suppose so."

June returns with our fries and drinks. "You want some ketchup?" she asks.

"Mayo," I say.

Mary scrunches her face. "Mayo on fries?"

"Don't knock it until you've tried it," I say.

"No thanks. Ketchup for me."

"I'll be right back," June says.

She returns seconds later with a bottle of ketchup and a bottle of mayo. I squirt some onto my plate and swirl a fry in it.

"That looks *so* gross," Mary says.

"You don't like mayonnaise?"

"Of course I do. I'm a New Yorker. I put it on all my deli sandwiches. But fries are for ketchup."

"Or hot sauce," I say.

She wrinkles her nose. "I don't think so."

"Or a mixture of mayo and hot sauce."

She chuckles. "Right. You grew up in New Orleans. It's making a little more sense now."

"Exactly. French Creole roots. Not many people know this, but mayonnaise originated in France."

She raises her eyebrows. "Really?"

"Well…I'm stretching the truth a little. It actually originated in Spain, but the French perfected it. A lot of the great sauces originated in France, though. Bearnaise. Hollandaise."

"Right." Mary grabs a fry and lets it hover over the mayo on my plate for a moment before ultimately choosing ketchup. "You said your grandmother owns a restaurant."

"That she does."

"I don't think I've ever had true Creole cooking," she says.

I pick up a fry, dip it in the mayo, as an idea surges into my mind. "Would you *like* to experience it?"

"Are you offering to cook for me?"

I shake my head. "Are you kidding? I can hardly boil an egg."

"Then you won't make me haggis?"

I chuckle. "I can't stand the stuff."

"And you call yourself a Scotsman?" she teases.

"I call myself American with a Southern mother and Scottish father."

"Your looks say differently."

"That's true." I run my hand down the sleeve of my Jacobite shirt. "My looks say Scotsman through and through. Maybe I need to stop wearing kilts."

"God, no," she says. "You look...*spectacular* in a kilt."

Her compliment warms me. Most people in Scotland no longer wear kilts day to day. I found, in the lifestyle, that they draw attention, so I wear them. Plus I've got damned good legs, if I do say so myself.

"So"—I clear my throat—"my offer to serve you a Creole meal."

"I don't know of any Creole restaurants here in the city, but I'm sure we could find one."

"I'm sure we could, but it might not be authentic."

"Then what are you suggesting?" she asks.

I reach across the table, grab her hand. The slight touch makes my groin tighten. I'm about to suggest something ridiculous, considering we just met twenty-four hours ago. Yet the words tumble out of my mouth with ease. "Come to New Orleans with me."

She drops her mouth open. "What?"

"You showed me part of your world last night. Let me show you part of mine."

The fry she's holding falls to her plate.

"I know I just told you how busy I am, and it's true. But I also said I have people who can take over for me. And right now, taking you to my grandmother's restaurant is way more important than anything else I could be doing."

"Ronan, I have a job."

Right. "You have any vacation time?"

"Two weeks," she says. "But my boss prefers more than a minute's notice."

"I wasn't suggesting we go today."

"When were you suggesting?"

"Tomorrow."

Her jaw drops again. "I can't just drop everything and leave."

"Fair enough. But would you *like* to go?"

"Well…yeah. I *would* like to. I've never been to New Orleans."

"I'm the best tour guide around. I grew up there. I know all the hidden places to go to that capture the true spirit of the Big Easy."

"You mean like Bourbon Street?"

I shake my head. "Absolutely not. Everyone knows about Bourbon Street. I'm talking about holes in the wall, where you can get the true feel."

She bites her lower lip. All I can think about is how I haven't even kissed her lips yet.

I haven't done any of the things I want to do to her.

And right now? I'd settle for simple vanilla sex just to have her.

What the fuck is wrong with me?

"I wish I could," she says.

"Talk to your boss tomorrow."

"The shop is closed on Sundays."

"Can't you call him at home?"

"My boss is a woman, and I suppose I could, but…" She bites her lip again.

Is she actually considering it?

New Orleans is a special place—a place where magic happens. Mary needs some magic in her life right now. She's floundering, in flux, and I want to help her. Because already I feel like she's helped me. She's shown me some of the beauty of my new home, and she's shown me some of the beauty of who she is.

"Sometimes," I say, "you have to grab the brass ring, Blossom. Sometimes...what will heal you is something you've never considered."

CHAPTER TWELVE

Mary

"Who says I need healing?" I say a little more harshly than I mean to.

"Don't take it the wrong way. But you said a scene went bad. You still go to the club, but you don't participate. Something's eating at you. Perhaps a change of scenery will help."

It's odd how strong the desire is to go with him. To run away to New Orleans with Ronan O'Connor.

New Orleans with a Scotsman.

Such a contradiction.

Though half of him comes from the South.

He's a half Creole baby.

I might be sacrificing my job if I take off. "All right. I'll call my boss in the morning."

"What if she says no?"

"Then I can't go with you, Ronan."

"What if I never make the offer again?"

My heart plummets to my stomach. Why is he affecting me so deeply? A spark of anger crawls at the back of my neck. "You're a businessman. A millionaire. You can do whatever you want. I'm a simple working girl, Ronan. My job means a lot to me. I like it, and I'm good at it."

He nods. "I understand."

"Thank you." I blow out a breath. His words are a relief.

But as he swirls his fries in mayo, which suddenly has become endearing to me, I realize that what I want to do—more than anything in the world—is go to New Orleans with him. Because there, I know I will learn all I need to know about Ronan O'Connor.

"Okay, you've talked me into it."

He raises his eyebrows. "You're going to New Orleans?"

"Not quite." I pick up my last fry, reach across the table, and swirl it in the pool of mayo on his plate. "But I'll try your fries and mayo." I bring the fry to my mouth.

It's exactly as I thought it would be.

Disgusting.

I force myself to swallow.

"Well?" Ronan's eyebrows are still raised.

"Never again. It was like eating a fry dipped in lotion."

He laughs then. A big raucous laugh. The first time I've heard him really laugh.

He normally looks so serious. As if he's a Dominant every minute, in all aspects of his life.

But I broke through.

I know then.

I will do whatever it takes.

Though it goes against every aspect of what I understand about myself, I'm going to New Orleans with him tomorrow. I'll convince my boss to give me the last-minute time off.

Nothing has felt quite right in my life since the botched scene with Jack.

This?

This feels right.

"Will you let me see you home?" he asks.

Why the hell not? I've already decided I'm going to New Orleans with him.

"Sure," I tell him.

He gestures to June for the check.

After our check is paid, Ronan rises and helps me from my chair. Most Dominants are polite like that. They treat women with the utmost respect.

Ronan is no different.

We leave the bar, and he hails a cab. Once we're inside, I give the cabbie my address.

We don't talk much during the ride, and he doesn't take my hand. In fact, our bodies aren't touching at all, but I'm hyper aware of him, so very conscious of the effect he has on me. My heart is thumping, and my flesh is warm.

"I'm not too familiar with the city yet," Ronan says when the cabbie drops us off in front of my apartment building.

"I'm lucky to have this place," I say as we walk in and I wave to the doorman. "When my father passed away, we found out he had this apartment as well as his residence. It's rent-controlled. I wouldn't be able to afford it otherwise."

That's not the whole story, of course. My father actually had my current apartment long before my parents' divorce, only we didn't know about it. He carried on with other women *and* men here, which led to the divorce. I didn't know about any of that then—my mother only enlightened me after his death. Since his death was also the death of my college career, because he was the one paying my tuition, I had to get over the thoughts of what went on at this place, move in, and find a job.

Now that I've made the place mine, it's cozy and functional.

"I don't understand the whole rent-control thing," Ronan says.

"It's kind of a mess. I can explain it to you if you're that interested."

"I am interested, but that will give us something to talk about on the plane tomorrow."

"I haven't said I'm going yet."

He pauses. "Forgive me for being so presumptuous."

We take the elevator up to my apartment. It's a studio, and my bed isn't made. It's in sight as soon as we walk in.

Which makes my nerves skitter.

Part of me truly wants to go to bed with Ronan, but he won't just take me to bed. That's too vanilla. He's only interested in a scene, and I don't play at my apartment.

My bed sits against one wall, adorned with a patchwork quilt and throw pillows, none of which are in the proper place, since it's unmade. A nightstand with a small lamp sits beside the bed.

Opposite the bed is my living area. A modest-size futon sits against the wall, and in the corner is a small entertainment center that holds a flat-screen TV. The kitchenette is laid out along one side of the studio and has a compact refrigerator, a two-burner stovetop with oven, and a microwave. My dining area is a tiny table with two chairs.

I walk the few steps to the kitchenette. "Would you like some water or anything? I'm afraid I don't have much alcohol, and definitely no Scotch."

"No, I'm fine. I won't keep you."

I don't know whether I'm relieved or disappointed. "Okay."

"I'm going to call you first thing in the morning," he says. "Be ready to tell me that you're going."

My cheeks warm.

He advances on me, caresses my cheek. "We both know you want to go, Mary."

Electricity sparks straight to my pussy. "Who *wouldn't* want to go?"

"If you do choose to go," he says, "it's all on me. The hotel, the plane fare, everything. Separate rooms, of course."

I hold back a gasp. "I can't allow you to spend that kind of money on me."

"Consider it a gift."

"From a man I hardly know?"

"From a man who wants to know you very much." He tips my chin. "I don't even know your last name."

"It's Sandusky," I babble. "My first name is actually Mariah. I've been called Mary my whole life. I already told you all this, didn't I?"

The almost-smile again. "Thank you for trusting me with your last name."

"I trust most Dominants who come into Black Rose. I know their vetting process. I know you're a good man, Ronan."

Besides, he hasn't so much as tried to kiss me.

I'm squirming just thinking about it—those firm lips on mine, prying them open, his tongue diving into my mouth.

But he's being a complete gentleman.

And my God… That makes me want him even more.

"Good night." He traces his finger over my bottom lip.

I tilt my face upward, close my eyes, and wait…for those lips…

But he leaves, closing the door behind him.

I sigh, clicking my deadbolt, and then I lean against the door and slide down until I'm sitting on the floor.

Damn.

• • •

I don't set my alarm on Sunday mornings, but I wake to the sun streaming through my window. I check the time on my phone.

Nine a.m.

Perfect. I can call Trish to see if I can get some time off.

"Hey Siri, call Trish McMaster."

The phone rings once, twice, three times.

"Mary?"

"Hi, Trish. I'm sorry to bother you on a Sunday."

"That's no problem. What can I do for you?"

"This is going to sound a little bit out of the blue, but I was wondering…is there any way I can have tomorrow off? Maybe the week?"

A pause. She's going to tell me to get fucked, and I don't blame her. Who do I think I am, anyway, asking for time off one day in advance to go off to NOLA with some guy I just met?

Finally, "You haven't taken any vacation yet this year, Mary, so you've got a lot of time available. Normally you give me a lot more notice, though."

My heartbeat accelerates. "I know. It's just that something has come up, and I really do need the time off."

She sighs. "All right. You never ask for any favors, so I'll make this work. But no more than a week, okay?"

A weight floats off my shoulders, but some anxiety about this impulsive decision remains. "You're the best, Trish. Absolutely. No more than a week. It might be less. I'll let you know."

"I appreciate that. Is there anything else you need?"

"No. And thanks again."

I end the call, and then I rise and pad the few steps into my small kitchenette where I start a pot of coffee.

Then I laugh out loud.

I just got a week off, and sure, Ronan said he was serious, but is he? I'm ready to jaunt off to a strange city with a man I hardly know.

A man I trust completely and implicitly.

What a strange life I lead.

If I don't hear from Ronan today, I'll simply call Trish back and say that my plans fell through. Not a big deal—

I jump at a knock at my door. Who the hell? On a Sunday morning?

I'm wearing shorty pajamas—pink and white. I walk to the door in my bare feet and look through my peephole.

I gasp.

Ronan O'Connor stands there.

"Ronan?" I say through the door.

He holds up a white paper bag. "I brought bagels."

I unhook my chain, unlock my deadbolt, and open the door. "What are you doing here?"

He walks in without an invitation. "Bringing bagels. Did you have breakfast yet?"

"No, but why are you—"

"I told you I would call first thing in the morning about our trip to New Orleans. I upgraded that to an in-person call with breakfast. Did you work it out?"

Suddenly, I'm feeling shy. My cheeks warm, and part of me doesn't want to tell Ronan that I worked it out. I feel like I'm being too bold.

I am still a submissive at heart, after all.

"Well?" he asks.

"My boss gave me the week." Then I add quickly, "But I realize we won't be gone for a whole week."

He looks me up and down. "Maybe we will. Who knows?"

Very strange from someone who has said he likes being in control.

"So...when are we leaving?"

"This afternoon."

Didn't he say he wanted to take me out tonight? I guess this is taking me out, all right. I look around my apartment, at my bed, my pot of coffee that's almost done brewing. "That doesn't give me a lot of time to pack."

He shrugs. "Who says you need to pack? We can get everything you need once we land."

I shake my head, chuckling.

"Something funny?"

"It's just...you're being very whimsical for someone who likes to be in control of everything."

He places the bag and cupholder on my small table, takes a seat on my futon, and puts his feet up on the steamer trunk I use for a coffee table. "Whimsical? I don't think anyone's ever used that word to describe me."

"What else would you call it? You invited a woman you barely know to go to your hometown out of state. Now you're saying we don't even need to pack."

He gazes at me. "I'm saying *you* don't need to pack, Blossom. I've already packed. And I plan on caring for your every need during this trip."

I'm frozen for a moment. Bound by his stare and his promises. He *is* in control, I realize, and he's calling me Blossom...

My coffeepot grinds to a stop, jolting me out of my head. "Would you like some coffee?" I ask.

"I don't drink coffee."

"You don't like it?"

"The Brit in me, I suppose. I got into the habit of drinking a strong tea at breakfast."

"I don't have any tea. Sorry."

"That's okay." He points to the cardboard cup holder with two to-go cups. "I brought some for us both. Plus poppyseed bagels with lots of schmear, of course, for my Manhattanite."

I smile. "All right. I'll try tea today."

Coffee is a morning ritual for me, but a nice cup of strong English Breakfast sounds pretty good. I'm not sure how it's going to taste with a bagel and cream cheese, though. Seems like we should be having clotted cream and scones or something.

Going to New Orleans is all about seeing new things, trying new things. I guess that starts right now with our breakfast.

I pull out a couple of plates and a knife for the cream cheese. "Are the bagels sliced?"

"Yes. I wasn't sure if you had a bread knife."

"I do. I love bagels. But pre-sliced is perfect. Now I don't have to dirty it up." I gesture to my small table in the kitchenette. "Have a seat."

Ronan rises from the futon. The table is tiny, and so are the chairs. For a moment I wonder if the chair will collapse under Ronan's weight. He's such a big man.

But it doesn't.

I bring over the plates and utensils while Ronan pulls the paper cups out of the holder.

"I like to drink my tea plain, but I brought some milk and sugar for you just in case." He pulls out a few packets.

"Plain sounds good."

I take the cup, letting it warm my hands. "You know? Let me get us some coffee cups. I don't feel right drinking tea out of a paper cup."

"As you wish."

I grab a couple mugs, set them on the table, and pour my steaming tea into one, inhaling the hearty aroma. "It's funny. I never drink tea at breakfast. But I love it in the afternoon or in the evening."

"You're such an American."

"Last time I checked, so are you."

"True. But I spent the last fifteen years in the UK. Plus, my father always had tea with breakfast when I was little." He flicks his gaze downward and back up. "When he was home, that is." He grabs a bagel, smears some cream cheese on it, and takes a bite. Once he swallows, he says, "New York bagels are unlike anything else. They're so chewy."

I grab one for myself. "They're the best, aren't they?"

"They are good. I'm not a bagel novice. We had them in Louisiana, but they aren't like this."

"Like you said, New York bagels are their own thing. You can't get them anywhere else."

He takes another bite and then sips his tea, raising one eyebrow. "Turns out tea is good with everything. I wasn't sure how it would jibe with the cream cheese."

"Isn't cream cheese like clotted cream?"

"No." He shakes his head. "Clotted cream is more like sweet butter. Another thing you should try."

"I get the feeling I'm not going find any of that in New Orleans."

"Probably not." He leans toward me. "I guess I'll have to take you to Glasgow."

I stop myself from gasping in surprise, but my eyes still widen. "Ronan, we've known each other for forty-eight hours."

"Have we now?"

The look on his face is unreadable. Does he feel the way I feel? As if we've known each other for a lot longer than two days?

I take a bite of bagel, trying to ignore the flutters in my stomach. I have no idea what's going to happen on this trip to New Orleans. Every step with him so far has been a surprise. And not knowing what's coming next just makes it that much more exciting.

CHAPTER THIRTEEN

Ronan

"They say this place is haunted," I tell Mary when the cab driver stops at the Cornstalk Hotel.

She laughs. "Oh?"

"You have your own room, but if the ghosts come and you're afraid, you can always bunk with me."

Her cheeks pink a little. "I suppose we'll see."

The driver opens the door for us, and I help Mary out of the cab. He grabs our suitcases from the trunk and sets them down. I hand him some bills. "Thank you."

"Not at all," he says with a smile.

I grab both of our bags, and we head inside. The Cornstalk Hotel is a boutique hotel located in the heart of the French Quarter, named for the cast-iron cornstalk fence that surrounds it. It's a historic building with intricate details, and it combines old-world charm with modern comforts. I walk with Mary into the lobby, which is filled with antique furniture and an ornate chandelier. I chose it because it seemed to fit what I wanted this trip with Mary to be—unique and unusual.

"Welcome, Mr. O'Connor," the desk clerk says as he wipes

his glasses with a cloth. "It's good to see you back. It's been a long time."

"Ten years at least." I usually stay with my grandmother when I visit, rather than a hotel.

"How are you?" he asks.

"Good. We have two rooms reserved. One for me, of course, and one for Ms. Mariah Sandusky."

He taps on his computer. "Yes, everything's in order. I'll find someone to take your bags."

"No need." I pick them up and turn to Mary. "This is an old hotel, so no elevators. Can you handle two flights of stairs?"

She looks at me with her mouth open. "Do I look like I can't?"

I gaze at her. Even after a long flight, she looks radiant. "You look like you can handle just about anything, Mary." I hand her the keys to both of our rooms. "We're on the second floor. After you."

She heads up the carpeted stairs, and they creak under her feet.

We reach the second floor, and Mary finds her room and unlocks the door.

"It's so strange to be using an actual key," she says. "Most hotels use cards now."

I glance around the hallway, at the rich wood paneling and molding, the vintage artwork, and the ornate carpeting. "Using a key card here would take away from the ambiance, don't you think?"

"Yeah. You're right." She walks into the room, and I follow her, setting her bag on the floor by her bed. "I've never stayed in a haunted hotel before." She looks around. "This is amazing."

She's right. The room has a classic and elegant vibe, with a cherrywood four-poster bed, matching nightstands, plus a writing desk and chair. The bed is adorned with a dark red comforter and plush pillows. Overhead is an ornate crystal chandelier, similar to the one in the lobby.

I stand close to her and whisper, "Don't be surprised if spirits visit you tonight."

"Somehow I doubt that." She lets out a chuckle.

"I guess we'll see." I walk to the door. "I'm going to my room to freshen up and change, and you should, too. I'll pick you up in an hour. Tonight, I'm taking you out for the best dinner of your life."

Her eyes light up. "At your grandmother's place?"

"The one and only." I take the other room key from her. "Enjoy your time alone. And don't let the ghosts scare you off."

I leave then, closing the door, and hear the deadbolt lock behind me.

Good. She's a smart woman. Always aware of keeping herself safe. A good submissive.

Damn. I need to help her find herself again. She's meant to be my submissive. I feel it in my bones.

I enter my room. It's a similar size to Mary's, but the decor is completely different. My bed is brass, with blue-and-green linens and mahogany night tables. My desk is an old rolltop, and my chandelier is slightly less elegant, with light green glass.

I brought a utility kilt with me, but I probably won't wear it. New Orleans is more a jeans and button-down kind of place. It's a good thing we're not here during Mardi Gras. Someone as beautiful as Mary would be inundated with beads. Inundated with requests to show her tits.

Which will *not* happen on my watch.

I always feel grimy after traveling, so I take a quick shower and change. There's an underground club here in the city. I'm no longer a member, but I know the owners, and I can get in anytime I want to. After a few days of showing Mary around, helping her see she can trust me implicitly, perhaps she'll consent to a scene there.

In the meantime, I could seduce her. We could have regular sex here in the hotel. I'd love for our first time to be at a club, though. I want it to be an actual scene. That's who I am, and I believe it's who she is as well.

One bad scene doesn't change a submissive. Doesn't change the soul of who she is.

I towel my hair dry and dress in a clean pair of jeans and a black Jacobite shirt.

I check emails, deal with some business, and then it's time to take Mary to dinner. I already called my grandmother to tell her we were coming. She promised me the best table in the house and a tasting menu that would give Mary the best of Creole cuisine.

I make sure I have my wallet and key, and then I leave the room, locking the door. Then I knock three times on Mary's door, which is directly next to mine, though not an adjoining room.

She opens it, and—

My God...

Black leggings, silver sandals, and a white tunic that shows a touch of the lace on her bra and her cleavage. Simple, really, but on Mary, it's elegant. Her auburn hair is pulled up into a messy bun, and on her ears are simple silver hoops.

I didn't think it was possible, but she looks even more beautiful than she did last night at the club in that burgundy dress.

"You look nice," she says.

I gaze at her, my groin responding. "You look amazing. Are you ready?"

She nods, and I hold out my arm. She links hers through it, and together we walk down the stairs and out of the hotel to the cab waiting for us.

"Where is your grandma's restaurant?" she asks.

"Near the underbelly."

"What does that mean?"

I narrow my gaze. "There's something I haven't told you yet about my grandmother."

She tilts her head. "What's that?"

"Not only is she the best cook in all of New Orleans, she's also a Voodoo priestess."

Mary's eyes nearly pop out of her head.

"Is that a surprise to you, New York girl?"

She smirks at me. "Ronan, I don't believe the hotel is haunted, and I don't believe in Voodoo."

"You don't have to believe in anything." I help her into the cab. "I only ask that you respect the fact that others do."

"Of course. I would never disrespect anyone's beliefs." She scoots to the opposite side of the backseat.

I sit down beside her, and the driver closes the car door. "My grandmother is very unique. In fact, you remind me of her."

She laughs a little. "I remind you of a Voodoo priestess?"

"Not that part, but that you're unique. Like the way you love the Rockefeller Center more than the Empire State Building."

"And the way I like ketchup on my fries?" She shakes her head. "I'm hardly unique, Ronan."

"I'll be the judge of that."

"Regardless," she says, "I'm sure I'll like your grandmother."

I squeeze her hand. "I have a feeling, Mary, that you're going to absolutely love her."

CHAPTER FOURTEEN

Mary

"So your grandmother is Creole?" I ask once the cab is moving. "Or Cajun? I don't really know the difference."

"That's a good question," Ronan replies. "The two words are often used interchangeably, but they're two distinct groups. The Cajun come from the French-speaking Acadians who were kicked out of Nova Scotia by the British in the eighteenth century. A lot of them settled in southern Louisiana and developed their own unique culture and cuisine.

"Creoles, where I come from, are a mixed-race cultural group who were born in Louisiana and are descended from French, Spanish, African, and Native American ancestors. Creole cuisine, in my humble opinion—though I may be biased—is more refined than Cajun cuisine."

"More refined?"

"It uses a lot of butter, cream, and wine."

"That makes it refined?"

"Okay, it just makes it delicious." He gives my hand a squeeze. "My grandmother uses a lot of fresh seafood, vegetables, and herbs. Sauces and gravies are also big in Creole."

"Interesting. What kind of things does your grandmother have on her menu?"

"Shrimp creole is one of my favorites. Her crawfish étouffée is amazing as well, though that's more Cajun than Creole. But she serves it anyway because it's popular around these parts."

My stomach lets out a well-timed growl. "What else?"

"Gumbo, of course. But don't worry about any of this. I've already told her what to serve us."

I give him a side-eye and lean toward him, lowering my voice. "I may be a submissive, Ronan, but I don't want you ordering for me."

"I'm asking you to trust my judgment. I grew up here. I know this food, and I know what my grandmother makes best. Let me ask you this. Is there anything specifically that you won't eat?"

"Brussels sprouts. And lamb."

"You eat all the other meats? Seafood? Mushrooms?"

"Yeah. I love most meat and seafood. Most vegetables. I'm not crazy about beets."

He nods. "I don't think there are lot of beets in Creole cuisine. Or Brussels sprouts. You're going to be fine, Mary. Please. Trust me."

I widen my eyes a bit at his use of the word *please*.

Dominants don't often use that word. It's understood that the submissive wants to please their Dominant. They don't have to ask.

Of course, we're not in a scene right now.

We're on a...date.

My God... How long has it been since I've been on a date? Not since Lucas...

"All right, Ronan. I'll trust you. And I will try everything.

But I reserve the right to not continue eating something if I don't like it."

"Of course. I wouldn't expect you to eat anything that you don't like. But I know you're going to love everything my grandmother puts in front of you tonight."

"I hope I do." I lean back a little, relaxing. "Tell me more about your grandmother."

"Her father was French, her mother African, but she was born here in New Orleans."

"That's so interesting."

"Do you know your ancestry?" Ronan asks me.

"Not really. I did some research once on my last name, Sandusky. There are two contradictory opinions. It could be from a Native American tribe or it could be Polish."

"Those are two totally different origins."

"I know. My father was no help. Of course now he's gone, but Sandusky, as you may know, is a city in Ohio, where the Wyandotte tribes lived. Some say it's an Indigenous peoples' name. Some say it's an Americanized form of the Polish name Sandowski. I honestly have no idea."

"What about your mom's side?"

"Her maiden name was Nelson, so, English."

"Or Scottish," he says. "Probably comes from the given name Neal which comes from the Gaelic name Niall, which means champion."

I raise an eyebrow. "You know Gaelic?"

"Just as a hobby. Once I moved back to Scotland after high school, I dabbled a little, mo leannan." He winks.

I resist the urge to call him a nerd. "Sounds like you dabbled more than a little."

"Not really. No one speaks Gaelic anymore, so it's kind of like studying Latin. It's a dead language but has its beauty."

"For someone who's half Creole you seem fully Scottish to me."

His face lights up. "I do love Scotland, for sure. While I was there, it truly felt like home to me."

"So you only came back because of the deal with Braden Black?"

He pauses a moment. Then, "It was a good time for me to return to the States. The business deal, of course, but there were other reasons."

Curiouser and curiouser. "What other reasons?"

"Maybe I'll tell you sometime, Mary."

The cabbie comes to a stop.

"But not now," he says, "because we've arrived."

CHAPTER FIFTEEN

Ronan

Chez Yvette looks the same as it always has. The Creole decor features bright colors and bold patterns, with red-and-orange striped upholstery in the waiting area. The walls are painted a warm terracotta.

The building is old, with exposed brick and wood beams that add historic character and warmth. The dining room is an eclectic mix of chairs, tables, and other furnishings—some wooden, some wrought-iron. I spent many an afternoon dusting those chairs when I was a kid.

Jazz posters, Mardi Gras masks, and vintage photos of New Orleans landmarks grace the walls, and potted palms and fresh flowers create a lush, inviting atmosphere.

My grandmother, Yvette Thibodeaux, comes toward us swiftly. She is in her late sixties, but she doesn't look a day over forty. Her light brown skin is still mostly free from wrinkles.

"Ronan, you gorgeous boy!" She grabs me in a ferocious hug.

Mémé, as I grew up calling her, is only a bit over five feet tall. I tower over her, but she grabs me as if I'm still a toddler running to her.

She pulls back. "Let me look at you. Just as handsome as ever. I'm so glad you're back in the States. But why are you up in New York when you could be down here?"

Before I have a chance to answer, she turns and grabs Mary's hands.

"And who might you be, you gorgeous thing?"

"Mémé, this is Mary," I say. "Mary Sandusky."

She reaches up to cup Mary's cheeks. "You are just beautiful, chérie."

"It's nice to meet you, Mrs…"

"Thibodeaux. Yvette Thibodeaux."

"I hope it's not rude to say this," Mary says, "but you look so young. You're absolutely beautiful."

Her brown eyes beam. "Good genetics, apparently. But I think it's also important to be young at heart. Ronan's mother's been trying to get me to retire, but I won't hear of it. I had her when I was merely fifteen, you know."

"So I've heard. It's amazing that you were able to accomplish so much and also raise a child at such a young age."

"Chérie, you do what you have to do. Ronan has told me to break out the finest on our menu for the two of you. I saved you the best table in the house."

I take Mary's hand and lead her to the table. It's a round table and can actually seat six, but Mémé has reserved it for us. Place settings for two are already on the table, seated close together so we can see everything in the restaurant.

"We're going to start," I say, "with turtle soup with a splash of sherry."

"With a Sazerac, of course," Mémé says.

"What's a Sazerac?" Mary asks.

"It's a classic New Orleans cocktail made with rye whiskey,

absinthe, Peychaud's bitters, and a sugar cube," Mémé says.

"Absinthe?" she asks.

"It's an anise liqueur. Tastes like licorice."

"I'll try anything once," Mary says. "Sure. Bring me a Sazerac."

"I will do that." Mémé smiles. "And your turtle soup will arrive a few minutes after the cocktails. I'll have Greta bring you some water as well."

"Perfect," I tell Mémé. "Merci beaucoup."

"De rien, mon cher." Mémé flits away, looking absolutely gorgeous in her bohemian-style skirt and blouse.

"She doesn't look like a Voodoo priestess," Mary says.

"Oh?" I raise my eyebrows. "What is a Voodoo priestess supposed to look like?"

Her cheeks redden. "I don't know."

"Did you expect her to come to our table and sacrifice a chicken or something?"

"Of course not."

"Voodoo is a religion, Mary—a religion that my grandmother takes seriously. The same as some Christians, Jews, and Muslims take their religion seriously."

"I didn't mean—"

"I know you didn't. It's not your fault that the word 'voodoo' has connotations that actual practitioners don't like."

"Actually, since we're here, I *would* like to learn more about it. More about everything here. The cuisine, the religion, the culture. I've hardly been out of New York."

"Really?"

She nods. "I'm kind of a homebody. I make decent money at the store, and the only reason I don't live paycheck to paycheck is because I have such good rent, thanks to my father. But as you know, being in the lifestyle can be expensive. Clubwear, toys, the rest."

"You have your own toys?" I ask.

"I get a discount at the store. So yes, I do."

"Do you ever use them?"

"On myself? No. And I don't take them to the club. I guess I just always thought it would be good to have them on hand if I ever... You know."

"Wanted to play outside the club?"

"Yes." She looks down at her napkin. "But that hasn't happened. Yet."

The word *yet* does not escape my notice.

She hasn't ruled it out.

The idea has merit. She's obviously struggling with playing at the club. Perhaps playing *outside* the club is an option to help her get through her issues.

A server I don't recognize brings our drinks.

I raise mine. "To us."

Mary picks up her drink and clinks it to mine. "To us."

She's never had a Sazerac, so I take the lead. I swish the liquid around in the glass, careful not to spill any. Then I let the floral aroma waft toward me.

"It's strong," I warn, "but it's delicious once you get used to it. Rye whiskey can be a little bit harsh compared to a single malt scotch, which is my favorite."

"I like a bourbon every now and then," Mary says. "Not a big fan of scotch."

"This will be harsh compared to a bourbon as well. You have to ease into it. The sugar cube has been soaked in the bitters, and the whole drink is muddled with some water and a twist of lemon. It will have a strong whiskey flavor, but the sugar and the herbal notes of the bitters will balance it. Let it sit on your tongue for a moment and enjoy the flavors. That'll ease the harshness of it going down your throat."

I take a drink, following my own advice. I let it sit on my tongue for a moment, easing the harshness of the rye, and when I swallow, it burns my throat in a good way.

Mary takes a drink…and then coughs.

"Okay?"

"Yeah. I didn't let it sit on my tongue first."

"Rookie mistake." I take another drink. "Try again. If it doesn't grow on you, I'll get you something else."

She nods, takes another sip. This time when she swallows, it goes down more easily, based on what I see from her neck and facial expression.

"Better?" I ask.

"Yeah." She twists her lips. "It's… I can taste licorice. It's almost a fresh taste."

"That's the absinthe and the bitters." I reach for the cocktail menu. "Would you like me to order you something else?"

She shakes her head. "I'm here for the full immersive experience. I'm going to eat and drink whatever you put in front of me tonight."

Her words arouse me. Words of pure submission. Words of letting me have control over this meal. Over her life—at least for the next couple of hours.

My groin tightens.

God, I want my cock inside her tonight.

I've waited long enough.

Then I erase the thought from my mind. Waited long enough? I've only known her for a few days.

She's worth it.

If I have to wait a year to have her, I will.

Did that thought really just cross my mind? I've never waited a year for a woman.

Mary takes another drink of her Sazerac. "You know? This definitely has promise."

"I'm glad you think so."

The server returns with glasses of water for both of us along with our turtle soup.

"Okay," Mary says when the server excuses himself. "Tell me what I'm about to eat. And be very specific."

"Do you want all the history?"

"Sure." She leans toward the soup and inhales. "Like I said, the total immersive experience."

"I've heard the story since I was a kid. My grandmother told us stories about all of her food. Turtle soup has its roots here in New Orleans. It was inspired by the turtle soup that was popular in France, where turtle meat was considered a delicacy. The original recipe here called for snapping turtle meat, which was readily available in nearby swamps and bayous."

She nods. "What kind of turtle is in this soup?"

"My grandmother still uses snapping turtle, but it's ethically sourced. Some restaurants that don't want to go to the expense use other meats."

Mary wrinkles her forehead. "Then it's not really turtle soup, is it?"

"No."

"I've heard of mock turtle soup," she says. "Is that what it is, then?"

"If you don't use actual turtle, then it's always mock turtle soup. But they still call it turtle soup, and with the same spices, they can mimic the flavor pretty well."

She stares at her bowl but doesn't reach for her spoon. "What else is in the soup?"

"Mémé uses a traditional tomato-based broth and seasons it with bay leaf, thyme, garlic, cloves, and black pepper. It's delicious. Rich and flavorful. She adds a touch of cayenne for a little bit of heat. Then the sherry adds a certain je ne sais quoi."

"What does that mean?"

"Je ne sais quoi? It means 'I don't know what.'" And I thought that was a common phrase in America, even for people who don't know a word of French.

"What do you mean you don't know?" she presses. "You just said it was a touch of sherry."

"True."

"So why would you say you don't know when you know what it is?"

I give her my stern and dominating look. "I don't think you're asking me that because you don't know the answer. I think you're asking because you're trying to put off actually tasting the soup."

Her eyes widen slightly, and her whole body responds by tensing. My cock throbs in my jeans.

Yes, Mary Sandusky is still a submissive.

She's still Blossom.

And I'm going to make her blossom. *Effloresce*.

Under my touch. Under my dominant hand.

Mary Sandusky will blossom into something she never even imagined she could be.

CHAPTER SIXTEEN

Mary

I take another sip of my Sazerac. This drink isn't for the faint of heart. While I enjoy a cocktail, I'm not a huge drinker. I never have been. When you're in the lifestyle, you must keep your faculties alert at all times. Whether you're a Dominant or a submissive or a switch, you need to always be in full control of your body. For a submissive, it's doubly important so that you can let your Dominant know if anything is going wrong.

So I don't drink a lot, and this drink is damned strong.

The problem is with every sip, it tastes a little bit better. It's growing on me in a way I never thought possible.

I'm also beginning to feel it. Only slightly, but that little tingle in my head… There it is.

And Ronan is right…

I'm putting off tasting the soup. I mean…it's turtle.

But I just told him I'm here for the immersive experience, so I'm going to immerse myself in this soup. I take a spoonful, bring it to my lips, blow on it, and…

I widen my eyes as the soup glides over my tongue. It's delicious, especially with the dollop of sherry. I take another drink of the Sazerac. It complements the turtle soup as if the two were made to go together, which they probably were.

When the server comes by and asks if we want another drink, Ronan raises his eyebrows at me.

"It's delicious," I say, "but I'd better stop."

"You sure?" Ronan asks. "Sazerac is excellent with all of the food that's coming. Or we could switch to a full-bodied, lusty red wine."

I think for a moment. I don't want to get even slightly tipsy tonight. "Tell you what. A small glass of wine with the main course sounds delectable. But as much as I like the Sazerac, I'm going to have to say no to further drinks."

"You heard the lady." Ronan hands his empty glass to the server. "But I'll take another."

Ronan is probably barely buzzed. The man is used to drinking top-shelf scotch, so one Sazerac probably does nothing for him. Plus, he's huge.

If he's a good Dominant, then he knows the unwritten rules as well as I do. You don't overindulge in alcohol or any other kind of mind-numbing substance if play is on the table.

Of course, I'm putting that cart way before the horse.

I haven't consented to a scene, and he hasn't asked for one.

Besides, that antique furniture at the Cornstalk Hotel is definitely *not* conducive to a scene.

Our server returns, clears the turtle soup dishes, and provides our next course.

"Shrimp remoulade," he says. "Enjoy."

Shrimp are arranged neatly in a shallow bowl, and a creamy, light yellow sauce is drizzled over them.

"So this is an appetizer?" I ask.

"Actually, I asked Mémé to create a tasting menu for us, including all of my favorite dishes. It just so happens that all of the dishes are excellent examples of Creole cuisine. This is shrimp remoulade—boiled shrimp with remoulade sauce, which is made with mayonnaise, mustard, and Creole seasoning."

"You and your mayo." I smile.

"Mayonnaise happens to be the best sauce out there. Combine it with mustard and some basic Creole seasoning, and you have a tangy goodness that you're going to love."

"I'm not a big fan of greasy sauces," I say.

"Mayonnaise isn't greasy. You said you eat it on sandwiches."

"Yes, it's a condiment, Ronan. Not a sauce. And yes it's greasy. Its major component is oil."

"Open your mind, Blossom." He gives me that almost-smile again, making my loins heat. "Mémé makes her own mayonnaise from scratch. She uses only cold-pressed avocado oil."

"Interesting. Not olive oil?"

"Extra-virgin olive oil has a very distinct flavor," he says. "She prefers avocado. Avocado oil, egg yolks, and just a touch of vinegar. Her mayonnaise is excellent, and I bet you'd love it on your fries."

"Are we having fries tonight?"

Ronan gives me a slight smile. "I don't think fries are on the menu."

"Then I won't be able to try this tangy remoulade sauce on my fries, will I?"

"Tomorrow. Tomorrow I will order you a great big order of fries with a side of remoulade."

"Okay. But when will we have beignets and coffee?"

"Tomorrow morning, of course. So you know what beignets are?"

"I'm a homebody, Ronan. That doesn't mean I don't read or watch TV."

"We'll go to Café du Monde," Ronan says. "Best beignets

in the big easy."

"Not here? At Chez Yvette?"

"Mémé does make a pretty good one. We could come back here tomorrow. But Café du Monde is a New Orleans staple."

"Okay, then Café du Monde, it is. This trip is all up to you, Ronan." I look down at the bowl of shrimp. "You're the expert."

"You *are* submissive, aren't you?"

I look over my shoulder and then lean across the table. "Was there really any doubt? But I'm not submitting to you because I want you to control me during this trip. I'm letting you take the lead because you're *from* here. You grew up here, and I know nothing about New Orleans."

A slow smile touches his lips. Yes, it's actually a smile this time.

He's so handsome, but so dark and broody. He doesn't smile much, and I've only heard him laugh once. Typical for most Dominants I know.

I'm going to make this man smile while we're here.

I'm going to make him smile at least twice every day.

"You have an interesting look on your face, Mary."

"Do I?"

"Yes. It's a bit mischievous. Seems like you're up to no good."

I smirk. "Maybe I'm not."

"Well, then, just be sure you don't take too many liberties. I may have to smack that sweet ass of yours."

His words travel straight to my pussy at lightning speed.

God...

I haven't felt like this since...

Have I ever?

Sure, I get turned on. I love a good scene. I love a good spanking.

But oh. My. God.

"Try the shrimp," he says.

Since I'm not sure how to eat it, I watch him take the first bite. Then I spear a piece of shrimp with my fork, swirl it in the sauce, and bring it to my lips.

A splash of flavors hits my tongue.

I love shrimp, first of all. I could eat shrimp cocktail at every meal.

But this is served hot, not cold, and the shrimp is cooked to perfection. It crunches slightly under my teeth, and it's not even slightly rubbery. And the sauce... The mayonnaise is cut by the acidity of the mustard, and the Creole seasoning... I don't know what's in it, but it's delicious.

Once I swallow, Ronan looks at me.

"Well?"

"It's amazing," I admit. "Absolutely delicious."

"Despite the greasy sauce?"

"Despite the greasy sauce." Which isn't greasy, but I don't say that. "How many courses are we having?"

"Eight."

My eyes nearly pop out of my head. "Do you really think I can eat eight courses?"

"I told you. It's more of a tasting menu. It will be just enough to satisfy you, and then we'll move onto the next course."

A sliver of excitement spurts through me. I do enjoy eating, but I rarely eat with a Dominant. I don't date. It's not who I am.

But I'm enjoying this date with this gorgeous Scotsman-slash-child of New Orleans who rarely smiles but whose voice sends electric pulses straight between my legs.

Our server comes by with Ronan's second Sazerac. He places the cocktail on the table and fills my water. "You sure I can't get you another drink, ma'am?"

I'm tempted, for sure. "No, thank you. But I will have whatever red wine the gentleman chooses when we get to our main course."

"Go ahead and bring her the wine now. In fact, we will have a bottle of whatever Syrah-based Côtes du Rhône my grandmother has available."

"Absolutely, sir."

"Côtes du Rhône?" I ask after the server leaves us.

"It's from the southern Rhône region of France, using the great varietals of Syrah and Grenache, mostly. Syrah is a bold grape, with spicy characteristics that pair well with the best Creole cuisine."

"You know a lot about food and wine."

"I know a lot about Creole food and the wines that complement it. I don't know a lot about Scottish food, because frankly, Scottish food isn't that exciting."

"You mean haggis?"

His lips curve upward slightly. "There's a lot more to Scottish cuisine than haggis. It's not as spicy and vibrant as Creole cuisine, but it's good in its own right. We get some great salmon from the coasts. And of course our shortbread is to die for."

"One day maybe you can take me out to a Scottish meal."

"I think I'd have to take you to Glasgow. Perhaps Edinburgh. If we go in the next month or so, we could catch the military tattoo."

His words should send me running. I've known him for how long? Two days? But already I crossed state lines with him. And the thought of him taking me to Scotland?

I kind of like it.

"What's the military tattoo?"

"It's a big festival with Scottish military bagpipes."

"That might be fun."

But I feel my cheeks burn. I don't want him to think I'm asking him to take me on another trip—this time overseas. He's already gifted me with this trip, which feels strange, but also good.

So I stop talking and finish my shrimp.

The server comes to take our plates, and then he brings the next course.

And God, it smells amazing.

"What is this?" I ask.

"The pièce de résistance," Ronan says. "Crawfish étouffée."

"I've never tasted crawfish."

"They're like mini lobsters, and they're succulent and delicious. You're going to love this."

I inhale the savory fragrance of onion, garlic, and seafood. "It smells wonderful. Very peppery."

"Three different kinds of pepper. Black pepper, white pepper, and cayenne pepper."

"So it's going to be spicy."

"Absolutely. But don't take a bite until"—he eyes the server, who's carrying a bottle of wine toward us—"we have some wine. Good man," he says to the server.

"Would you like to taste, sir?" the server asks.

"I think the lady should taste."

I widen my eyes. "Really, Ronan, you should taste. I don't know anything about wine."

"There's no big secret to wine tasting," Ronan says. "Wine snobs would tell you otherwise, but frankly, isn't the most important thing that you enjoy it?"

"You mean rather than contemplate the nuances of it?" I smile.

"Exactly."

The server shows me the wine bottle. I'm not sure what I'm supposed to say. Then he hands me the cork.

Ronan nods. "Sniff the cork."

I obey.

Yes, *I obey.*

And right now, sitting with Ronan, if he told me to get under the table and give him a blow job in this public restaurant, I'm pretty sure I'd obey that, too. The way he looks at me with those smoldering blue eyes. My panties are already melting.

The server pours a tiny amount of wine into my glass.

I've seen people taste wine before. I pick up the glass, swirl the liquid, notice its color.

Red. It's the color of red wine.

I sniff it.

Smells like wine.

And then I take a taste.

And it tastes...like red wine.

But it is also quite good. It's bold, with a touch of spice, and it makes my mouth slightly dry. That's the tannins. I do know a little bit about wine. Just a little.

I look at the server. "It's delicious."

I put my glass down, and he fills it halfway. Then he fills Ronan's.

Once the server is gone, Ronan picks up his fork. "Now, take a taste of the étouffée. Make sure you get a crawfish in this first bite. Swallow it, feel the pepper going down your throat, and then take a drink of the wine."

I obey him, and oh boy—the sauce is peppery, but in a good way. Such a different peppery from Thai or Indian cuisine, which I eat a lot in the city.

Way different.

I take a drink of the wine, and it coats my throat so smoothly, easing the pepper while complementing it at the same time.

"Well?" Ronan asks.

"I've never experienced anything like that before."

"What do you mean?"

I lick my lips. "It's almost as if... And I know this is impossible, but it's almost like I can taste it not only on my tongue and in my mouth, but in my throat as well." What I don't say is how erotic the experience is. Simple eating, but Ronan has made it into a turn-on.

"That's the pepper combo. Simple peppers, individually. But together, they create something explosive."

"Delicious."

"Can you taste the crawfish?"

"I can. It's...rich."

"We'll have to go to a crawfish boil while we're here. Crawfish is delicious in étouffée, but you can't beat it by itself with just a little bit of drawn butter. So good."

"I feel like you're trying to fatten me up on this trip," I joke.

"I like a little meat on a woman, Mary." He gives me a wink.

"I'm at a weight that works for me," I say.

"Oh yes." He burns me with his gaze. "It definitely works for you."

CHAPTER SEVENTEEN

Ronan

Our next course is Mémé's famous red beans and rice, and she adds a spicy kick to it.

My bright idea was to introduce Mary to the best of Creole cuisine, but we're only on plate number four, and now I just want to be alone with her.

I don't even know what to expect. She's made it clear she doesn't want a scene. That's not where her head is at these days.

That will change. Already I know this. But I won't force it. I'm not that kind of a Dominant. I don't get off on forcing my submissive to do something she doesn't want to do.

No.

What draws me to domination is the control. The control I never had as a child who wanted nothing more than to have his parents home for more than a few days at a time.

I learned what I *didn't* want as an adult. No family, no children. Simply a relationship where I was in control and I called the shots. Never would I put a child through that feeling that he wasn't important to the two people who were supposed to love him the most.

I've already got a hard-on underneath the table. And being in jeans instead of my kilt...it's damned uncomfortable.

"Something I recognize," Mary says. "This is red beans and rice."

"Good eye."

She smiles coyly. "Not so good. I recognize red beans, and I recognize rice. Plus there's some sausage, too. Is it andouille?"

"The one and only."

Mary has only taken a few sips of her wine. She's serious about not drinking too much. I respect that a lot.

"This wine is going to be great with red beans and rice, and of course also with the jambalaya that comes next."

"I'm glad these are small servings," she says. "Or I'd be done by now."

"That's what a tasting menu is. A series of small plates."

"It's been great, Ronan. Really. I can't thank you enough."

"No thanks are necessary. I'm happy to do it."

She gazes at me then, her head slightly cocked, her eyes slightly narrowed.

She's wondering what I expect in return.

She'll be surprised to know I expect nothing.

But I do hope...

I want to get her in bed so badly. I'll engage in vanilla sex if that's what it takes. Me on top of her, thrusting into her sweet little cunt.

I take a bite of my red beans and rice. There's no cream in the dish, but it always has a creamy taste to me. Creamy, spicy, delectable.

Same as I imagine Mary's pussy will taste.

My God...

I look at her then. "Would you like to get out of here?"

"But this is only the fourth course."

"True. And I can't disappoint my grandmother."

"Why are you in such a hurry, Ronan?"

"I want to be alone with you, Mary. If that's not what you want, I can accept that. But it's what I want. It's what I've wanted since I first laid eyes on you."

She looks down, pushes her red beans and rice around on the small plate. "Ronan...I don't know that I'm ready to go there. A scene."

"I just want to be alone with you. I didn't say we need to have sex. Or play. Or do a scene."

Of course, that's what I ultimately desire. But with Mary, I wouldn't mind strolling through the seamy side of the New Orleans underbelly. Showing her where the vampires live, where the ghosts haunt.

She takes a bite of her red beans and rice. "Delicious. I'm not sure which is my favorite. I guess if I had to choose, I'd say the crawfish. This is a close second. Along with the shrimp and the turtle soup. Which I guess is everything."

"That's the marvel of Creole cuisine. It's all so delicious, you don't really have favorites. It's funny that Mémé didn't prepare shrimp Creole tonight. That's one of my favorites."

"You mean you didn't request it?"

"No. I just asked her to put together an eight-course meal showcasing her best, and I have to admit, she is doing that."

"So jambalaya is next?" Mary says after swallowing her bite of red beans and rice.

"Yes. And then fried catfish and grillades and grits. Dessert will be Mémé's famous bread pudding."

"Not bananas foster?"

"Bananas foster is delicious and originated here in New Orleans, but bread pudding is more of a Creole favorite. Mémé does it like no other. Her whiskey sauce is legendary."

"Creole seems to use a lot of alcohol in cooking. First the sherry in the turtle soup. And now the whiskey sauce for the bread pudding."

"Probably no more than any other cuisine. Creole has a lot of origins in French cuisine, though, and the French use a lot of alcohol in their cooking."

"Do they?" she asks.

I nod. "Bananas foster may be a flambé treat, but the French originated the flambé. With crepes suzette."

"You know so much about cooking, Ronan. Have you ever thought of going into the culinary arts?"

"God, no. I hate cooking. Can't even boil an egg. I learned all this stuff from Mémé. I spent a lot of time with her when I was a kid. This restaurant was basically my home."

"But your parents…"

"Were never home," I say, and I hope to leave it at that. "But I do owe my parents a lot. Now that my father's retired, I run the business."

"Do you enjoy your work?"

"I do. Some days more than others. I'm a bit of a micromanager, but I'm learning to delegate. I like what I do. It's a challenge. But it's still work, Mary. It's not play."

She bites her lip at the word *play*.

"I know that." She looks down at her plate, spears a piece of sausage on her fork. "I can't thank you enough for this trip."

"I told you before, Mary. I have no expectations other than that you enjoy yourself. And that maybe we get to know each other. Whether that includes any time in the bedroom doesn't matter to me."

The words are so odd.

All those years with Keira, and I thought we had something special. A Dominant-submissive relationship with no expectations of anything more. Then she grew to want more, but I didn't.

Yet here I sit with a woman I barely know. Who I desperately want to know, and who I'm willing to go the distance for.

Any other woman who intrigued me but didn't want to do a scene? I'd move on.

There's something about Mary.

I keep my lips from curving up at the movie reference in my head.

But there is something about her—something special, something intriguing, something captivating.

Something almost…extraordinary.

She's beautiful, yes. But is she the most beautiful woman I've ever laid eyes on? No.

She has a lovely and hot body. But is it the hottest body I've ever laid eyes on? Granted, I haven't seen her naked, but based on what I have seen? No.

Her tits are luscious, but not the biggest.

Her legs are long and shapely, but not the longest and most shapely.

Perhaps it's that spray of freckles across her nose.

Or her hair, darker red than my own but still blazing.

Or her deep brown eyes. Eyes that look like they can see straight into my soul.

More likely it's her fragility. Someone hurt her. Changed her. Caused her to lose something. I want to help her find it. Find herself again. And the more I get to know her, the more I'm drawn to her. The more I want to get inside her to help her heal.

And damn, I want to get inside her physically as well. Big time.

Our server comes by, clears the dishes, and then brings the

jambalaya.

Mémé's jambalaya is wonderful. Her classic rice dish is made with a variety of meats that include chicken, sausage, shrimp, and pieces of catfish along with peas and corn and carrots.

I bring a forkful to my mouth, expecting my taste buds to explode.

But I don't taste anything.

Because as I stare at Mary, all I can think about is getting my tongue between her legs.

I know she is going to be creamier than the red beans and rice and sweeter than the bread pudding and more robust than the rich whiskey sauce.

Somehow...

Somehow I will taste her.

"My God, it's like each dish is more delicious the last." Mary smiles.

Fried catfish is next, which is delicious and succulent but bland compared to the last spicy dishes.

Then grillades and grits—thinly sliced beef and pork simmered in tomato-based gravy and served over creamy grits.

And they *are* creamy.

But not as creamy as I know Mary's pussy will be.

Mary finishes her glass of wine. "I'm not sure I can eat another bite, Ronan."

"You can. You've got to try the bread pudding."

"Is it really made with stale bread?"

"Yes. The best cooks don't waste anything. Stale bread, eggs, milk, and sugar. And then, of course, Mémé's special whiskey sauce."

"What kind of whiskey does she use?"

"Usually bourbon."

"You mean she doesn't use scotch for you?"

A smile tugs at my lips. "Scotch would not be right for the whiskey sauce. You need the caramel taste of a bourbon."

She lifts her eyebrows. "Not the dirty flavor of a scotch?"

"Yes, I know. You're not a fan."

"It honestly tastes like dirt to me."

"Perhaps I'll make a scotch drinker out of you," I say.

"Somehow I doubt it. Though I did enjoy the Sazerac. The rye was harsh, but it didn't taste like peat moss."

"You may not agree if you drink it straight. You get a lot of floral and sweet from the bitters and sugar."

"It was delicious."

"Tomorrow I'll take you for a Pimm's cup. That's another famous New Orleans cocktail, and they're very refreshing and delicious."

"I'm not a huge drinker, Ronan."

"I know that. I can tell. But you have to try one Pimm's cup. It's more of an afternoon drink."

"All right. As I said, I'll defer to your expertise while we're here."

I gaze at her face then. Take in her beauty.

In a way, it's a very innocent beauty. The girl-next-door beauty. Even though I know that she, as a seasoned submissive, is far from innocent. But perhaps she's innocent in other ways. In the art of cuisine and libations, for sure.

The odd thing is…

I want to know more about her. And not just in the bedroom.

Which is odd, considering I couldn't give the same to Keira, who I care for, and with whom I shared a good chemistry as a Dominant to her submissive.

I have no idea if Mary and I have any chemistry in that way.

I desperately want to find out.

CHAPTER EIGHTEEN

Mary

Back at the hotel, I'm surprised that I don't feel bloated. We had quite a large dinner, but the portions were small, and though I was getting full, I feel fine now.

"Tomorrow," Ronan says as he sees me to my hotel room door, "I'll knock on your door at ten a.m. We'll go to Café Du Monde for beignets and coffee."

Disappointment threads through me. I'm not ready for this evening to end.

Ronan cups my cheek and strokes my jawline. "Good night, Mary."

"Good night."

He turns away.

"Ronan?"

He looks over his shoulder at me. "Yes?"

"I..."

"What is it?"

"Never mind. It can wait."

His gaze darkens. "Do you want me to come in your room, Mary?"

"Yes. I do."

"All you had to do was ask."

He comes back, takes the key from me, and unlocks the door. I walk in, and he follows.

Then he cups both my cheeks. I can't resist a face holder. Especially when searing blue eyes are gazing into mine.

"What do you want, Mary? Tell me, and it's yours."

"I don't kiss," I say bluntly.

"That's a shame. You have beautiful lips."

"I mean...I don't kiss when I play. I don't like to get that personal with a Dom. It's not something I've ever really enjoyed, anyway."

"Then you haven't been kissing the right people."

"Maybe not," I admit. "I've only been in one real relationship before I became a submissive, and that was in high school. Then in college I got involved..." I sigh. "I just don't kiss."

"What is it that you don't like about kissing?" he asks.

"I don't know. It's so...personal."

"That it is." He trails a finger over my bottom lip. "And that's not what you want."

"No. Not really. I'm a submissive. I play with several Doms, though not at the same time. It works for me. But you..."

"I what?"

"Something. I don't know. You make me want something else."

He trails his finger over the shell of my ear. "What is that? Because you've made it clear you're not interested in a scene."

I gaze downward. "It's not that I'm not interested. It's that..."

I'm not sure what to say. My aversion to kissing isn't making sense to me at the moment, because all I can truly think about is Ronan's lips on mine.

He tips my chin upward. "I think I can change your mind about kissing."

I open my mouth to object, but—

His lips come down on mine.

My first kiss in...how long?

He tastes like a dream—sweetness from the bread pudding, boldness from his after-dinner coffee. And his tongue. God, his velvety tongue, twirling with mine. It's a deep and passionate kiss. Already my legs are wobbling, but his strong arms hold me steady.

I have no toys here.

Nothing to make a scene for him.

Even if I did, I wouldn't dare do anything on this antique furniture. It's not made for that.

Still he kisses me, walks forward until my back is against the wall.

His cock grinds into my belly. He's hard, so hard.

All I can think about is him inside me. That gorgeous cock between my legs.

Already I know it's gorgeous.

And already I know—

But I stop thinking. I let myself go, soft moans coming out of my throat as he pushes me against the wall. I melt into the kiss without meaning to, and just when I don't ever want it to end—

He breaks the kiss, trails his lips to my ear, nipping my earlobe.

"What do you think about kissing now?" he whispers with a groan.

I try to form the words, but I can't. All that comes out of my mouth is a soft whimper.

"I see," he whispers, his breath hot on my ear. "I'd like

nothing more than to kiss you again."

"Please..." I sigh.

This time he slides his lips over mine in a quick brush. "Except I'm afraid I may not be able to stop with a kiss."

I look beyond him at the bed. "I... This room... It's not set up for..."

"A scene. I know. But you're not ready for a scene, are you?"

I bite my bottom lip, savoring the flavor of him still on it. "I don't know, Ronan. I don't know what I'm ready for. I like being a submissive, but..."

"You'll always be a submissive, Mary. It's part of who you are. But if you want to have sex, there's no harm in that."

"I have sex all the time during scenes."

"I know, but that doesn't mean you have to have sex tonight. Or tomorrow, or ever again if you don't want to."

"Would you just kiss me again?"

"No, Mary. I won't."

"But Ronan—"

He slides his fingers over my lip, quieting me. "If I kiss you again, I'm going to fuck you, Mary. So if you don't want to go there, I won't kiss you again."

But I *want* to go there.

I want to go there more than anything.

I want to feel his lips not just on my own but everywhere else on my body, especially between my legs.

It's been so long...

So long since I've had regular sex with a man.

"I do want it, Ronan. Please..." I wrap my arms around his strong neck. "Make love to me."

His lips are down on mine again. Then his tongue—my God, that talented tongue—it's everywhere in my mouth all at once. Yet it's not too much. He uses just the right amount of tongue so that the kiss is perfect, passionate, and raw but not violent or slobbery.

It's perfection.

How did I ever stop kissing? How did I think I no longer needed to be kissed?

My whole body is on fire with passion and desire. It's a slow burn. I'm not used to a slow burn.

I'm used to a scene, where I'm tied up, tantalized with toys, and then fucked hard.

Where I don't climax until I'm commanded to.

Right now? I almost feel like I could come from this kiss alone.

His hard cock, still bound in his jeans, pushes against me, and I grind into him, finding the right spot on my clit to rub against his erection.

God…

I moan into his mouth as my flesh tingles with the sensation.

My clit is ready. I think I can come from dry-humping alone.

But then he breaks the kiss. "You want to come, don't you?"

"My God, yes."

"I'm afraid I can't let you do that. Not yet."

"Yes, sir…" I breathe out.

"I'm a Dominant by nature, as you are a submissive. So while this will be vanilla sex, you will still not come until I tell you to."

"Absolutely, sir."

He brushes his lips over mine. "Good girl. I can't wait to get my cock inside that sweet little pussy of yours, Mary."

I gasp.

"Are you all right?"

"Yes. I'm just not used to being called by my real name in these situations."

"Do you prefer me to call you Blossom?"

"Yes… I mean…" I look deep into his fiery blue eyes. "No. No, Ronan. I want you to call me Mary. It doesn't make any sense, but from your lips, it seems…right."

"Then Mary you will be." He trails his lips over mine, giving me chills.

Then with a *whoosh*, he pulls me into his arms and carries me to the bed, where he undresses me slowly and methodically.

I can't recall the last time a man undressed me. Usually I arrive at the club in lingerie or leather gear, and I strip for the Dom. Or he rips my clothes from me.

This is so different.

And I'm enjoying it.

He sets me on the bed, and then he takes his own clothes off, again slowly.

I watch, my eyes wide. He's as beautiful as I knew he'd be—porcelain skin, scattered reddish hair on his gorgeous pecs, abs like granite, legs like Thor, and between them…

I lie on my back, and he hovers on top of me, kissing me again. We kiss for a long time, slowly and passionately. He trails his finger down my abdomen, and then he breaks the kiss and moves his lips down my body, ending between my legs.

He looks at me there for a moment. But only for a moment, just enough for me to want more.

Such a gentle touch for a Dominant. So different from what I'm used to.

But he becomes more dominating as he comes toward me, kneels next to my head, his cock hard and ready.

"Suck me, Mary."

I obey without question because that's what I do as a submissive.

And frankly? He has the most beautiful dick I've ever seen.

A few shades darker than his fair skin, it's large and straight, with two veins marbling it in an exquisite pattern.

A drop of fluid squeezes out of the head, and I lick it off with my tongue, savoring the salty maleness. Then I take the head between my lips, suck on it gently.

And then not so gently.

I don't speak because normally I'm told not to speak during a scene.

But is this a scene? Truly?

Then I let the thought fall away. I just want to enjoy this.

I continue to suck on his head, then I take more, adding my fist to increase the friction.

But he abruptly moves away from me, his jaw clenched. "Can't wait any longer."

He moves off the bed, grabs a condom packet out of his jeans, sheathes himself quickly, and then returns, placing me on my hands and knees.

He enters me swiftly from behind, burning through me as if he's made of one solid flame.

My God…

He's not even touching my clit, but already I know I'm going to come.

Harder, faster, harder, faster…

I hold back.

I could come, but I don't. He told me not to.

I want to cry out in ecstasy, surrender to this passion igniting inside me.

And I'm ready, so ready…

"That's right, baby," he growls above me. "Feels so good to fuck you. You're so tight—tight and perfect. You want to come?"

"God, please…"

"All right, Mary. I want you to come. Now."

At his command, I explode. I fall forward, my chest hitting the bed, as he continues to pound me.

The contractions start in my pussy, radiate outward through my whole body to my fingers and toes, and then they plummet back—back to my core where my pussy pulses and pounds and my whole world seems to center between my legs.

"That's right. You come for me. *Come.*"

The orgasm continues. I scream into the pillow, balling the bedding in my fists. He pounds me, pounds me, pounds me...

Until—

He thunders into me, releasing with a growl.

I stay there, my ass in the air, my chest on the bed, my arms stretched out, grasping fistfuls of the comforter.

Don't want to move. Don't ever want to move.

I relish the fullness, until Ronan withdraws.

He turns me over so that I'm lying on my back.

He hovers above me, his dick still hard and dangling between my legs.

"Oh, Mary. I haven't gotten to suck those nipples yet."

I shudder at his words.

I don't know if I can come again. That last one was so incredible that it took all of my energy, and I'm lying here like a limp fish.

But then he trails his finger up over my breast, plucking one nipple.

And my pussy reacts.

Tingles shoot through me, and I know I'm ready again. Ready for whatever he offers.

He straddles me, keeping his weight on his thighs.

He cups my breasts, plucks at my nipples. With each twist, each tug, my pussy pulses, ever ready for another climax.

"I want to taste these nipples," he says. "I want to taste your pussy. Dive into it. Suck all the cream out of it until you're begging me to stop."

"Please..."

"But the same rules apply," he says. "No climax until I tell you."

I nod. "Yes, sir." I'll agree to anything at this point. Anything, as long as I can have another orgasm.

"You're so beautiful, Mary." He twists a nipple. Then he leans down, takes it between his lips, and sucks.

I sigh—a soft sigh of contentment. Of need. Of want.

He plays with the other nipple with his fingers as he sucks the first one.

Then—

"Oh!" I gasp.

He bit my nipple. Bit it ever so quickly and just hard enough. Just hard enough to make my clit throb.

He switches then, moves his lips to the other nipple, trailing his fingers up to the first one to continue his play.

Tug, pull, nip, suck.

My God, my nipples are on fire.

I'm ready...

Ready to come again...

On the brink...

But I won't go over. I won't go over until he lets me.

Then he trails his hand over my abdomen between my legs, massages my clit, and then thrusts two fingers inside me.

"Come," he says against my nipple. "Come now."

I shudder under him. His thumb is rubbing my clit while two fingers are inside me, massaging my G-spot and fucking me. He knows just what to do, where to touch.

How does he know my body so well already? Is he just that

good? Or is it something more?

Doesn't matter.

Doesn't fucking matter at all.

He goes back to my nipple, licking, sucking, and still he plows into me with his fingers.

Then he flips me over. He pushes my thighs upward so my ass is in the air.

"So beautiful," he says.

He wets his fingers in my pussy juices and then slides one finger over my asshole.

I've had anal sex many times, but I've never wanted it more than I do right now.

"I'm going to put my finger in here, Mary. And when I do, the dynamic between us will change."

I don't know what his words mean. I don't care in the moment. All I want is his finger in my ass. Drilling in and out of it.

He massages it gently, and then quickly, he breaches the tight rim.

I cry out at the invasion, but once he's past the tightness, all I can think about is how good it feels, his finger in my ass and then his other hand playing with my clit.

"Such a tight little ass, Mary. I'll fuck it soon. But not tonight."

I whimper at the loss, but he's already fucked me once. Perhaps he can't.

But already I know I can.

Ronan O'Connor is good for twice in one night. Possibly even three times.

So why would he hold back?

I don't care.

I don't care because it feels so good with his finger in my ass and his other hand at my clit.

I'm ready, ready to—

"Come for me," he commands.

Once the pulse starts again in my pussy, he moves his hand from my clit, forces two fingers into my heat.

He drills me in both holes in perfect tandem.

And I come.

I come for the third time...

And I know I've still got many more left.

CHAPTER NINETEEN

Ronan

Mary is the most responsive submissive I've met in a long time. And she's so susceptible to commands.

I believe I may have found what I've been looking for.

I just need to get her over the hump.

Over whatever scared her away from scenes.

I've gained her trust.

But have I really?

She knows how well members are vetted at Black Rose Underground. She knows she has no reason *not* to trust me, as I have no reason not to trust her.

In fact, I didn't need to use a condom. I could've fucked her without one, and I doubt she would've been upset. Monthly testing is required at Black Rose Underground, and birth control is required for women who aren't in monogamous relationships.

But that would've been presumptuous of me.

Next time, though, there will be no condom between me and her tight pussy.

There will be no condom between me and her tight ass.

My cock is straining. I could do her again.

But I won't. I'll hold back. I'm going to taste that pussy. I'm going to give her a fourth orgasm. Perhaps even a fifth if she's up for it.

Then after that, I'll let her sleep.

Because I think, more than anything, this woman needs to relax.

I'll make sure that happens.

Before I take her again, we have to talk.

I pull my fingers out of her pussy and ass, and then I head to the bathroom. I wash my hands quickly and then wet a washcloth with warm water. I return and move Mary onto her back, spread her sweet legs, gaze at her delicious pussy. So pink, so swollen, so wet with her glistening cream.

I clean her gently, take the washcloth back to the bathroom, return.

"I've tasted you a bit," I say, "but now I want to feast on you, Mary."

She sighs, closing her eyes.

"Open your eyes," I command. "Watch me eat your delicious pussy. Never take your eyes from mine."

She opens her eyes in obedience, locking her gaze to mine.

I swipe my tongue over her wet slit, taste her delicious, tangy juices.

I want to start slow, tease her a bit. But I can't. I suck her labia into my mouth, lap up her pussy juices.

I munch on her, devour her, slide my tongue up to her clit every now and then, but I can't wait to get back to her beautiful pussy.

When I finally command her to come, she does, and I push her thighs forward, baring her asshole to me. I slide my tongue over, force it into a point, and probe her.

I probe her sweet little ass.

God, I'm hard.

I could easily slide into her cunt right now. Into her ass.

But no. No. No.

I must hold myself in check.

Because…if anything is to work between us, we need to have a solid understanding.

As her orgasm comes to a close, I pull her thighs down, move toward her, kissing her nipples along the way and then tugging on her earlobe. "Sleep now, Mary."

Her eyes flutter closed.

She's not asleep yet, but she will be.

And I have a feeling that she hasn't had a good night's sleep—a full night's sleep—in quite some time.

• • •

I wake to a pounding on my door. I glance out the window. It's still dark.

I rise, wearing only my boxer briefs, and race to the door.

"Ronan!" A harsh whisper.

I open the door quickly. "Mary, what is it?"

"I swear to God, I don't believe in any of this stuff," she gasps out. "But one of the lights in my room is flickering."

I peer outside my hotel room door. "It's an old building. It's probably just old wiring."

"Ronan, you said this place was haunted."

I cross my arms. "And you said you didn't believe in those things."

Mary looks down the hallway, rotating her gaze. "I don't, except… It's freaking me out."

"Let's go see what's going on." I pull on my jeans and head to her room. Sure enough, the chandelier over her bed is flickering.

"Isn't that weird?" she says. "I turned it off."

I walk to the light switch, and sure enough, it's in the down position. I flip it up, and the flickering stops, leaving the light on.

"I can't sleep with the light on."

I flip the switch off. The chandelier goes dark. "It'll probably be okay now. It's an old building, Mary."

"What if…"

I place my hands gently on her shoulders. "You're going to be fine. Would you like to switch rooms?"

"Have you had any flickering in your room?"

"No."

"I just…" She looks down and then back up, her cheeks blushing. "Maybe you could stay here with me. Or I could stay in your room with you? I'm not saying I want to—"

I nod. "I understand. There doesn't seem to be any haunting in my room, so we'll stay there. Gather whatever you need."

"Thank you," she breathes, her shoulders dropping. She grabs her phone and her purse. "Everything else will be okay until morning."

I lead her to my room next door and lock up.

She climbs into my bed, and I climb in on the other side.

I wanted her to get a good night's sleep. I had her good and relaxed, but then the damn chandelier had to flicker.

We can always sleep in. I was going to pick her up at ten to get beignets, but that can always wait until the next day. I will not wake her up until she wakes up herself.

She needs her sleep.

I spoon up against her, ignoring my hard cock, and kiss her shoulder. "Go to sleep, Mary."

She closes her eyes, and within a few moments, her breathing has become shallower, and I know she's succumbed to slumber.

I move away from her, lying on my back, staring up at my own chandelier.

"Are you here?" I ask.

The light flickers on for moment.

"I thought so. Try not to scare her, got it?"

The light flickers off and stays off the rest of the night.

The Cornstalk Hotel is one of my favorite places in New Orleans. The place is presumably haunted by the ghosts of former residents and visitors, including a woman who is said to have jumped from a balcony to her death and a Confederate soldier who haunts the hotel's courtyard.

I learned, growing up here, not to discount the rumors.

Is there a ghost here? Did he or she truly answer me with a light flicker?

Maybe.

Maybe not.

But I keep an open mind—and an idea comes to me. One that will make Mary's stay here memorable indeed.

CHAPTER TWENTY

Mary

When I wake up, I'm not sure where I am.

Then I remember. New Orleans. With Ronan. In his room. I came here because a ghost—er...a *light*—flickered in my room.

I don't know what time it is, but I do feel rested, despite the fact that I freaked out in the middle of the night.

I'm relaxed now—as if I'm floating on a soft cloud. A chandelier flickering would have no effect on me in this moment.

But in the middle of a dark night, in a strange hotel that's rumored to be haunted?

Even after that mind-blowing sex with Ronan, I was still freaked.

He's not beside me in bed, but I hear the shower running in the adjacent bathroom.

I'm tempted to walk in and join him.

My God, who am I?

This is all *so* not me.

I was perfectly happy living my submissive life. Having no relationship, getting my pleasure from my scenes at the club.

HELEN HARDT

But then the scene that went wrong…

It wasn't even that bad, from a purely factual standpoint, but it affected me. And I can't deny that it did just because it seems like it shouldn't have.

The shower stops, and a few moments later, Ronan walks out, a towel around his waist.

His red hair is wet and hangs around his shoulders in damp waves. God, he's beautiful. Magnificent even. Already my pussy reacts, especially when I remember those glorious orgasms last night.

"Oh good, you're awake," he says.

"What time is it?"

He squints at the sun coming through the filmy drapes. "About nine thirty, I think."

"We were supposed to leave at ten."

He shrugs. "True, but I wanted you to get your sleep."

"Why?"

He walks toward me, looking scrumptious. "Because, Mary, I feel like it's been a while since you've had a night of uninterrupted sleep. Am I wrong?"

"You're not wrong."

"I was hoping to give you that last night, but I suppose our ghostly friend interfered."

My heart races and my nerves jump. "You really believe it was a ghost?"

"Maybe."

"The wiring?" I ask.

"Most likely."

I nod, still unsure. "Thanks for letting me stay here with you. I did sleep like a rock."

"You're welcome to stay in my room with me every night, if you wish. You make the rules."

"That doesn't sound like something a Dominant would say."

"You know as well as I do, Mary, that the true power in the relationship belongs to the submissive."

I sit up in bed. "I've never seen it that way. I see it as a balance of power between the two."

"Yes, I can see that as well." He walks to his suitcase that sits on the floor, riffles through it, and pulls out a pair of boxer briefs. "I think you and I need to have a talk."

"What about?"

He slides the underwear on under the towel and then drops the towel to the floor. "About what we both want out of this."

The dark blue stretchy fabric of the boxer briefs perfectly accents his muscular thighs and perfect ass—not to mention the beautiful bulge in front. My skin sizzles, but I ignore it. "What if all I want is to be with you for a few days? What if I want to sit this one out, so to speak?"

He frowns. "What do you mean by that?"

"Taking a break from the club scene feels pretty good, Ronan. Having vanilla sex was…nice. It's been a long time for me. I never thought I'd want it again, but—"

He holds up his hand to stop me. "Last night was very enjoyable. I won't say that it wasn't. But Mary, a vanilla relationship isn't what I want."

My heart drops. "I know that, Ronan."

"I would like you to be my submissive," he says. "But until you're ready to get back into that scene, I don't want you to think this relationship is something that it isn't."

"I don't think anything of our relationship, Ronan."

But I'm lying.

And I'm sure he knows I am.

I could fall in love with this man. And I never thought I wanted to be in love again.

. . .

Sometimes when your heart is broken, and you realize it will never be whole again, you find ways to patch it.

That's what Brenda says, anyway.

"Perhaps it's best that we end this," Lucas said to me that last night, after I confessed my love to him.

Lucas was my first Dominant. We met in college, though he wasn't a student. He was a professor. Never my professor, but he saw something in me. He groomed me into the submissive I became.

And I did something really stupid.

I fell in love.

I'm not the only woman to get screwed over by someone she thought cared for her.

Far from it. Lucas and I were different. I should've seen that from the start.

But I was young, innocent, naive.

Ignorant.

I'd never been in love before. I'd never even had sex before.

Lucas took my virginity—and he took it in a gentle and sweet way. It wasn't until months later that he introduced me to the BDSM lifestyle.

I was taken aback at first. Creeped out, for sure. But I was falling in love with this older, experienced man, and I wanted to please him.

So I allowed him to teach me, and I found I was a natural submissive. I grew to enjoy the lifestyle. But with Lucas, I wasn't simply a submissive. I was his lover, too. We didn't only play scenes together.

We had regular sex, too. Vanilla sex, he called it. And it was enjoyable for both of us—at least I thought it was, even when he said we were no longer dating in the traditional sense. That we were Dominant and submissive, nothing else.

Still, I thought he loved me.

With Lucas, I felt I had it all. The love that I thought I needed, and the sexual satisfaction that came from submitting in a club environment. Plus we kissed. We kissed all the time. And I loved the kissing.

I learned my hard limits with Lucas. He was good to me. But it only lasted until I left college. After two years, when my father died and I couldn't afford to go back, Lucas ended things—and his timing was impeccable. I'd just confessed that I had fallen in love with him.

Then I realized what his true fetish was.

As a professor, he fetishized students. He was very careful. He made sure to find a student who wasn't interested in what he taught, which was sociology.

I intended to be a business major, so I fit the bill.

I considered going to the dean and reporting him for dating students at the school.

He told me it was okay, as long as they weren't students in his classes, but a careful reading of the university's rules indicated otherwise.

"Mary, don't do it," Brenda said. "All it will do is keep the wound open. It will fester. You may take Lucas down, but you'll do more harm to yourself. It's better to move on."

She was right.

So I moved on.

I left school when my father died, and I found employment at Treasure's Chest, made peace with the fact that I wouldn't finish college—at least not yet—and I began to do some research on how I could continue in the lifestyle but stay out of a relationship.

Because I was done. No more love. And no more kissing.

I could have the sexual satisfaction I craved, the submission I craved, but steer clear of relationships.

They only lead to heartache.

CHAPTER TWENTY-ONE

Ronan

"I think I want to go home, Ronan," Mary says to me after wiping the powdered sugar from her lips.

We're back at Mémé's for beignets—Mary's request, because she wanted to see Mémé again—but I am planning to take her to Café du Monde tomorrow so she can get the full experience she said she wants.

Or perhaps not…if she chooses to leave now. Disappointment wells in me. After the night we had, why does she want to leave?

I put my beignet down on the plate and glide my napkin over my lips. "Why? I haven't shown you any of the sights yet. Don't you want to see the graveyards? They're legendary."

"Of course, I would love to see everything. So far, this place is spectacular. It's everything you said it was and everything I've read about it. But I—"

She bites her lip, looks down at her plate, which is full of crumbs and powdered sugar. She takes a sip of her café au lait and wipes her mouth again.

"Tell me what's going on, Mary."

"I'm not sure I can give you what you want," she says.

"I see."

"But let me be honest with you. I have no intention of leaving the lifestyle. I enjoy it, and I'm good at it. I like being a submissive."

"We can go as slowly as you need to," I say.

"I appreciate that, but that's only..." She shakes her head. "Never mind. I just think it's better if I leave. I'm perfectly capable of getting on a plane by myself and flying back to New York. I want you to stay, Ronan. Visit with your grandmother. Enjoy your old stomping grounds."

This makes no sense. "Have I done something wrong?"

"No. You've been a perfect gentleman."

"Maybe that's the issue."

She lets out a nervous chuckle. "No, that's not the issue at all. I have to tell you that I think a scene with you would be... fucking amazing. I think you could take me places I've never been. But I don't see that future for us, Ronan."

Even I am shocked at how fiercely I feel the dagger of her words puncture my heart. "Why not? I get that you had a bad experience. I understand this isn't easy for you. I get that it's going to take time for you to get back into the club scene. I'm willing to wait, Mary, because I think you might be my perfect submissive."

She sighs. "That's where you're wrong."

"Why do you say that?"

"Ronan"—she clears her throat—"I will never be your perfect submissive."

"I disagree."

She draws in a breath. "My God, you're going to make me spell it out for you, aren't you?"

"I'm not going to make you do anything, Mary."

"Ronan—"

"Give me one day. Spend the day with me—and the night—and then tomorrow morning, if you still want to leave, I will personally put you on a plane to New York."

She takes a bite of beignet, chews, swallows, and wipes an adorable smudge of sugar from her chin. "You're not making this easy. The fact is that I *want* to stay."

"Then what's the problem?"

She clams up.

I don't know what's truly bothering her, and I think it's time she was honest with me.

"Tell me," I say. "Tell me about the scene that went bad."

Her cheeks redden.

"It wasn't anything terrible," she says. "I've told you that much. But it happened because the Dominant I was playing with was beginning to have feelings for a woman."

"A woman other than you, I assume?"

She nods. "Yeah. He and I are just friends."

"Still?"

"Yes, of course. He's a good guy. He was so apologetic. He felt terrible about what happened. He took excellent care of me afterward."

Okay, that all makes sense. But I'm still missing some pieces to this puzzle. "What are your hard limits, Mary?"

"Edge play, of course."

"Edge play means different things to different people."

"Gunplay. Breath play. Blood sports."

"I don't engage in any of those, either," I say.

"But I like to be beaten hard, Ronan. Very hard. As long as no blood is drawn."

"I think I see what you're getting at."

"He didn't mean to, but his head wasn't in the game. He wasn't focusing. He knows that, and he took care of things. And it's not so much that I'm afraid it will happen again. He and I won't play together again. I wouldn't have anyway, but he's in a monogamous relationship now."

"And are you afraid my head won't be in the game?"

"No. Not at all. I'm pretty sure your head is always in the game, Ronan."

"It is."

She pauses, looks down at her hands. "I'm not sure I can explain it any better than that."

"I think you probably can, Mary."

"You're right." She crosses her legs and takes a sip of coffee. "I'm just not ready to."

Fair enough. I'm not going to push her. "Then will you spend the day with me? And the night? And if you're still not ready to tell me tomorrow, I will put you on a plane myself."

She swallows and then licks her bottom lip.

And my cock reacts.

"All right," she says. "I'll spend the day with you."

"Perfect." It's hard not to smile from ear to fucking ear. "What would you like to do today?"

"Whatever you think we should. You're the expert."

I nod. "Would you excuse me for a moment?"

"Of course." She reaches for her café au lait and brings it to her lips.

I head to the bathroom.

But Mémé waylays me. "You look disturbed, Ronan."

"I'm fine."

"You like that young woman," she says bluntly.

I look over my shoulder and sigh. "She's an enigma."

She reaches up, grabs my shoulders so I'm facing her again. "Yes, and you could never resist a challenge, could you?"

"No, Mémé."

"Don't you think it's about time you settled down?"

"That's not who I am."

Mémé reaches up again, standing on her tiptoes, and pinches my cheek with a smile, like she used to when I was a little boy. "You might be surprised, chéri."

CHAPTER TWENTY-TWO

Mary

I was able to patch up my heart after Lucas, as Brenda advised. But it's not whole. I don't think it will ever be whole again.

The botched scene with Jack got me thinking about emotion. About how it can really screw you over.

And that's where the problem with Ronan comes in—the truth that I couldn't tell him.

I don't know the man, but I allowed him to whisk me off to New Orleans. Something I would never do.

It's like that botched scene with Jack opened up something in me.

My emotions remembered that they were there, and they started bubbling to the surface.

Fear.

Fear that another scene might go wrong.

Other emotions, too.

Envy.

I find myself envying Brenda and Dalton and what they have.

Then...

I can't call it love. No one falls in love in forty-eight hours.

But extreme like. Extreme like and attraction to Ronan O'Connor.

He's made it damned clear where he stands. He's not looking for love or even extreme like. He's looking for a submissive to play with. That is simple. That is all.

And I can't fault him for that.

It's what I wanted for so long.

All of this because of a damned botched scene. It wasn't the first botched scene I ever participated in. It was the reason the scene was botched—because Jack was suppressing emotion for another woman.

In some strange way, his suppression of emotion brought out my own.

I'm scared.

I'm scared that being a part-time submissive may not be enough for me anymore.

I never thought I'd want what Brenda and Dalton found.

But perhaps I do.

And if I do, this thing with Ronan must end, or I'll end up with a shattered heart again—and this time will be worse because it wasn't whole to begin with.

I widen my eyes when Yvette takes a seat at our table across from me where Ronan was sitting.

"Good morning, Mary."

I look down at my empty plate. "Good morning. I loved the beignets."

"Thank you. I'm very proud of them." She smiles. "What do you think of my grandson?"

I have no idea why she's asking, what she expects me to say. "He's…great."

"He's a good man." Yvette glances toward the restrooms.

"My daughter doesn't have the best marriage with Ronan's father. They're still together, but it's mostly in name only. I saw much more of Ronan while he was growing up than his father ever did. The man was off globetrotting, spending most of his time in the UK and continental Europe. Making lucrative business deals when he should've been at home attending to his wife and child. When Simone went with him, as she sometimes did, Ronan was here alone."

Again, I don't know what she expects me to say. "Ronan hasn't told me much about his childhood."

"My grandson never learned what's important in life. Family, children, someone to love."

"Oh?"

"He works too hard. He micromanages. And now that he's back in the States, I'm going to make sure he stays happy."

She reaches across the table, takes my hand, and slides something into it. A small piece of paper and a tiny cloth pouch.

"What is this?" I ask.

"A simple love spell," she says. "You are falling in love with my grandson, are you not?"

My cheeks burn. "I hardly know him."

"Yet you flew across the country with him."

"I know. I sort of got whisked away," I admit. "I'm not naive. I know women should be careful. But I felt safe with him."

A slow smile spreads across Yvette's pretty face. "Why do you think that is?"

I can't tell her why it is. I can't tell her that we're both members of the same underground club in New York City and that the members are vetted very carefully. That's why I feel safe with Ronan. The only reason.

"I..."

"You don't have to answer that." She squeezes my hand. "I

see it in your eyes."

"You see what in my eyes?"

"I see my grandson's future. I believe it lies with you, Mary. I could be wrong, but it's unlikely. I'm almost never wrong when it concerns matters of the heart."

I touch the pouch, let the silk caress my fingers. "Ronan told me you practice Voodoo."

"I do. It's my religion. I learned it from my mother, and she learned from hers. My own daughter wasn't interested. So I guess it dies with me."

"That's kind of sad."

"It is." She looks up. Ronan is returning from the bathroom. "Put that away now. It was lovely talking to you."

I secure the little packet she gave me in my purse before Ronan sees it.

"Mémé," he says. "What's going on here?"

"I'm just having a little talk with the lady. Telling her about the beignets." Yvette rises.

"No, please sit," Ronan says. "If you have time, that is. I'm showing Mary the city today. We'd both love to have your opinion on the best things to see in only one day. What are the must-sees?"

"You know what I'm going to tell you, Ronan. St. Louis Cemetery Number One, of course. The resting place of Marie Laveau."

Ronan nods, letting out a low chuckle. "Of course."

"We have some amazing cemeteries here in the city," Yvette continues. "Some of them are aboveground cemeteries, which we call cities of the dead. St. Louis Cemetery is like that. It's one of the oldest cemeteries in New Orleans, dating back to the eighteenth century. You can't go right in. You have to take a guided tour."

"Oh," I say.

"But it just so happens that my friend Beatrix is a tour guide there, and all it will take is a phone call. I can get you in today."

. . .

Yvette's friend Beatrix is a gorgeous woman with silver hair but not a wrinkle on her smooth, dark brown complexion.

She embraces Ronan and kisses him on each cheek. "You're as handsome as ever." She smiles. "And who do we have here?"

"Bea, this is Mary."

I hold out my hand. "It's nice to meet you."

"That's no greeting!" She pulls me into a hug. A waft of sugar and wildflowers hits me.

She smells homey.

"You two are lucky," Bea says. "No one else signed up for this tour, so you get a private showing. Let's go in."

Ronan grabs my hand—I try to ignore the sparks that shoot through me—and we follow Bea into the cemetery.

"We're not alone here," Bea says. "Spirits are among us, but don't be frightened. No one means you any harm."

A chill runs through my body at Bea's words, and I grasp Ronan's hand a bit tighter.

"First," Bea says, "a bit of history. You already know all this, Ronan, but I want to give your lady friend the full picture."

"Absolutely," Ronan agrees.

Bea smiles, showing bright white teeth. "St. Louis Cemetery Number One was established in 1789, and it is the final resting place of many notables, including the famous Voodoo queen Marie Laveau. The cemetery is divided into squares, and each square contains rows of aboveground tombs and crypts."

"Why are they above ground?" I ask.

"New Orleans sits below sea level, and the water table is very high. If people were buried underground, their caskets would often float to the surface during heavy rains. Aboveground tombs were built to keep the deceased dry."

Eerie images of floating dead bodies swim through my mind.

"Since it's just you two," Bea continues, "where would you like to start?"

"Marie Laveau," Ronan says.

"Of course. But as you know, Ronan, there is some controversy over whether Marie Laveau is actually buried in this tomb. Some historians believe that the tomb belongs to her daughter, who had the same name."

We follow Bea to a white rectangular structure with a raised base surrounded by a fence. Colorful Mardi Gras beads, along with coins, flowers, and candles, rest at the bottom of the tomb.

"Marie Laveau was a famous Voodoo queen who lived in New Orleans in the nineteenth century."

"What are all the beads for?" I ask.

"Those are offerings left by visitors."

"Offerings for what?"

"From those who seek her favor or guidance, or for those offering simple prayers. Legend has it that if you draw three X's on her tomb, make a wish, and leave an offering, your wish will come true. It's illegal now to deface the tomb in any way, but you can still leave an offering. We prefer offerings that are biodegradable, but some visitors still leave coins and beads."

I don't believe in any of this stuff, but I feel a sense of peace at the tomb. I wish I had something to leave because I could sure use some guidance right about now.

We continue the tour, and some of the tombs are truly beautiful and ornate with sculptures of religious symbols, angels, and each one is unique. Some are gray stone, and some white.

"Families would often commission sculptors to create intricate statues and designs to honor their loved ones. Some tombs even have stained-glass windows and decorative ironwork," Bea explains.

"That was amazing," I say to Ronan when our tour has come to an end.

He drapes a strong arm over my shoulders. "I'm glad you enjoyed it. What else would you like to do while you're here?"

I think for a moment before I answer. The love spell in my purse... Marie Laveau... Leaving an offering for guidance...

"Could I have a moment with Bea, please?"

"Sure." He removes his arm and walks among the tombstones.

"Yes, love?" Bea says to me when Ronan is out of earshot.

"Could you take me back to Marie Laveau's tomb?"

"Of course. Do you wish to make an offering?"

"I do."

As we walk, I look again at all the gravesites, think about the people buried here on this hallowed ground. When we reach the tomb, I turn to Bea.

"I don't have anything biodegradable to leave."

"A coin or two is fine," she says. "Or simply your good thoughts or a prayer. She will hear you."

I walk toward the tomb, reach into my purse, my fingers grazing the silk bag, and pull out my wallet. "How many should I leave?"

"It's not the gift that matters," Bea says. "It's what the gift represents. What is in your heart."

I nod and grab two quarters from the zippered compartment of my wallet. I set the coins among the wealth of other gifts.

And I make my wish.

When we return to Ronan, leave the cemetery, and bid goodbye to Bea, I grab his hand.

"What did you think?" he asks.

"I think...I'd like to learn more about Voodoo."

CHAPTER TWENTY-THREE

Ronan

"Voodoo?" I ask.

"Yeah. I mean, it means something to your grandmother. It's a huge part of the city's culture. Of its history."

This woman never ceases to surprise me. I know exactly where to take her—the New Orleans Historic Voodoo Museum. Mémé took me there often when I was a kid, and it's located in the heart of the French Quarter, offering a fascinating look at the history and traditions of Voodoo in New Orleans.

A half hour later, we're entering the museum, complete with dim lighting and an eerie atmosphere. Mary's eyes widen as she gazes at the walls adorned with various artifacts and artwork related to Voodoo, including dolls, masks, and ritual objects.

"You want to watch the short film about Voodoo in New Orleans?" I ask.

"Yeah, if you don't mind."

She watches with rapt attention, taking in the information I've known my whole life. Voodoo is interesting and intriguing for sure, but I don't put any stock in it or any other religion.

One of the highlights of the museum is its collection of

Voodoo artifacts, including traditional Voodoo dolls, gris-gris bags—small fabric pouches that contain talismans—and other ritual objects. I've seen all this before, but Mary seems completely mesmerized.

Another section of the museum focuses on the role of Voodoo in New Orleans' music and cultural traditions.

And of course, there's a whole section on Marie Laveau herself.

After an hour, my stomach is growling. The beignets didn't last long, and it's past lunchtime.

When I open my mouth to suggest something to eat, Mary says, "I'd like to shop. Maybe get a souvenir."

"Look around you. There are souvenir shops everywhere."

"No. I mean a Voodoo shop."

I try not to drop my jaw. "All right. I'll call Mémé and ask her to recommend the best place."

She grabs my arm. "Perfect, and then I want to see more of the city. Show me everything. I'll even try that Pimm cup you were talking about."

"You mean Pimm's cup."

"Right. Yes."

I text Mémé quickly, and she gives me an address to a shop not too far from where we are.

As we walk into Odette's Botanica, I inhale the smoky aroma of incense. The smell is familiar. Mémé burns it all the time. The walls of the small shop are lined with shelves filled with candles, herbs, oils, and crystals.

Mary walks in with her eyes wide.

"Good afternoon," a young woman with blue hair says. "Welcome. Can I help you find anything?"

I nod to Mary.

"I'm really just looking," Mary says. "I was just at the

Voodoo museum. It's all so interesting."

The woman smiles and walks out from behind the register. "I'm Veronica."

"Mary." She shakes Veronica's hand.

"We have a large selection of Voodoo and spiritual supplies," Veronica says, "including candles for different intentions and purposes, such as love, prosperity, and protection. You can also find herbs and oils that are commonly used in Voodoo and other spiritual practices, as well as crystals and other items believed to have spiritual and healing properties."

"Wonderful," Mary says. "Is it okay to just look around?"

"Of course. And if you're interested in learning more about Voodoo and spiritual practices, you can sign up for one of our workshops or classes. These classes cover a range of topics, including Voodoo history and traditions, herbalism, and candle magic."

"Amazing," Mary breathes. "I'm from New York. This is all new to me."

"How long will you be here?" Veronica asks.

Mary sighs. "I leave tomorrow, so I'm going to cram everything I can in today."

I open my mouth to mention that she doesn't have to leave tomorrow, but then I think better of it.

I can't push Mary into doing anything she doesn't want to do.

She gazes over the shelves, picks up a crystal wand, and strokes it with her fingers.

"That's rose quartz," Veronica says. "For love."

Mary's cheek pink, and she sets the crystal down. "Do you have any books about Voodoo?"

"Of course." She pulls a paperback off one of the shelves. "This is a good one for beginners."

Mary glides her hands over the book's glossy cover. "I'll take this." She retrieves the crystal wand. "And this. It's just so beautiful."

"Absolutely. Anything else?"

"Just these two for now, thanks."

Veronica rings up Mary's purchases, and I hand her a credit card, but Mary stops me.

"No, Ronan. I want to pay for these."

"I'm happy to," I say.

"I know, but you've paid for everything so far. Let this be for me."

She's resisting. Even after our amazing vanilla sex, she's still resisting.

I vow to be understanding.

When we leave the shop, I take her on a whirlwind tour of the city. We start at Jackson Square, the heart of the French Quarter, where we see the iconic St. Louis Cathedral, the oldest cathedral in North America.

My stomach is nearly empty by the time we hit the French Market, a bustling, open-air marketplace that features a range of vendors selling everything from handmade crafts to fresh produce. We walk along the streets of the French Quarter, taking in the colorful architecture and historic landmarks, my favorite of which is Napoleon House.

"Here's where we get a Pimm's Cup," I say. "And a sandwich for me."

"Oh!" She gasps. "I guess we should eat, shouldn't we? I've just been so involved in everything. I can't believe you grew up here. This is simply the most marvelous place in the world."

We step inside the historic building, which is characterized by high ceilings, exposed brick walls, and antique furniture.

"This place was originally intended to be the residence of

Napoleon Bonaparte during his exile, but he never actually lived here."

"It's all so fascinating."

A host leads us to a table, and within a minute, a server appears.

"What can I get you today?"

"Two Pimm's cups," I say, "and a muffuletta for me. Do you want something to eat, Mary?"

"What's a muffuletta?"

"It's a sandwich that originated here in New Orleans. It's sesame bread filled with layers of Italian cold cuts, cheese, and a tangy olive salad."

"Sounds delicious."

"Make that two," I say to the server.

"Right away. I'll get you some water, too."

"Great, thanks." I turn back to Mary.

"So what exactly is a Pimm's cup?" she asks.

"It's a refreshing drink made from Pimm's No. 1, which is a gin and herbal liqueur, lemonade, lemon-lime soda, and a cucumber garnish."

"That does sound good."

"You'll love it." I look into her brown eyes.

The word "love" isn't lost on me.

CHAPTER TWENTY-FOUR

Mary

Back at the hotel, I shower, washing the day away but keeping the memories.

How have I never left New York before?

There's so much more to life than one place.

New Orleans is seamy, exciting, full of life and culture.

Once I'm done, I towel off, let my hair fall over my shoulders, and squeeze out some of the moisture. My reflection catches my eye in the mirror, which is foggy from the shower. It's blurred, so I grab a towel and wipe it off.

And I see myself.

I see myself as I am—naked, damp hair, no makeup.

And I want Ronan to see me like this. I haven't let any man see me without makeup since Lucas. I always wear makeup to the club. Dark lipstick, smoky eyes, lots of mascara to accentuate my already naturally long lashes.

But now I see myself. I see myself as I truly exist. My lips are full and pink, my skin is fair, freckles are sprayed across my nose and cheeks, and my eyes are big and brown.

My hair, the reddish-brown of a dark terracotta, much

darker than Ronan's.

And my body. Firm in all the right places, with medium-size breasts and long legs.

The only thing made up on me is the burgundy nail polish on my fingers and toes.

I wrap the cushy white robe around my shoulders, securing the belt.

Then I leave the bathroom and head to the back bedroom. The chandelier above the bed is flickering again.

But I feel no fear this time. Not after a day of wandering the streets of New Orleans, learning about the culture and of the myriad ghost stories.

Probably faulty wiring in such an old building. But if it's not? Whatever spirit is in my room means me no harm. I know that now.

I jerk at a knock on the door.

"Who is it?"

"It's me, Mary."

Ronan's deep and sexy voice.

I open the door, as my true self.

He gapes at me. "My God. You're beautiful."

I warm from the top of my head down to the tips of my toes. He looks just as amazing. His hair is also damp, and he's wearing a khaki kilt and a simple white T-shirt. His feet are bare.

"I'd like to invite you to my room," he says.

"Oh? And what excitement awaits me there?"

"Come with me, and you'll find out."

I don't even have to think about it. I put my hand in his, lock my door behind me, and follow him to his room.

I spent the night here last night.

The covers are turned down, and one red rose lies on

the pillow where I slept. I walk toward it, not waiting for any kind of permission, bring the flower to my nose, and inhale its sweetness.

"How did you know roses are my favorite?"

"I didn't. I'm glad they are."

"Mmm." I inhale the sweet fragrance again.

"Does the ghost in your room still frighten you?" he asks.

"No."

"Good, because there's a ghost in this room as well. And we're both going to fuck you tonight."

I widen my eyes as my pulse goes into overtime. Something coils in my gut. Is it fear? Or is it desire?

Or is it a combination of both, with underlying raw and aching need?

"I don't have any bindings here, Mary, so the ghost will bind you. You'll be able to feel the silk around your wrists. The straps will hold your hands above your head, attaching you to the rungs of the headboard."

"But—" I stop abruptly. I was going to point out that the headboard has no rungs, but he's creating a fantasy for me. A scene.

And although I'm still a bit apprehensive about scenes, I want more than anything to play along. I want to be with Ronan.

I want to be here.

I want to see what it's like to be his submissive. For the first time in a long time, I want to submit. I feel my sexual fire coming back.

"Take off your robe, Mary."

I obey, untying the belt, parting the plush terrycloth, letting it fall from my shoulders into a white heap around my feet.

"Now lie on the bed, your hands above you, clasping them together."

I walk to the bed, lie down on the cool and crisp white cotton sheet, goose bumps erupting on my skin. I raise my hands above me, clasping them together.

"Feel the silk against your wrists, Mary. The ghost is binding your wrists."

I close my eyes, concentrate, and yes... The wisp of cool silk against my wrists. I feel it.

"Open your eyes," Ronan commands. "Do you see him?"

"No."

"If you concentrate, you may catch a glimpse of him. If you don't, that's okay. He's going to secure your wrists to the headboard now. You won't be able to move your arms at that point. Are you ready?"

"I'm ready, Ronan."

"Concentrate," he says, his deep voice hypnotic. "You'll feel him secure you to the headboard. You can try to move, but you won't be able to."

"Yes, sir."

I close my eyes again, concentrate, and then—I know it's my imagination, but—

A soft *click*.

Soft *click* of a leather binding being secured to the headboard.

I let a smile spread across my lips.

"Very good," Ronan says. "Very. Good."

He comes back with a silk handkerchief. "I'm going to blindfold you now, Mary. That way, you won't know whether it's me or the ghost tantalizing you."

I close my eyes. "Yes, sir."

"Good girl."

The coolness of the silk floats over my eyes, and I lift my head so he can tie it behind me.

My arms don't move. They are secure.

Ronan's lips brush over mine. "No talking," he whispers. "Unless it's to say your safe word. Can you tell me what that is?"

"Tesla," I say softly.

"Good. That's the only word I want to hear come out of your mouth. You may moan, shriek, any nonverbal communication. But no speaking unless you need to say your safe word. But already I know you won't need to use it."

I sink into the cool sheets, my sight taken from me, my wrists bound and my arms secured above my head.

Will he secure my feet? I don't know, and I can't ask. I'm submitting to him. Allowing him to take my sense of sight, allowing him to bind me by his sheer will alone.

A sliver of apprehension glides through me, but it is quickly replaced by pure arousal. Already I can feel my pussy getting wet, getting ready for him.

"I don't normally share my submissives, Mary, but I've known this ghost for a long time."

I simply nod, playing along.

"He will only do what I allow him to do to you. And I know you will be pleased."

Something cold touches the tip of one nipple.

I recognize the feeling. It's an ice cube.

"Such beautiful tits you have, Blossom."

My submissive name. *Blossom.*

Funny. I like it better when he calls me Mary.

My nipples are hard, so hard.

"Have you ever had both of your nipples sucked at the same time?"

I shake my head, careful not to use words.

"You will tonight."

The ice cube trails to my other breast, swirls around my other nipple. I gasp at the coldness. I want lips on them. Teeth biting on them, tugging at them. I want them twisted hard. If only Ronan had some nipple clamps here at the Cornstalk Hotel. But that will no doubt have to wait until we get back to New York.

Yes... When we get back to New York...

I'm looking forward to it. Getting back to the club. Going into a private suite with Ronan. Doing a scene together.

My God...

My nipples are protruding, so ready. I want so badly to beg him to suck them, but I don't dare speak.

I obey my Dominant.

I obey him gladly. Because I know when he finally puts his mouth on my nipples, finally gives me what I desire, it will be all that much better.

"Jean-Pierre," he says softly, "suck Mary's nipple."

Jean-Pierre? The name of the ghost? I stop myself from smiling.

Then I gasp as my left nipple is sucked between two firm lips.

They could easily be Ronan's lips. My hips rise from the bed of their own accord.

"Do you like it?" Ronan asks. "Do you like it when Jean-Pierre sucks your nipples?"

I moan, nodding.

Ronan can't speak. He can't speak with his lips around my nipple.

What is happening?

Surely I would know if Ronan were using his fingers on my nipple.

"Good, my lovely Blossom. I will suck the other nipple

now. Two pairs of lips on your nipples at the same time, sweet Blossom. I want to hear all the moans. All the groans. I want to know how this makes you feel."

Then my nipple between Ronan's firm lips.

Lips, yes. So good. While the other nipple... Someone is sucking on it, pulling on it with teeth.

Both my nipples being tormented at the same time. Have I ever felt anything more luxurious and erotic?

I moan. I want to speak. I want to tell Ronan how good it feels.

But I don't. I will obey. It's what I do. I submit.

I obey.

God, it's torture, not being able to tell him how good it feels. Two pairs of lips on my hard nipples, sucking, licking, tugging.

One pair of lips pops off my nipple. I whimper at the loss.

"You're so beautiful, Blossom. Your breasts are rosy and flushed, your nipples so hard, your areolas scrunched up. Jean-Pierre will continue with your left nipple, but I'm going to see to other things."

I don't know what Ronan is able to do with his fingers. How he's making it feel like a mouth. How will he continue doing it when he's between my legs, sucking me? He has long arms, for sure.

But then I forget. I forget reality. And I imagine the ghost of a young Creole man named Jean-Pierre sucking my nipple between his firm, plump lips.

I imagine his big cock. Ready to plunge into me when Ronan tells me it's okay.

And then I feel Ronan's tongue between my legs.

Velvety and firm, he licks me. Sucks my pussy lips, twirls his tongue around my clit.

So, so good.

I imagine his cock driving into me while the ghost of Jean-Pierre still plays with my nipples, slides his tongue over my body.

All the while I can't move my arms, can't see what's happening.

I don't think I've ever been as turned on as I am right now. I literally cannot move my arms, so strong are the invisible binds.

I relish the sounds of Ronan eating my pussy. The slurping and sucking is music to my ears, and I lift my hips, grinding my pussy against his stubble, his firm lips, his jawline.

"You taste like a fantasy," he growls against my flesh, and then he shoves his tongue inside my cunt, and my God, with both my nipples still being sucked, back and forth from one to the other, I'm ready, so ready, but—

"No," he snarls against me. "Not yet, Blossom. You don't come yet."

Yes, sir, I say inside my mind.

Because his command is that powerful, the orgasm stops in its tracks. I stop at the edge of the cliff, my toes digging in the ground.

I will not jump.

I will not fly.

Not until my Dominant commands that I can.

But my God...

My body is on fire, my flesh is searing, blazing. My nipples, the sucking feels so good, so good, and it travels down, straight to my pussy. And all I can think about—all I can dream—is—

"Good girl, Blossom. You've earned it. *Come.*"

A finger slides into my pussy, and I clench around it, my orgasm shattering me. Imploding me into the bed. I unscrunch my body and fly off the cliff, soaring, soaring, soaring...

All the while...

The ghost sucks my nipple. Sucks my fucking nipple.

While Ronan finger fucks me, twirling his tongue over my clit...

My *God*.

I scream, yell, moan. I say nothing in words, because there are no words.

Even if I weren't under Ronan's thrall, I'd have no words to describe the ecstasy that I feel.

"Let her nipple go now, Jean-Pierre."

The ghost's lips slip from my nipple.

And as I come down from my climax, Ronan's teeth tug at my earlobe.

"We're going to fuck you now," he says to me in a whisper. "Both Jean-Pierre and I."

I nod.

"Do I have permission, Mary? To take your ass?"

I nod again.

Please, yes. Please take my ass, Ronan.

"Good. Jean-Pierre will be in your pussy, and my hard cock will plunder your ass. Have you ever had a double penetration before?"

I shake my head.

"Are you looking forward to it?"

I arch my back, nodding.

"Good. So am I."

He kisses my lips then, shoving his tongue between them. The kiss is raw, firm, and drugging, and I know it for what it is.

A prelude for something amazing to come.

We kiss for a few timeless moments, and I savor the taste of my own pussy on his lips.

When he breaks the kiss, I let out a soft whimper, but then I remember what's coming.

My first DP.

Ronan…and a ghost.

Ronan's lips trail down my neck, over the tops of my breasts, down my abdomen to the tip of my clit, where he licks it sweetly.

Then he spreads my legs, pushes them forward so my ass is in the air.

He swipes his tongue over my ass.

"Sweet hole," he growls.

Something warm slides between my butt cheeks.

"Some lube," he says.

Lube, yes. I'm no stranger to anal sex. A lot of Dominants love it, and so do I.

"I'm going to slide a plug into your ass now, baby," he says. "To get you ready for my cock."

I nod, sucking in a breath for the invasion that I know is coming.

Then I feel it, the tip of cool stainless steel against my flesh. He slides it in, and once the bulbous part is past the rim, I let out a breath.

"That fills you up nicely. You'll be ready for my cock in no time."

Lips trail over my thighs then. Full lips.

"You like that," he says. "You like when Jean-Pierre kisses your thighs?"

I nod, biting my lip.

How is he doing this? I know it's not a ghost. I know Ronan is making it all possible.

I don't care how he does it. Because I'm so ready.

"I'm going to take the plug out of you now. Remember, you're bound. You cannot move your arms or hands."

Indeed I am bound. I won't move.

In my own head, I can't move.

He slides the anal plug out of my ass.

"So gorgeous. Do you realize you just winked at me, Blossom?"

I warm all over, arch my back. I wish I could pull my thighs up, make the opening even wider for him.

And then...

The tip of Ronan's hot cock nudges against my asshole.

"I'm going to go in first, Blossom. Let you get used to my invasion of your ass. Then Jean-Pierre will enter your pussy."

I suck out a gasp. I'm ready, so ready. I can't say this, but he knows. He sees the cream trickling out of my pussy the same as I can feel it.

"I know you're not a virgin in this hole. I kind of wish you were, Blossom. I'd love to be the first man to take this beautiful ass."

You'll be the last...

The words fly into my mind, yet I don't know where they came from.

But I stop thinking at all when he breaches my rim, taking my ass in one swift thrust.

I cry out, but not in pain. Only in pleasure. Of the sheer fullness of my hole filled by this amazing man. This perfect Dominant.

Then the tip of a warm cock nudges my clit.

I open my eyes, ready to gasp, but of course I see nothing. I'm blindfolded.

How is he doing this?

But then I don't care. I don't care because the ghost cock slides into my pussy, and I'm full, so full. I open my mouth, hoping another ghost cock will slide inside it.

It doesn't, but for a moment I imagine all three of my holes are filled.

How I'm submitting...

Submitting to Ronan...

And to a ghost.

Ronan fucks my ass, and in tandem, the ghost fucks my pussy.

When Ronan goes in, the ghost comes out.

And my God, every part of me is throbbing. Every part of me is nerves going crazy, dancing.

Dancing, jumping, twirling...

Every part. Every fucking part.

Is it the ghost nudging my clit with his cock?

Who cares? It's all so amazing and good and perfect and ecstatic. I'm in nirvana, coming so close to paradise.

Ready to jump... Ready to jump... Ready to jump...

And then—the deep voice of my Dominant.

"Come, Blossom. Come now."

I tug on my invisible bindings, arch my back, try to move my ass in tandem with both the thrusts.

It's all impossible, but I try, because at his urging, I'm shattering, I'm coming, I'm flying off the precipice and into the sea of ecstasy.

And all I want...

All I want in this very moment—and in all the moments to come—is for this feeling to never end.

Time suspends itself. In my head I see Ronan fucking my ass, the ghost kneeling in front of him, fucking my pussy.

The ghost... He's blond, blue-eyed, and his teeth... They're pointed like a vampire's.

My God...

He's good-looking...

But nothing compared to Ronan.

Ronan, who's all man. Not a ghost, but a true living man,

his cock invading my ass as it's never been invaded before.

"Come again, Blossom."

Electricity surges through me once more, picking up where the previous orgasm left off...

I squeal, I scream, and I turn my head from side to side, wailing.

Because this feeling—this ecstatic feeling of double penetration—the invisible bindings, the blindfold, the ghost...

It's so pure and perfect, and I'm so happy to submit.

To submit to this man...

In this moment... I never want to submit to another.

CHAPTER TWENTY-FIVE

Ronan

Mary hasn't moved her wrists or her arms, despite the fact that nothing is holding her there. She's bound by my will. By the invisible chains of our ghost.

I'm ready...

So ready to come inside this tight little ass.

I want to hold off, but—

"God, Blossom..." I grit out. "We're both ready. We're both ready to come inside you."

I release into that tight little ass, my cock contracting, my balls scrunching, and with every pulse into her, I lose something of myself.

Something that I'm glad to give.

She will be mine. Mary. Blossom. Mariah Sandusky.

She will submit to me. Exactly the way I want her to.

She will be *mine*.

I stay inside her for a few precious moments, and then I pull out, keeping my trickery a secret.

Because, of course, no ghost was fucking her. No ghost was sucking on her nipples.

I laid the groundwork, and her imagination did the rest.

"Lie still," I say.

I hate to leave her, but I must take care of her after anal sex.

I go to the bathroom, wash myself, and wash the toys I used. I bury them deep in my suitcase before I head back to the bed and slide the warm washcloth I brought over Mary's ass and pussy. Then I remove the silk from her eyes.

"I've taken off the invisible bindings, Mary." I take her arms, massage her wrists gently, as I would if she'd truly been bound, and then pull her up into a sitting position.

"You may speak now."

Her eyes well with tears. "I can't even believe it, Ronan. I can't believe how incredible that was."

"This is only the beginning, Mary. I will take you places you never dreamed of going."

"You already have." She wipes the perspiration from her brow. "You brought me here to New Orleans. And the scene we just did together? It's the most aroused I've ever been. That double penetration… My God."

"You liked?"

"How did you…"

I place my fingers over her lips to quiet her. "Let it go, Mary. Remember it for what it was, for what you felt. Don't take away the mysticism."

She smiles then—a big, wide smile—and I'm not sure I've ever seen her look so beautiful. Her skin is flushed from the sex, from the orgasms, and her lips are swollen and pink. Her nipples are still hard and probably slightly raw from everything I put them through.

I can't wait to get clamps on them.

That *will* wait, though. That will wait until we get back to New York, back to Black Rose Underground.

She melts against my chest.

"Do you still want to go home tomorrow?" I ask.

She pulls back and meets my gaze. "I do, Ronan. I do... because I want to go to the club. Black Rose Underground. And I want to submit to you there."

I cup her cheeks, bring her toward me, and kiss her lips, sliding my tongue between them.

We're both sated, so this kiss is gentle. A simple meeting of mouths.

But the odd thing is?

I'm feeling something different.

Something strong and potent.

Something unique...and foreign.

From a gentle kiss.

I break the kiss. "Would you like to go back to your room?"

"I'll stay here with you, if it's all right."

"It's all right."

I don't normally let a submissive sleep with me, but that ship has sailed. Mary already slept in my bed last night.

I narrow my gaze. "Perhaps the ghost of Jean-Pierre will visit you during the night."

She snuggles into my shoulder. "Jean-Pierre is wonderful, but I only need you, Ronan."

CHAPTER TWENTY-SIX

Mary

Once I'm back at my Manhattan apartment the next afternoon, I think about calling my boss and telling her I can work the rest of the week, but I decide against it. I've already got the time off, paid vacation, so I may as well use it.

Tonight I'm meeting Ronan at the club.

He asked to pick me up, but I decided I needed to approach the scene the way I normally do.

I get to the club myself, and I get home myself.

We'll take it slow.

Because even though we've been together twice now, I still fear that being at the club will bring back the haunting memories of the scene that went wrong and all the emotions they stir up.

It's best for me to stick to my particular regimen. We meet there. We play. I go home.

Already I know the scene will be amazing. Probably different from anything I've done before.

Of course there won't be double penetration. I never play with more than one Dominant at a time, and there are no ghosts at Black Rose Underground.

I chuckle to myself. *Ghosts.*

One day he may reveal his secrets to me. But do I really want him to? I could figure it out. It's not that difficult.

But then I lose the fantasy.

The fantasy of a ghost haunting a New Orleans hotel and fucking me along with Ronan.

I love the image in my mind.

And I don't want to lose it.

Besides, I have something else in mind for today.

I'm going to visit the State University of New York. I've decided to finish my degree in business. I might like to own my own business someday. Maybe my own lingerie and toy store, or better yet, an online business. Or perhaps I'd like to change my major. Maybe psychology, so I can counsel people in alternative sexual lifestyles.

Ronan makes me want *more.*

There's a scholarship program called the Excelsior Scholarship that allows eligible students to earn a free college degree at City University of New York or State University of New York.

I don't know if I'll be eligible, but it doesn't hurt to check it out. I fire up my laptop.

But then I'm interrupted by my phone. It's Brenda.

"Hey, Bren," I say into the phone.

"Hey yourself. What were you thinking, coming back early?"

I'm not sure how to answer. Part of me wishes I were still in New Orleans with Ronan. I only got one day of sightseeing, and there was so much more I wanted to do there. But my choice was to come home after one day, and I still think it was the right one.

"I don't know. It just seemed weird, going on a trip with

someone I barely know."

I know him now. In the biblical sense, and in another sense as well. He shared a lot of himself with me on our short trip. Plus I met his grandmother, a remarkable woman.

I smile to myself. I still have her love spell in my purse.

Sure, I don't believe in any of that, but she does. And for some reason she thinks I'm the one for her grandson.

I suppose we'll see about that.

"Did the two of you hit it off?" Brenda asks.

"Oh, we hit it off."

"Oh my God… I bet New Orleans has some spectacular BDSM clubs."

"We didn't get that far," I say.

"Oh…"

I say nothing.

"You didn't…"

"I did, Brenda. I don't know what I was thinking. Well, I know what I was thinking the first night. I was afraid my room was haunted."

Brenda lets out a laugh. "Come on, Mare. Seriously?"

"Well, yeah. We were staying at this hotel that's supposedly haunted. The chandelier above my bed flickered on and off during the night after I'd already turned the light switch off."

"And you didn't think—"

I interrupt her. "Yes, I know. Old building. Old wiring. Yada, yada, yada."

"Are you sure you didn't just want to join him in his room?"

I have no answer because part of what she says is the truth. Had I not had Ronan to run to, I would've dealt with the faulty wiring or the poltergeist or whatever the hell it was myself.

"I'm not going to sit here and psychoanalyze myself on the phone with you."

Brenda laughs. "You don't have to. I'm happy to do it for you. I think you like this guy, Mary. I think you like him, and I think it's scaring the hell out of you."

"Why would that scare me? I've always liked my Dominants."

"Yes, you have, but at the risk of sounding like a middle schooler, I think you *like* him like him."

She's not wrong, and it *does* scare the hell out of me. I haven't let myself have feelings like this in a long time. Not since Lucas.

So why not change the subject?

"I'm thinking about going back to school. Finishing my degree."

"That's great," she says. "I always felt bad that you didn't finish with me and graduate."

"I hated leaving school," I admit, "but it turned out to be the best thing for me at the time. It got me away from Lucas. That was such a toxic relationship."

"Yeah, it was. I'm not one to say I told you so…"

"No, you never did, and I appreciate that."

"I *am* going to say something now, though."

I roll my eyes, knowing well she can't see me.

"I saw that," she says.

"What are you talking about?"

"You rolled your eyes."

"I did not."

"Oh, spare me, Mary. I know you better than you know yourself. And that's why I need to say the following. Don't screw this up with Ronan."

"What is there to screw up? I don't date."

"No. And it's served you well for the last five years. But you've had scenes go bad before, and they never affected you like the one with Jack did."

"So?"

"So...I think maybe your subconscious is telling you that you want something more now."

Brenda's not a psychologist. She's a paralegal. So she doesn't know crap.

But we have been friends since we were eighteen, and she is right about one thing. I have been a little envious of what she and Dalton have found together.

But I hardly know Ronan.

The problem is...

I *want* to know him. I haven't been able to get him out of my head since I first laid eyes on him, and now that I've had him sexually?

My God, I felt things that I thought were dead in me forever.

I felt things I never wanted to feel again.

Now that they've edged into me? All I can think about is more.

God, I'm fucked. In every sense.

"I'm seeing him tonight at the club for a scene," I tell Brenda. "We'll see how it goes."

"Dalton's still out of town," she says. "You want me to be there?"

I open my mouth, ready to tell her yes. *Please be there.*

But I'll never be able to deal with this if I can't meet it head on. I've already been alone with the man. I've already allowed him to dominate me.

There's no reason to be apprehensive at all.

"As much as I want you there, I think I'd better go alone," I say. "I'm never going to get over this hump if I need a security blanket, you know?"

"I do know. Dalton comes back to town Friday, so maybe we'll see you both at the club this weekend."

"Maybe. We'll see how everything goes."

But already I'm looking forward to the weekend. I'm thinking about all the scenes Ronan and I can play out together. And all the scenes I can't even conceive of because they're in his head, not mine.

I'm looking forward to it.

I'm excited just thinking about it.

And that...is the problem.

CHAPTER TWENTY-SEVEN

Ronan

"What are you doing here?" my administrative assistant, Jennifer Morgan, says. "You were supposed to be gone all week."

"You know me. I micromanage."

It feels pretty good to be back. I hate leaving my business in the hands of others, even those I completely trust, like Jennifer.

"I read through the notes from the meeting with Braden Black yesterday," I say. "I should've been there."

"Why? Everything went smoothly."

"I know. I should've at least teleconferenced in." I shake my head. "I'm here now."

I'm not sure what I was doing. Taking a virtual stranger to my hometown and leaving my business in the hands of, yes, perfectly capable businesspeople, but they're not me.

"Well, since you're here"—Jennifer hands me a manila folder—"you can sign these documents yourself. I was going to have Brody do it. He's got your power of attorney."

Brody is my legal counsel. He's an American, but he was with me in Glasgow. So was Jennifer, who's also an American, as well as my second-in-command, Sabrina Ellis. They've all been with me in the business since I took over for my father. They're all sitting in my office with me.

Besides Brody, Jennifer, and Sabrina, I hired four others once we relocated here a month ago. They've all proved to be invaluable.

So yes, I trust them implicitly.

But still… They're not me.

"All right." I grab a pen. "So I checked my calendar. It looks like once we get these documents signed, we can move forward with hiring an architect to design our hotel."

"Correct," Sabrina says. "I've been looking into that. I found a good firm. Or what I thought was a good firm. But Braden Black recommended someone else."

"Why?"

"He wouldn't say why, only that he thought the first firm skated on ethics a bit."

I nod. "Let's go with Black's recommendation."

"That's what I figured you'd say. I've already set up a meeting for next week."

"Now that I'm back, can we move it up?" I grab my phone and open the calendar app. "This afternoon, if they're available?"

"Jennifer?" Sabrina says.

"I'll get right on it." Jennifer whisks out the door to her own office next to mine.

"I know I originally wanted this resort in Las Vegas to have a Scottish theme," I say, "but I'm rethinking that. What do you think about a New Orleans theme?"

"It's not exactly original," Sabrina offers. "The Orleans already has that theme."

"Yes, I know. But I was thinking of really diving into the culture. Recreating some of the cemeteries, the seedier side of

New Orleans."

Sabrina shakes her head. "Ronan, we've had these plans drawn up for a year. Now that you've purchased the property from Braden Black, redesigning everything will take more time, and that will take more money. Besides, a Scottish theme, with all the dealers and employees wearing kilts? There's nothing like that now in Vegas."

I sigh. She's right, of course. I just enjoyed getting back to my roots the last couple days.

But Scotland is also my roots. This way my company will offer something that isn't currently available.

"You're right," I defer.

"Why the sudden change of your mind?" Brody asks.

"Just my time in New Orleans. You know I was raised there. It'll always be home to me. Even though I look like I belong in a tavern in Scotland." I laugh.

"How about a restaurant?" Sabrina says. "We all know that Scottish food in general isn't anything exciting. You've already planned to have five restaurants in the hotel. Why not devote one of them to your grandmother's Creole recipes?"

"I love that idea. Give yourself a raise, Bree."

Sabrina laughs. "If I did that every time you told me to, you wouldn't be able to afford me."

"We'll have one Scottish restaurant because it's a Scottish-themed hotel. I believe most people will go there to see the hunky waiters in kilts."

"Are you saying you're only going to hire male waiters?" Brody asks.

"No. Federal law won't allow me to do that, which I know is your point, Brody. But we're going to put the women in kilts as well. A uniform."

"Good." Brody chuckles. "I know we've been in Scotland

for a long time, but I didn't think I had to educate you on Title VII."

"Nope. You don't. Besides, women in kilts are pretty sexy, too."

Jennifer knocks and then walks in. "Good news. The architects are able to meet with us today. But we have to go to them."

"Not a problem. Have Philippe bring the car around."

"You want anyone else at the meeting?" Jennifer asks.

"Just Brody and Sabrina. And I'd like you there to take notes, Jen."

Jennifer makes a note on her iPad. "The meeting is set for three o'clock, so I'll have Philippe ready at two."

"Two? How far away is this place?"

"It's uptown. But you know how traffic is in New York."

"We could always take a cab," Sabrina says.

"No. We'll take the car. Philippe needs to continue learning his way around New York."

I quickly scrawl my signature on the documents and hand them back to Brody.

"All right. I've got about a million emails to respond to, so I will see all of you down in the lobby at two."

"You got it, boss." Sabrina stands.

The three of them exit my office, and I get back to work.

My phone sits next to me. I can almost see it pulse, as if it has a heartbeat.

I want to call Mary. She took the week off from work, and I'm going to see her tonight at the club.

So why do I want to speak to her so badly?

Damn.

I miss the woman.

And that's unlike me.

I left Keira because she wanted more than I could give. She and I were together for five years, but apart from our scenes together, she wasn't part of my life. My life consisted of work, work, and more work with my weekend excursions to the club my only interactions with her. They were very pleasurable for both of us. She was a good sub, and I was very attracted to her.

But I didn't get that squishy feeling.

That squishy feeling that I didn't even know existed until I met Mary.

I grab my phone and shove it in my top desk drawer.

Except I still know it's there.

I still want to call Mary.

I suppose it won't hurt to text her. I grab my phone out of the drawer and pull up her number.

Hi there. I'm looking forward to tonight. I hope you're having a good day.

Then I hit send.

I read back over the text.

My God. Could it be more boring?

I wait for the three dots to begin moving to signal that she received it and is texting me back.

But she doesn't.

So I shove my phone in my desk drawer and return to my business at hand. Only an hour to go before my staff and I leave to meet the architects.

And only eight hours to go until I meet Mary at Black Rose Underground.

CHAPTER TWENTY-EIGHT

Mary

I sit alone at the bar at Black Rose Underground, wearing the little black dress I wore the first night I met Ronan. Normally, if I'm waiting for a Dominant to meet me before a scene, I dress a little more scantily. Some of the Dominants I play with like lingerie, fishnet stockings, and garter belts. Others like a corset. Some like nothing at all. I've only sat at the bar completely nude once. It's not really my jam. But there are others who stay naked once they get to the club. I look over my shoulder, and my gaze is drawn to a woman dressed in nothing but rope.

It's a work of art, but I don't gawk. No one at Black Rose gawks at one another. We admire the beauty—the feast for the eyes—and we look and we smile. But we never stare.

Darius, a Dominant I've played with on more than one occasion, approaches me. "Good evening, Blossom."

"Hi, Darius."

His gaze homes in on my neck. "Are you up for a little something?"

My cheeks warm as my hand absently wanders to my neck.

I'm not collared, which is why Darius can approach me.

"I'm meeting someone," I say.

"That's too bad. Someone amazing, I hope."

"More than amazing."

He looks into my eyes. "It's been a long time, Blossom. I've missed you."

Darius is a good Dom. "Yes, we've had fun."

"But you haven't missed me?"

The truth is...no. I haven't missed any of my Dominants. Not since the scene with Jackson. "I've missed our talks."

He frowns. "I see. How have you been, Blossom?"

"I've had a difficult few months." Not a lie, but I leave out the life-changing two days in New Orleans.

"I'm sorry to hear that. Do you want to talk about it?"

We all sign confidentiality agreements as members of Black Rose Underground, so there's no way that Darius knows what went on between Jackson and me. That's the way I like it.

"It's not a big deal. I had a scene go too far. But the funny thing is, it's not the first time that's ever happened. I'm not sure why it affected me so profoundly this time."

"Maybe you've come to the tipping point."

"What's that?"

"It happens to most submissives at some point."

Then why haven't I ever heard of it? "You're going to have to explain that."

"I don't have any hard evidence or statistics. My findings are purely anecdotal. But I've been a Dominant here at Black Rose for quite a while, and before that, a Dominant at another club. And I found that most submissives like you—those who stay out of relationships and just come to play—eventually want something more."

"What about Dominants? Don't you want more?"

He shrugs. "Maybe someday. But right now, this suits me fine. I'm a workaholic in my day-to-day life, so I don't have time for a real relationship. Plus, I'd have to find someone who shares my proclivities in the bedroom."

"I think you could probably find that person here."

"But most single ladies who come here are like you, Blossom. They come because it's what they prefer, too. A no-strings-attached way to practice what they enjoy in the bedroom and not have it mean anything." He shakes his head. "I take that back. I know it means something to you. It does to me as well."

I smile at him. "It's okay, Darius. I know what you meant."

"Who are you meeting?"

"A new member. He's only been here a couple of times."

Darius grins slowly and nods. "Ah. I know who you mean. The Scotsman."

My cheeks warm. "He looks the part, doesn't he? He's actually American. He was born and raised in New Orleans."

"I think I see him now, actually." Darius leans over and whispers in my ear. "Make sure he puts a collar on you, love."

So much for the rule of not staring and not gawking.

I *do* stare.

Because Ronan walks in, wearing his O'Connor tartan, like he did the first time we met. Shoes, hose, and no freaking shirt. Just like he did the first time I laid eyes on him.

The first time I fell under his spell.

God, he's beautiful.

He zeroes in on me and heads toward me.

I'm only drinking water.

Darius makes his escape, nods at Ronan as he approaches me.

"Who's that?" Ronan asks.

"His name is Darius. He's a Dominant."

"Did he ask you to play?"

"He did, but I told him I was meeting you."

He raises an eyebrow. "What was he whispering to you?"

"If you must know, he said that you should put a collar on me."

He pulls a velvet choker out of his sporran. "I should've given this to you when we landed. My mistake." He burns me with his gaze. "Believe me, Blossom, it will not happen again."

The soft velvet from Ronan is cool against my throat.

"Are you just drinking water tonight?"

"I only allow myself to have one drink before a scene, and I wanted to wait until you got here."

"Good enough." He motions to the bartender.

Freddy is on duty tonight. He's a broad-shouldered young man, shirtless as per the rules here at Black Rose.

"Good evening, Blossom. And you are..." He nods to Ronan.

"Ronan," he says. "I'll have a Macallan fifteen-year, neat."

"Coming right up, and for you, Blossom? A lemon drop, I assume?"

I ponder a moment. "Freddy, I'm going to try something different tonight. Make me a Sazerac."

Freddy's eyebrows rise. "I think I can safely say that you are the first person since I've been working here who has ever ordered that."

"Do you know how to make one?"

"I know how to make everything, beautiful."

Ronan goes rigid beside me at Freddy's endearment. But Freddy calls all women beautiful. Besides, I'm not exactly his type. He's in a relationship with another bartender, Leon.

Freddy turns to prepare our drinks, and Ronan touches my cheek.

"So...a Sazerac."

"Yes. I enjoyed it. I didn't think I would, but I did, and... I don't know. I feel like I want one. I feel like..." I shake my head, let out a nervous laugh. "I'm not making any sense."

"It's all right. I know what you're saying. New Orleans gets inside your soul. You weren't even there for very long, but you can't wait to go back, can you?"

"You're absolutely right. How did you know?"

"Are you kidding me? I grew up there. The place is a part of me. I may look the part of my Scottish heritage, but I'm equal parts Creole."

"I really enjoyed meeting your grandmother," I say. "She's one of a kind."

"That she is, Blossom."

He's using my club name here, which he should.

But I long to hear my given name from his full lips again.

Freddy returns with our drinks. "One Macallan fifteen-year neat, and a Sazerac for the beautiful lady."

"Thank you." Ronan shoves a bill toward Freddy.

Freddy pockets it. "And thank you."

An open bar is part of our club membership, but we're still expected to tip the servers and bartenders.

I take a sip of my Sazerac. It's good but...different.

Ronan raises his eyebrows at me. "So...?"

"Delicious. But not like the one at your grandmother's."

"Everything always tastes a little bit better in the Big Easy. I had a good time with you, Blossom."

"I did too. I mean..." I stir my Sazerac. "Not every submissive can say they've been fucked by a ghost."

His lips curve slightly upward.

I wonder what it would take to get a huge smile out of him.

"You look beautiful tonight."

"Thank you. So do you." I grin and take another sip. "Isn't it funny that we both wore the same thing we wore when we first met?"

"Oh, yeah," he says. "That *is* what you're wearing."

"You're such a man. Men never notice things like clothing, do they?"

"We notice it more when it's lying in a heap on the floor."

I smile.

So strange how mere words affect me. I'm not used to that.

I gesture to his tartan. "Why did you wear the same thing?"

"It was clean."

I let out a soft chuckle. "You're something, Ronan."

"So are you, my sweet, fragrant Blossom." He leans toward my ear. "And I do mean sweet and fragrant."

Tingles shoot through me, and I'm ready. So ready for what he has in store for me. We haven't discussed the scene, but he already knows a little bit about what I like. I imagine we'll set some limits before we go back. Or maybe we won't. Part of me wants to be surprised.

Ronan shoots his scotch back in one gulp.

But he doesn't ask Freddy for another.

"You want me to finish this?" I ask.

"You go at your own pace," he says. "Tonight isn't just about me. It's also about you. I'm going to show you how to please me. And I'm willing to take all the time you need."

My heart nearly skips a beat. Everything he says makes me shudder. Makes me quake with excitement and arousal. He's the Dominant, so yes, it *is* about me pleasing him and about me submitting to him. But as a submissive, I help make the rules.

Unless I've known a Dominant for a while and have played with him more than once, we always have a talk before the scene. It's standard operating procedure.

But I almost hope I don't have that talk with Ronan.

I'm willing to let him do whatever he wants to me. After all, he already knows my hard limits. And I know him well enough to know he won't try to breach them.

He knows my safe word. We've already been together twice. He knows my body.

He's been inside my ass, and I don't normally let a Dom in my ass until we've been together several times so I know that I have his complete trust.

But with Ronan...

Already I know I'll go wherever he wants tonight. I'll go into the most forbidden, erotic, taboo fantasy if that's what this man wants.

Because what he wants is ultimately what I want.

To please him.

With every cell in my body, I want to please Ronan O'Connor.

More than I've ever wanted to please any Dominant before. Even Lucas.

I finish my drink. "I'm ready when you are...sir."

CHAPTER TWENTY-NINE

Ronan

My groin tightens. All I can think about is getting Mary back to a room. I was able to reserve one of the larger private suites. When we arrive, the lights are dimmed. In the corner is a king-size bed covered in red silk.

"Turn around, Mary," I command.

She turns, her back to me. I thread my hands into her soft hair.

"I'm going to braid your hair."

"Why?"

"That's for me to know. You be quiet now."

Her hair is soft and silky as I braid it, and it feels wonderful against my fingertips.

Once it's braided, I slide my hands over her thighs, gliding her dress up and over her hips and ass.

A moment later, the dress is off, and only her panties cover her.

I set her on the edge of the bed, and then I bind her hands with handcuffs.

She lies on the bed, her nipples hard and turgid.

Then I remove her panties.

I climb on top of her, hover over her. Kiss her neck, her lips. Her nipples.

So much more I could do to her in this place, but what I want is her. Now.

I shove my dick into her.

I fuck her hard, fuck her fast...

"My God, Ronan!"

I'll punish her for speaking, but not now.

Now I need to—

"Fuck..." I release inside her.

God...

For a moment I think I could stay inside her forever.

But Mary squirms beneath me, and I realize I need to punish her for speaking.

I rise as the last of the orgasm drains from my body. Then I stare down at her, her pussy swollen from my attentions, her nipples hard, straining toward me. Her hair braided.

She'll find out why I braided it now.

"Rise," I say.

She obeys, sliding her beautiful body off the red silk and standing before me.

"I need to punish you now. Do you know why?"

She nods.

"I'd like you to speak for a moment. Tell me why."

"Because I spoke without permission."

"Smart girl."

I grab her by the braid, yank her head back, exposing her milky neck. I slide my lips over it, my tongue. Nipping at her, biting her.

She groans.

"This isn't your punishment, Blossom. This is only because

I love your neck so much."

I move her to the wall, where instruments hang from various hooks.

I cover her eyes with a red silk blindfold.

I take her hand, remove the cuffs, and then lead her to a table and help her lie down. I use leather bindings to secure her to the leather-topped table, and then I spread her legs, binding them to the table as well. She's laid out only for my pleasure, and she can't see.

I kiss her lips, jamming my tongue between them.

Then I grab a vibrator, float it over her nipples, down to her clit.

She trembles. "Oh..." She moans.

"Are you frustrated? Do you want to come, Blossom?"

She nods her head almost violently.

"That would be a punishment, then."

I set the vibrator down, find a riding crop, and—

Whomp!

I bring the leather down onto her breasts.

Her capillaries burst, and her chest becomes even rosier than it was. *Whomp!*

This time over one nipple.

Whomp!

And then the other.

Whomp!

This time right over her clit.

"My God!"

"Mary, Mary. You're defying me, aren't you?"

She presses her lips shut.

I brush mine over them. Then I head to her ear, nipping her lobe. "What am I going to do about that?" I move away from her and slap the riding crop over her pussy once more.

She groans out in ecstasy but does not say any words, simply bites her lip.

"I could turn you around," I say. "Lock you in this position with your ass facing me. I could flog it until it's red and juicy. Then I could fuck you. Fuck that sweet asshole like I did the other night."

She groans.

"But that wouldn't be punishment. You've spoken twice now without permission, Blossom."

I should continue the punishment. But the fact that she spoke? It has me more aroused than ever. Why would I be aroused by such defiance? Blossom is not a new submissive. Which means...

She truly can't help herself.

I put down the riding crop, grab the egg-shaped vibrator once more.

"I'm going to bring you to the edge, Blossom. You haven't climaxed yet, and I think maybe... I think maybe you won't."

She bites her lip, whimpering.

I turn on the vibrator, feel it against the palm of my hand. Through this vibrator, I will feel everything Blossom feels.

It's a secret shared by most Dominants. When we use toys, it's only an extension of ourselves. The energy vibrates through the toys and into our bodies.

When a riding crop comes down on my submissive, I feel it. The energy travels through the leather and into my body.

And my cock grows harder. Each time.

But with Mary? I'm harder than I have ever been.

Normally, I'd be able to restrain myself. I wouldn't have fucked her on the bed. Not after she spoke out of turn.

What is happening to me?

But I stop thinking about it. I'm here to do a scene with

Blossom. And in a scene I will do it. I will punish her, whether I want to or not.

I slide the vibrator between her legs.

Set it on her clit, watch her squirm.

And when she starts groaning, I remove it.

She whimpers.

Vibrator on clit.

Moaning.

Remove it.

Whimper.

I continue this for the next couple of minutes until she finally cries out, "Please, let me come!"

I stop myself from smiling. "What am I going to do with you, Blossom? You can't obey a simple command to be quiet. Are you this defiant with all your Dominants?"

She shakes her head vehemently. Bites on her lip to keep from speaking.

"What is it about me that makes you want to defy me so much?"

She keeps her lips glued shut.

"Very good. Do not speak again, or you will not like the consequences."

I'm hard again. Hard again for her. And I yearn to turn her around and fuck that tight little ass.

But first I must tease her a bit more.

I bend down, flick my tongue over her clit.

She gasps out loud.

I savor her, her tangy and fruity flavor. The musk travels through my nose and infuses my body with her.

The tantalizing taste pleases my tastebuds.

Oh my God. I must have her.

But I *can* restrain myself, even if she cannot.

I slide my tongue across her slit, sucking all the cream out of her.

"My God, Blossom. Such a delicious pussy. Beautiful, dazzling, and delicious." I continue sucking on her, swirling my tongue around her clit, and then nibbling on it until she's ready to come...

I move away, nibble at her thighs, shove my tongue into her wet pussy.

She's gasping above me, whimpering, pleading, though not in words.

I tease her again, twirl my tongue over her hot clit, give it the slightest suck...

"Ronan, please!"

I rise, head to the bureau, and grab two nipple clamps.

"You just won't obey, will you?" I slide one clamp onto her nipple, and she gasps.

"Nipple clamps," I say. "I will pinch those nipples until they're ready to pop off."

She bites on her lips, whimpering.

She'll enjoy nipple clamps. She enjoyed me biting her nipples hard in New Orleans. This isn't really a punishment for her, and I know this. So does she.

The punishment will be that she doesn't come.

I tighten the clamps and then yank on the chain between them.

She lets out a groan.

"Does that feel good to you? Nipple torture?" I step back a moment and simply gaze at her. "Blossom...you look so beautiful right now. I could fuck you. I could let you come. I could nibble on that hard little clit of yours until you shatter into pieces. But what kind of punishment would that be?"

She whimpers again, biting her lip to keep from speaking.

I yank on the chain again, and she quakes.

"If you can stay silent for the rest of the scene, maybe I'll let you come."

She bites her lip again, whimpering.

I give the chain between her nipples another good yank, and then I slide my tongue down her abdomen, over her vulva, licking her clit.

Time to see how much she can take. Truly.

"I command you not to come," I say. "You will *not* come. Do you understand me?"

She nods, her eyes blindfolded still. Her cheeks are red, as are the tops of her breasts. I stand back a moment, simply regard her, her beautiful body. Then I decide.

I am going into that ass again.

But not until I get it good and red.

"I'm going to unbind you now, Blossom. Then I'm going to help you stand and turn you to face the wall, where I'll bind you again. If anything is uncomfortable to you, use your safe word. Do you understand?"

She nods.

Quickly, I unbind her, bring her to her feet, and bring her to the wall, where I click the bindings into place once more.

Her nipples are still clamped, and I can reach around and yank on the chain if I want to.

But the first thing I want to do is look at that puckery little asshole.

I kneel down, position myself between her legs, and swipe my tongue between her cheeks.

Her legs are far enough apart that the cheeks are already spread a bit, giving me easy access to that beautiful little hole.

"You taste like cherry pie," I say against her cheeks. "Delicious, Blossom. Fucking delicious."

I rise then, grab the riding crop I used before, and then…

Slap!

I bring it down upon her gorgeous little ass.

Slap, slap, slap!

She moans, and her ass turns a delectable pink. I kneel again, tongue her sweet hole, and then grab the vibrator. I shove it between her legs, touch her clit as I continue my tongue's assault on her ass.

She squirms—or she tries to—shoving her ass against me as much as she can.

She's whimpering, moaning.

And I feel her pussy is ready.

She's ready to come—so I end the vibration.

That whimper of loss comes out of her throat.

I move over to the bureau, grab some lube, warm it in my palm.

Then I slide against her ass and breach it with a finger.

She gasps.

"Do you like my finger in your asshole?"

She nods as she whimpers.

"Do you know how good it felt to fuck you in the ass, Blossom? It was the most amazing sensation. I'm an experienced man, but you have the tightest ass I've ever been inside."

This woman… I could say she was made for me. But I don't even know her.

That's not what I'm looking for anyway.

I wipe the thoughts from my mind as I lube up my cock, ready to slide it slowly into her ass.

Then I grab the vibrator once more and touch it to her clit.

She quakes.

I slide my tongue over her neck, reaching her ear. "Are you ready? Are you ready for me to fuck your ass?"

She nods.

"Good girl."

I brace myself, bend my legs, reach her ass. She sticks it out as much as she can, ready for me.

I slide my cock between her ass cheeks, and then, quickly, I breach the tight rim of her asshole.

She sucks in a breath. I wait a moment. And then I thrust all the way in.

Sweet, sweet heaven.

I wait—wait until I can feel her body relax a bit—and then I slide out and back in.

I've already come once, so I was thinking it would be a little longer before I came again.

But already I can feel my balls scrunching up to my body, my cock ready to explode.

Still, she hasn't come. That will be punishment enough.

In, out, in, out—until I can take it no longer.

I shove myself into her ass, releasing.

CHAPTER THIRTY

Mary

I'm dying a slow and perfect death.

My clit is on fire—throbbing inside already.

But I cannot disobey his command not to come.

With one word, I could come.

I've disobeyed him already. I've spoken not once, not twice, but three times. And he's punished me for it.

He may not let me come tonight.

Though I could go home after the scene and masturbate myself to climax, already I know I won't.

I won't because he told me not to.

And obeying him... Submitting to him... Giving no one but Ronan control of my pleasure...

It feels right.

So fucking right.

He withdraws from my ass, and I listen to his footfalls as he walks to the bathroom in the suite, turns on the faucet, and then returns. A washcloth slides between my ass cheeks.

"You're something amazing," he growls against my thighs as he washes me.

I want to tell him everything I'm feeling, how I'll never come again unless he tells me to. How this is "something amazing" that I've never experienced. Not with any Dominant. Not even with Lucas.

But I'm putting the cart before the horse. We don't know each other, and he's probably not feeling anything like that.

After all, he left Scotland to come here.

He won't be able to give me what I'm craving.

But Brenda and Darius were right about one thing, and I know it now as much as I know my own name.

The reason that scene with Jack affected me so profoundly is because I'm ready for more. I'll always be part of this lifestyle, but I'm ready for a commitment. To commit to one Dominant.

But Ronan isn't ready for that.

He will be playing with other submissives, and that...

Jealousy slices through my heart.

Something I haven't felt in so long. Thought I'd never feel again. Was perfectly content never to feel again *because it sucks*.

It feels like your heart is literally cracking in two.

Once he's done cleaning me, he unbinds me, and then he removes the blindfold.

"You may speak now, Blossom."

But I say nothing.

I'm not sure what to say.

I could beg for an orgasm, but I already know he won't give it to me. Until he tells me to come, I won't.

What the hell is wrong with me?

I've been punished before by a Dominant withholding orgasm, but each time that happened, I took care of myself that evening once I was home.

I won't do that tonight.

I won't come until Ronan commands me to.

"Do you want to come?" he asks.

I open my mouth, ready to say yes, but the words that actually emerge surprise even me.

"Not unless you want me to, sir."

My God, has he broken me?

He brings his hand to my cheek, gently caresses it. "That's the right answer, sweet girl."

He picks me up into his arms then, carries me over to the bed where I was handcuffed, and spreads my legs.

He slides his tongue over my pussy, nibbles on my clit as he thrusts two fingers into me.

Then he meets my gaze from between my legs. "Come, Blossom. Come for me."

It happens then.

Stars burst inside me, filtering out through my fingers and toes into the universe, taking me to nirvana.

It surprises even me how quickly I come at his simple words.

And I know...

I'm certain of only one thing...

This is the best orgasm I've ever had...even better than what I had in New Orleans.

And I won't have another until he tells me I can.

• • •

When Ronan sees me home, I expect him to give me a kiss good night, but he doesn't.

Which further cements what I fear.

Despite our whole New Orleans junket, we are not lovers, perhaps not even friends. We are a Dominant and a submissive who play together.

That's all.

And I do something that I almost never do.

I cry.

Not full-blown, racking sobs or anything. Just gentle weeping with tears landing on my pillowcase.

I jerk upward as a thought spears into my head.

The love spell that Yvette gave me is still in my purse.

I don't even believe in that kind of stuff.

But what are spells anyway? Are they not just a prayer in a different form? I don't follow any one religion, but I do talk to God. I ask for forgiveness when I've done something bad, I give thanks for all the good things in my life, and on occasion, I ask for something.

I've never asked for someone to fall in love with me.

That seems to be crossing the line. Things I ask for are simpler. I ask for people who are suffering to find happiness. If I'm short on money one month, I ask for a little help. Sometimes it comes and sometimes it doesn't, but I always get by.

I open the little packet Yvette gave me.

And then I smile.

What's written on the paper is not a spell at all. It's a simple message.

Dearest Mary,

I know you and my grandson haven't known each other for long, but I see something when he looks at you. I see something I've never seen in him before. I believe you're the one. You were placed in his path and he in yours. Don't force it, and if you're not feeling what I believe you are feeling, feel free to ignore this note. But I have a sixth sense about these things. You don't practice Voodoo for a lifetime and not see the signs of impending love. Inside the sachet are rose petals and peppermint leaves and a small crystal of rose quartz. A talisman to attract love. Keep it with you.

Because even if it's not Ronan, I can see that you're ready for love, Mary. And it will come to you.

Avec amour,
Yvette.

CHAPTER THIRTY-ONE

Ronan

After a solid morning of meetings, I end up having to fly to Vegas the next evening.

I want to take Mary with me.

So crazy. I already took her to my hometown, and I'll be working during all my waking hours in Las Vegas. I won't have any time to spend with her.

But damn...I don't want to be so far away from her.

"Get a grip," I say out loud to myself.

She's not mine—although that's the word that comes to my mind when I think about her.

I'm not cut from that cloth, and neither is she.

If I *were* cut from that cloth, I would be making a life with Keira in Glasgow right now.

Except...

I feel something for Mary that I never felt for Keira. Which makes absolutely no sense. I hardly know the woman.

But I feel as if—as my grandmother would say—we are souls that have encountered each other before, during different lives.

"Absolutely not," I say, again out loud.

Jennifer knocks and opens the door. "Your flight's all set. You leave tonight at seven p.m. from LaGuardia. First class seat on United."

"Perfect. Thank you." I close my mouth and then open it, ready to ask her to get Mary a seat on the same flight, but then I close it again quickly.

I need to stay focused.

Normally I wouldn't even tell a submissive that I'm leaving, but I feel like I should let Mary know.

I send her a quick text.

Afraid I won't be able to meet you at the club this weekend as planned. I have to fly to Las Vegas on business. I'll be back Sunday.

I wait for her reply.

It doesn't come.

She's probably just busy.

Except she's probably *not* busy, because she took the rest of this week off.

Still…it's not my business. Perhaps she won't be upset at all that I'm going to be gone this weekend.

And if that's the case, I need to take that as a sign. That whatever this is that I'm feeling for her is nothing.

Nothing more than meeting a new person that I have a lot of rapport with.

Leave it at that.

Jen comes in again. "Your lunch is here. Do you want me to set it out for you?"

"Yeah, please. Thanks."

Jennifer opens the bag of takeout and sets it out on the little table on the other side of my office. "From the kosher deli down the street," she says. "Turkey and avocado with bacon on sourdough. Potato salad and freshly brewed iced tea."

"Perfect. Thank you."

"Not a problem. I'm going to lunch now. I've got my phone on me if you need anything."

"Great. Have a good lunch."

I rise, walk over to my small table, and take a sip of the iced tea, cooling my parched throat.

I've been thinking about Mary since last night. Since I left her at her apartment without so much as a good-night kiss.

I wanted to kiss her. I wanted to kiss her and stay the night with her in her bed.

But I've already spent two nights with the woman—and that is two nights too many.

I pick up half of my sandwich, take a bite. Delicious. I haven't been in New York long, but I quickly found that there's no better delicatessen anywhere.

The creaminess of the avocado works so well with the smokiness of the bacon and the mild flavor of the turkey. But the best is the sourdough bread. Freshly baked every day. You can't find bread like this anywhere else, not even in San Francisco, and certainly not in New Orleans. Of course, I'd defy anyone to find a beignet in New York. At least one that's worth eating.

I finish my lunch quickly, sit back down at my desk, and continue working. I've got a lot to get done before my flight tonight.

Then the ding of my cell phone.

Mary has responded to my text.

Have a safe trip.

That's it.

Have a safe fucking trip.

What did I expect? She's a submissive, and I'm a Dominant. We don't owe each other any further explanation.

Damn.

I thread my fingers through my hair.

I'm going to miss her like crazy, which makes no sense at all.

Again, I consider asking her to come along, but again, I stop myself. It's a work trip. I'm going to be busy. I won't have any time to spend with her.

Except for nights… In her room…

God…

What is *wrong* with me?

I hardly know the woman.

I have to get home to pack, so I finish up what I'm working on and go back to my hotel suite.

"Shit," I say out loud.

I had an appointment with my realtor Saturday morning to look at potential apartments in the city.

I text her quickly and cancel, saying I have to go out of town.

Then I pack my bag and call Phillipe to take me to the airport.

All the time, I'm thinking about how much I'm going to miss Mary.

And her simple, impersonal response. My hands itch. They want to pick up my phone and give her a call.

But I resist the temptation. Resist the urge.

It's not what she wants.

And it shouldn't be what I want.

• • •

I had Jennifer book me at the Orleans Hotel.

I want to look at it, see what I would've done differently.

I gained three hours on the flight, so it's only eight p.m. here.

But I have no desire to research the hotel this evening.

No.

My desires lie elsewhere.

CHAPTER THIRTY-TWO

Mary

I feel pretty shitty after I hit send.
Have a safe trip.

That's all I said to Ronan, but I wanted to say so much more. I'm deeply disappointed that we won't be together this weekend at the club.

Today is my last day of vacation time. I was going to spend the day registering for classes online, but I desperately need to get out of my apartment, so I decide to take the subway to the university itself.

Why register online? I can register in person. Maybe talk to an admissions counselor. Find out what my options are. Back-and-forth question and answer is always better face-to-face.

I have two years of college under my belt. I quickly send an email to my university to have them sent to me.

I dress in the only pair of conservative black slacks I own. For work, I usually dress in jeans and a top from the store, sometimes a corset.

My mother once told me that every woman should have a

navy-blue skirt, a pair of black dress pants, a crisp white blouse, and a pair of black pumps, because you never know when you're going to need to look professional.

I choose not to wear the pumps. I slip on a pair of black flats instead because I'll be walking.

The black pants and the crisp white blouse—a cotton blend— still fit me perfectly. I pull my hair up into a high ponytail with a black scrunchie, apply a touch of lip stain, blush, and mascara, and I'm ready to go.

• • •

"May I help you?" a young woman asks when I walk into the administrative building at the school.

"Yes, hi. I'd like to find out what my options are for finishing my degree. I have two years toward a business degree at Mellville."

"You can do all that online. You didn't have to come in."

"Yes, I know. That was my original plan, but I have the day off today, and I thought why not visit the campus? See if it's a good fit."

"Absolutely." She hands me a map of the campus. "We do have a tour today. Graduating high school seniors always tour on Fridays. You can join the tour that leaves in an hour."

"I'd like that. Thank you."

"And I'll see if one of our admissions counselors is available as well. Give me a moment."

"Thank you," I say again.

The receptionist taps on her computer. "It looks like one of our counselors does have availability. Why don't you have a seat and I'll give him a call and see if he's willing to talk to you?"

"Thank you. I appreciate it." I move to the small waiting

area, take a seat on the sofa, and pull my phone out of my purse.

For the life of me, I don't know what people did to look busy before cell phones.

A few moments later. "Miss?"

I raise my eyes to the receptionist's voice.

"I can go ahead and take you back to the counselor."

"Great, thank you." I rise and follow the woman behind the reception desk to a hallway of offices.

She knocks on one of the doors.

"Come in," a man's voice says from the other side.

I cock my head. No way...

She opens the door.

"Hey, Luke. This is the young woman who wants to talk about registering."

Luke? My stomach drops.

He was Lucas to me.

That was five years ago, when I was a student at Mellville... and he was a professor.

I resist the urge to drop my jaw.

He rises, moves to shake my hand. "Good morning, I'm Luke Tedesco."

Really? Does he really *not* recognize me?

"Mariah Sandusky." I hold out my hand.

"Thank you, Regina," he says to the receptionist.

Regina nods, leaves, closes the door behind her.

"Mary..." he says.

I snap my hand back and turn toward the door. "We don't have to do this."

"Wait—you want to finish your degree, right?"

"I think I can probably find another college."

"Don't be silly." He sits down at his desk, taps on his computer. "Are you working full-time?"

"Yeah."

"We have lots of night programs available. Or you could take advantage of our extensive online programs as well." He reaches under his desk and then sets a few brightly colored pamphlets in front of me.

I take a seat as he gestures, fidgeting with my hands.

"This doesn't have to be awkward, Mary."

Too late.

He's still as good-looking as I remember. Tall, with sandy-blond hair and blue eyes. But those eyes I once found so mesmerizing are nothing compared Ronan's.

I was young, innocent, and naive, and I fell in love with a professor—a professor who introduced me to my submissive side.

Is he still in the lifestyle? I've never seen him at Black Rose Underground. If I had, I probably would've found another club.

"Do you have your transcript with you?"

"It's online. But I—"

"As I recall, you were an excellent student, Mary. It's a shame you couldn't finish school."

"My father died. You know the story."

He presses his lips together for a second. "Yes, I remember. Still, a shame. You left without so much as a word."

"I didn't have a choice."

"Something could've been worked out. We could've found you a scholarship."

Do I have to spell it out for him?

"I had to leave, Lucas. You and I both know why."

He narrows his gaze. "I believe that's the first time you've used my name."

He's right, of course, and my cheeks warm. In the past, I referred to him only as sir.

"I'm no longer your submissive, Lucas. I'll refer to you as I like."

"Five years..." He stares at me. "You're still as beautiful as you always were."

"I'm here to discuss registering at the university."

"Of course you are." A snakelike grin crawls across his face. "You could've done all of this online, you know. I think you knew I was an admissions counselor here, and that's why you came in."

This time I do let my jaw drop.

Is he fucking serious?

"Don't feign surprise, Mary. You and I both know what's going on here."

I rise then. "This meeting is over."

He stands and grabs my wrist from across the desk. "Don't go. We have a lot to talk about."

I yank my wrist away from him. "Don't touch me again, Lucas. And unless the thing we need to talk about is my registering for classes, I assure you we have *nothing* to discuss."

"Don't you ever wonder what might've happened between us?"

"Nothing would've happened. You made it quite clear. We were Dominant and submissive, and that was it. If I hadn't left? We would no longer be in any kind of relationship."

"That's where you're wrong."

"Think what you want, Lucas. This meeting is over."

I leave the room, taking care not to slam the door, though I want to.

I whisk by the reception desk.

"Everything okay?" the woman says.

"Actually, no. I will *not* be enrolling in classes here."

She opens her mouth and says a few words, but I don't listen.

I leave the building and the campus as quickly as I can.

. . .

On my way to the subway station, I stop at a coffeehouse. What I really need is a drink, but it's way too early for that. I walk in, get in the line, which is about four people deep, and open my purse to grab my phone. My hand brushes against the talisman from Yvette.

I pull it out, let it sit in my palm. It's light. I feel like I'm holding nothing. But inside the little silk packet is rose petals, peppermint, and rose quartz.

The mint and floral scent infuses me with energy.

Yvette seems to think Ronan needs more. I sure want more.

But I don't think he does.

I'm staring at the talisman when the person behind me says, "Excuse me, ma'am. It's your turn."

Startled, I drop the talisman. The stranger behind me picks it up and hands it back to me.

"Thank you," I murmur.

"May I help you?" the cashier asks.

"I'd like a vanilla latte, please."

She grabs a cup, but then I have a change of heart. "Wait a minute. No. Café au lait. Do you have coffee with chicory?"

"Coffee with what?"

"Never mind, just café au lait."

She blinks. "I'm not sure what that is."

"Make her a regular latte," the gentleman behind me says. "Just coffee and steamed milk. That'll be close."

The cashier looks at me with her eyebrows raised.

"Sure, that's fine," I say.

"Caffè latte is the Italian version of a café au lait," the man says.

"Is it? I had never really heard of café au lait until I went to

New Orleans recently."

"New Orleans?" He smiles. "I love the Big Easy."

I smile too, pay for my coffee.

Then I take a seat to wait for my drink to be made.

The gentleman, who's very nice-looking with blond hair and blue eyes, approaches my table. "You mind if I join you?"

I'm not really looking for company but... "Sure, why not?"

"Thanks." He takes a seat, removes the lid from his coffee, and lets the steam escape.

"Black?" I ask.

"Oh yeah. I love New Orleans, but I always drink my coffee black. Even at Café du Monde. Everybody drinks café au lait except me."

"When were you last there?" I ask.

"A couple months ago. I had a business trip."

"Oh? What do you do?"

"I'm a corporate attorney. I work for Black, Inc." He holds out his hand. "I'm Tom."

Black, Inc.? Where Ronan is doing business...and he's familiar with New Orleans. Shit, does this guy know Ronan?

I take his outstretched hand. "Mary."

At almost the same time, the barista yells, "Mary!"

That elicits a chuckle from Tom. "I guess I could've waited another second. Then I would've known your name without asking."

I force a smile, rise, and go fetch my latte. I bring it back to the table, remove the lid, and take a sip, wiping the mustache from my mouth with a napkin.

"Well? Anything like café au lait?"

"It's good. But no. Coffee with chicory was something else. I've never had anything like it."

"It is good," he agrees. "I'm sure some of the coffee houses here have it. Or you could order it online. I order mine straight from Café du Monde. They ship it."

"Duly noted." I take another sip of the latte. It is delicious. Simple, strong coffee with steamed milk. But the chicory is definitely missing.

Funny how I'll never look at coffee the same way now.

Or a few other things.

"So what do you do, Mary?" Tom asks.

"I work at Treasure's Chest. It's a boutique shop that sells clubwear and lingerie."

He tilts his head and smiles. "Oh, yeah. I've walked by it many times. Maybe one day I'll come in and say hi."

"Sure."

But he won't. Men never walk into a lingerie shop unless they know what else we sell there.

He checks his watch. "I've got to get to a meeting. It was nice meeting you." He pulls out a card. "Give me a call anytime."

"What for?"

"In case you'd like to go out."

Perhaps it's the submissive in me, but I never ask men out. "I'm afraid you'll have to call me if you want to go out," I say.

"Happy to do that. But I don't have your number."

I'm not sure why, but I pull my business card out of my purse, my hand grazing the talisman again. I don't want to be rude. "This only has my work number, so you'll have to call me there."

"Thanks. You'll hear from me. So nice to meet you, Mary."

I watch him exit the coffeehouse.

And though he's good-looking, and I'm pretty sure he *will* call me, I won't be going out with him.

I don't date.

I hadn't wanted to date anyone in a long time.

Until I met Ronan O'Connor.

CHAPTER THIRTY-THREE

Ronan

Black Rose Underground has several sister clubs throughout the United States that honor our memberships. Clubs that are vetted as carefully as Black Rose is.

One of them is in Las Vegas, and I decide to pay it a visit Friday evening.

Maybe a scene with a willing submissive will get my mind off of Mary and her text.

Maybe it will get my head back where it needs to be.

To work. To play at the proper times.

I didn't bring any of my club gear or any of my kilts to Vegas. I had to pack quickly, and I brought only business attire. I wear black pants, black dress shoes, and a white button-down. I remove my tie.

I haven't been to any of the sister clubs because I just became a member at Black Rose.

Las Vegas is different from New York.

Definitely a different vibe, but a leather club is a leather club. If the owner of Black Rose Underground says this club is okay, it's okay.

I walk in, and the atmosphere is livelier than Black Rose. Black Rose's decor is red and black with a solid wood bar, very classy.

This club screams Vegas.

Neon lighting, a large dance floor, a black lacquer bar.

And sex out in the open.

The few times I've been to Black Rose, I haven't seen that. People who want to have sex out in the open go to one of the exhibition rooms. Those who prefer privacy—as I do—reserve a suite or playroom.

But on the black lacquer bar located in the back of the main room, a naked woman sits, her legs spread, and a man sits on a barstool, eating her out.

Men are visual creatures, so my groin tightens, even in light of the obvious health code violations.

I look around, taking in the debauchery.

Yes, definitely Vegas.

A topless server with fake tits that look like cereal bowls approaches me, smiling broadly. Her hair is bleached blond, and her face is round and pretty. "May I help you?"

"Absolutely. I'll have fifteen-year Macallan, neat."

"Come have a seat at the bar. I'll get it for you."

I nod and follow her.

There are only two open seats at the bar, one of which is right next to the man eating the woman.

I choose the other.

The server walks behind the bar and then holds out her hand. "I'm Lindy. I haven't seen you here before."

"That's because I've never been here before. I'm a member at one of the sister clubs in New York City."

"Oh. What brings you to Las Vegas?"

"Business."

Lindy grabs a glass from under the bar. "Happy to have you. Would you like someone to show you around the club?"

"That's all right. I'll just look around myself. But thank you."

"Never a problem." She winks and smacks her lips. Then she pours my drink and slides it toward me. I take a fifty out of my wallet and hand it to her.

"Wow. Thank you." She winks again and then turns her attention to another person at the bar.

I didn't notice her at first, but the person at the bar is a woman. She's dressed in an emerald-green minidress, fishnets, and platform slides.

She turns to look at me.

Her eyes are green, a striking similarity to her dress. Hair is dark brown.

"Good evening," she says.

"Good evening."

"I'm Aurora." She holds out her hand.

"Ronan." I take her hand.

She's a beautiful woman—more classically beautiful than Mary even—but not so much as a spark passes between us.

Still, I came to get my mind off of Mary, and Aurora is indeed gorgeous. Totally my type, even more than Mary is.

"You look like Jamie Fraser," she says.

"Right. The *Outlander* guy." Good thing Mary enlightened me.

"Are you Scottish?"

"Half," I say.

"What's your other half?"

"French Creole."

She giggles. "No way."

"Way," I say monotonically.

I feel like I'm back in college at a fucking frat party.

"I'm a mixture of Irish and Armenian with a little bit of Greek sprinkled in," she says.

I nod. "Yeah, you do look that part. The green eyes of the Irish."

"On my Armenian side, all their eyes are brown." She bats her eyelids.

"Your eyes are striking," I say.

"Yours are too. The color of the sky."

"Thank you." I watch her finish her drink. "Can I get you another?"

"I'd like that."

I signal to Lindy. "Another for the lady, please." Then I turn back to Aurora. "What are you drinking?"

"Old-fashioned. My drink of choice."

I nod. "I like an old-fashioned. It reminds me of a sweet Sazerac."

"What's a Sazerac?"

"It's a Creole cocktail made with rye whiskey. It's delicious, but it can be harsh."

Aurora motions to Lindy. "Instead of an old-fashioned, could I try a Sazerac?"

Lindy looks through her bottles and shakes her head. "Oh gosh, I'm sorry. We're out of rye."

"Bummer," Aurora says.

"Just imagine your old-fashioned a little bit harsher, with floral undertones," I say.

"Absolutely." She gives me a dazzling smile.

"You live here in Las Vegas?" I ask.

"I do."

"What are you doing here in the club? Are you looking for play?"

She smiles slyly. "Always."

"It would be my pleasure if you would join me. Assuming you're a submissive."

She pouts her lips. "Can't you tell?"

"I had a feeling, but it's always best to ask."

"You have Dominant written on your forehead in indelible ink, Jamie Fraser."

Does she really think that will turn me on? For me to be compared to some fictional character because I happen to resemble him slightly?

I finish my drink, set the glass on the counter. I pull another bill out of my wallet and slide it over for Lindy.

Any other time, a comparison to a fictional character probably wouldn't bother me. Why tonight?

Aurora is beautiful, elegant. And available.

And I'm suddenly no longer interested.

I'm not sure I ever was.

Fuck. I'm lying to myself.

I *never* was.

I'm interested in playing with only one woman, and she's back in New York. That fact in itself isn't unusual. Keira and I were exclusive in our play.

No. What's unusual is that I find myself thinking of Mary during the day, during work, when we're not together at the club. I want to protect her—and not just as a Dominant protects his submissive. Something about her has affected me on a visceral level. It's why I invited her to New Orleans...and it's why I can't stop thinking about her now.

Mémé always wanted me to settle down, to have a family, but I resisted because I was determined never to put a child through what I went through. A child is a gift. He or she shouldn't be something that a parent tosses aside for the sake of a career. I'm married to my career. I micromanage. How does a wife and child fit into that scenario?

Answer—they don't.

I couldn't give Keira what she wanted because I didn't feel that way about her. But Mary? I'm feeling things so foreign, so unusual, that it's making me reconsider my life's path.

"Afraid I can't stay, after all," I say to Aurora.

She places her hand over mine.

A serious no-no for any submissive.

Perhaps the rules are different here in Las Vegas. I don't know, and I just realized I don't really want to know.

Admittedly, this place is a feast for the eyes. Sex going on in front of us. No bondage play, though. Mostly just regular sex out here in the open.

"It was nice to meet you." I rise, walk out of the club, not even bothering to look back.

Aurora is beautiful, no doubt. The type I usually go for.

But Mary...

Sweet and passionate Mary...

Damn it all to hell.

I'm having feelings I have no business having.

And after I just left Keira for the same reason. Except with the two of us, *she* was the one having feelings. I leave the club and head back to the Las Vegas strip.

No one ever sleeps in this city. It's too late to get into any of the worthwhile shows.

So I simply walk by all the pimps hawking their women.

"Want to see a good show?" one of them asks me.

"No, thank you," I say.

Pamphlets gets shoved in my hand, photos of women.

Not interested. I could've had a woman more beautiful than any of them at the club.

I head back to my hotel, walk around the casino. I'm not a huge gambler, but I enjoy some blackjack now and then.

I sit down at one of the tables, play a few hands, lose three hundred bucks.

Okay. Now I'm done.

I head back up to my bedroom. And I do the unthinkable.

I call Mary.

It rings once, twice, six times before it goes to voicemail.

"Hi, this is Mary. I'm so sorry I missed your call. Please leave me a message and I'll get back to you as soon as I can."

Just the sound of her fucking voice makes me hard.

I open my mouth, but I don't know what to say.

So I don't leave a message.

I wish I could take the call back.

It's Friday night. Where is she?

At Black Rose without me? We don't have any understanding between us. She's free to do as she pleases.

Most subs like her spend Friday and Saturday evenings at a club.

Damn.

Jealousy spears into my gut.

I've got to do something about this.

I can't leave Las Vegas, though.

I have meetings all through tomorrow. Then I leave on Sunday.

So I text Mary.

I return Sunday afternoon.

I'm coming to see you at your apartment. Be there.

CHAPTER THIRTY-FOUR

Mary

"He's got some nerve," Brenda says after I read Ronan's text.

We're having drinks at her place, waiting for Dalton. His flight lands in an hour, and then he'll come to Brenda's place in a cab.

At which time, I will exit.

But I need a friend tonight.

I initially came to vent about my accidental meeting with Lucas, but we quickly shifted the subject onto Ronan.

"Who does he think he is?" Brenda says, shaking her head.

"He's a Dominant."

"Yes, but he's not *your* Dominant. He's only your Dominant when you're doing a scene together. What the hell happened between you two in New Orleans?"

"I'm not sure. I think…" I shake my head vehemently. "Seeing Lucas today brought it all back. What it's like to have feelings for a Dominant when they're not returned. I can't go back there, Bren. I just can't."

"It's interesting that Ronan is taking his time with you. Are you sure he's not having feelings himself?"

"No. If he were, he wouldn't have canceled a date at the club via text." I did see his call on my phone, but he didn't leave a voicemail, either.

"That's true…" Brenda takes a sip of her wine. "I still say he has a lot of nerve."

"Agree one hundred percent."

I'm playing the part, for sure. But inside, I desperately want to obey Ronan. I want to be at my place Sunday afternoon when he gets in. I want to be ready for him, naked, holding my wrists out for him to bind.

What the hell is wrong with me?

I never wanted to be a full-time submissive.

Even Brenda and Dalton don't practice the lifestyle full-time. They only play at the club. At home, they have normal sex. Brenda told me.

"So, back to Lucas," she says.

Anger seeps into me. "There's nothing else to say about Lucas. He's still a dick. I'm not sure how I ever developed feelings for him in the first place."

"Innocence." Brenda takes another sip. "Innocence is the biggest fault when you're young and innocent."

I wrinkle my forehead. "Uh…what the hell did you just say?"

"Hell, I don't know. I've had a lot of wine."

"Of course you're young and innocent when you're young and innocent," I nearly snap. "I can't believe you thought I would want to go back to that."

"Ease up, Mare. That's not what I said and you know it."

I let out a breath. "Sorry. You're right. I'm not angry with you. I'm pissed about Lucas, but mostly I'm upset about Ronan."

Brenda takes another sip of wine. "Why isn't Lucas teaching

anymore? Why did he leave Mellville?"

"I don't know, and I don't care."

"You mean you didn't ask?"

"Hell, no, I didn't ask. All I could think about was getting out of there. I certainly won't be taking classes there."

"I think it's great that you want to finish your degree, though."

"Yeah. I never gave it any thought until—" I cock my head. "Until what?"

"Until...Ronan." I inhale slowly and then let it out in a heavy sigh. "I don't know why, but he makes me want to be a better version of myself."

A slow grin spreads across Brenda's face. "You *are* having feelings..."

I rub my forehead. "But I hardly know him. I was with Lucas for nearly two years before I developed feelings. They developed slowly. It doesn't make any sense that I'm feeling this stuff when I've known Ronan for a mere week."

"Love is a funny thing."

"Who are you to talk? You and Dalton had been playing together for a year before you decided to act on the feelings developing between you."

"True." Brenda sets her glass of wine down and looks at me, her expression serious. "Love is different for everyone, Mary. Don't fight it. You're falling in love with the guy. Face it."

I shake my head. "I can't. I can't go back there. I can't go through what I went through with Lucas again."

"Ronan isn't Lucas."

"Ronan is more of a Dominant than Lucas could ever hope to be. The man isn't looking for a relationship. He's made that clear."

"Mary, if he isn't looking for a relationship other than at

the club, why is he demanding to meet you at your apartment?"

I take a long sip of wine.

Brenda makes a valid point. On the other hand—

"Because he's a demanding motherfucker. He's a Dominant."

"Right. And you're a submissive. At the club. In the bedroom. Not in real life."

"No... And I never thought..."

Brenda drops her jaw. "Oh my God. Don't tell me you're considering being a submissive in real life?"

"I don't know what I'm considering anymore." I set my wineglass down a little too harshly, and a few drops splash out. I quickly wipe them up with a tissue. "Nothing seems to make sense. What I liked so much about playing solely at the club was I didn't have the headache and heartache of a relationship to deal with in everyday life. I go to work. I sell clothing and toys. I teach classes a couple nights a week. Friday and Saturday nights, I go to the club, usually pick up a scene. That's it, other than going to the gym with you. That's my life, and I was content. I *am* content."

"Is content all you want?"

"Content is amazing. I have you. I have some other friends. That's the only workout my emotions need. Friendship."

She frowns. "So if something happened to me..."

"I'd be devastated, of course. It would rip my heart out. You've been my bestie since we were eighteen years old. But it's different, and you know it."

"Yes," she says, a dreamy look on her face. "It's definitely different."

I don't need to be clairvoyant to know she's thinking about Dalton and the love they share.

It's been a long time since I saw that look on my own face. Not since...

Then I wonder... This thing with Ronan. It's happening so quickly, and I know better than to let my emotions rule me. Most likely it's just intense attraction.

But I've experienced intense attraction before, at the club with certain Doms. But that's all it was. Purely physical. Chemistry.

I never take it home with me.

"Emotion is not a bad thing," Brenda says.

I stop myself from rolling my eyes. "Did I say it was? I feel emotion for you. For my other friends. For my mom. I just don't want the kind that can fucking shatter your heart into a million pieces."

"'Tis better to have loved and lost than never to have loved at all," Brenda says, that dreamy look still on her face. She pours herself another glass of wine.

"Easy for you to say. You're right at the beginning of an amazing relationship. What if you lost Dalton?"

She stops pouring and nearly slams the bottle down. "Don't say things like that. He's on a fucking airplane right now."

"See what I mean? You'd be devastated. And I'd be there for you, but no friendship in the world can make up for the loss of a love like you and Dalton have."

"Mary..."

"You'd be heartbroken if something happened to me or to one of your other friends. One of your parents, your sisters. It wouldn't be the same as if something happened to Dalton. Those are things you don't recover from, Brenda. And I don't want to be in that situation."

Brenda glares at me, drinking her wine.

"Don't get pissed. I'm only stating the truth, and you know it. Dalton's fine. He's going to be here in about an hour. Then the two of you can have crazy monkey sex all night, and I'll go home and..." I shake my head.

Brenda softens. "You're going to wait for Ronan to get home on Sunday and come to your place."

I say nothing.

I say nothing because she's fucking right, and we both know it.

• • •

I lower my gaze, not looking at Lucas until he instructs that I can.

"Look at me, Mary."

I raise my gaze to meet his. "Thank you, sir."

"And thank you, Mary."

I swallow, still meeting his gaze. I have to tell him about the feelings I'm developing. I have to, because if I don't? Things will never change.

My heart is slowly breaking.

"May I speak, sir?"

"Yes, of course."

I fall to my knees, take his hands in mine, still meeting his gaze. Very strange, because normally when I'm on my knees, I'm not allowed to look at him.

"What is it?" He pulls me to my feet.

He's right. It's better this way. If I'm going to speak about what's been happening to me lately, we need to be on equal footing.

"Sir"—I clear my throat—"I was wondering... I was wondering if perhaps we could go out sometime. Maybe to get dinner."

Lucas furrows his brow. "That sounds like a date, Mary. Once we entered this lifestyle, we agreed we were no longer dating."

"I suppose it could be a date." I look down. "Or it could be two friends having dinner."

"We're not friends, Mary."

His words slice into my heart like a sharp knife.

We're lovers, playmates, partners in many ways. We don't play with other people. We both made that commitment to each other when we began this journey. I've learned so much from this man, and I've enjoyed the path it's taken me on. I'm a submissive at heart. It's what I like in the bedroom. I like bondage, and I like being dominated.

And while I understood that it may not be a long-term relationship...I always thought we were friends.

"You don't consider me a friend, sir?"

"Mary, we defined the parameters of this thing between us when we ended our dating relationship and began this one."

"Yes, I understand that. I've learned so much from you, sir. I've enjoyed it, and I found out a lot about my sexual proclivities. But I'm almost twenty-one."

"Yes, I've been looking forward to your birthday."

"You have?" Happiness surges through me.

"Yes. Because once you're twenty-one, I can take you to a club."

That happiness? It fizzles into something I can't name and settles in my gut.

"Well, yes," I say. "I've been looking forward to exploring the clubs as well."

"Playing privately in the club won't be much different than playing privately at my home."

Lucas has his own dungeon, complete with many tables and toys and other paraphernalia.

"What is the difference, then?"

"It's a different experience. You'll meet others like yourself.

Have conversations. You can play in public or in private."

I gulp. "In public?"

"If you're an exhibitionist by nature. Which I happen to be, Mary."

Play in front of others? I gulp again. So much Lucas and I haven't talked about. But still… Just being near him makes me giddy. His kisses melt my heart.

And of course our playtime… Well, I don't have anything to compare it to, but the orgasms are amazing, and he knows all my hotspots.

But I've been watching my friends date. I hear them talk about their boyfriends and girlfriends. I can't say anything. I can't say anything because Lucas is a professor here. He's not my professor, but we agreed when we started that we'd keep this thing under wraps.

"You know I can't be seen with you in public," he says.

"You just said we might be doing something in public at the club."

"Yes, I did. But no one associated with the university frequents the club I go to. We will be perfectly safe there."

Perfectly safe…

"You mean *you* would be perfectly safe, sir. I wouldn't be safe at all."

"Of course you would be. I would never let anything happen to you, Mary."

I shake my head, tears welling in the bottoms of my eyes. He doesn't get it.

"I don't know how else to say it, sir. I'm falling in love with you, and it's killing me."

"Mary…"

"Tell me you feel the same way, sir. You must."

"I assure you that's not true. I'm sorry, Mary." *He sighs.*

"Perhaps it's best that we end this."
  And right there.
  In that moment.
  Ice forms around my heart.

• • •

I wasn't sure that ice could ever be melted, but Ronan...
  I can't allow it.
  I text him quickly, after I get home from Brenda's.
  I don't take orders from you.
  Then I hit send.

CHAPTER THIRTY-FIVE

Ronan

This feeling overwhelming me is anger. Rage. But something else as well.

Why would I demand that she be at home so I can come straight to her apartment when I return from Las Vegas?

It's unlike me, and if I'm ready to have a relationship with someone, shouldn't it be with Keira? Someone I've known for five years?

Why would it be with someone I barely know—someone I just met? Hell, I don't even know what her favorite color is.

Which is why I'm having Phillipe drive me straight to Mary's apartment from the airport.

I have news. News I don't particularly like, but news that perhaps makes everything for the best. I found out yesterday that I have to relocate to Las Vegas for the next year. It's the micromanager in me. This project needs someone in town to oversee it, and I'm new in the States. I can't ask Sabrina to do it. She has a family in New York. And frankly, I don't know anyone else who I trust enough.

I want Mary to come with me. I stalk toward her apartment

and knock on the door harshly.

No one answers.

Damn her.

Where the fuck is she?

I grab my phone. I didn't answer her text from the other day. I figured I would make more of an impression in person.

But what kind of impression am I trying to make anyway? I'm a Dominant, that doesn't equate to a domineering bastard.

But that's what I'm acting like.

I can't seem to turn it off.

Mary is mine.

Mine, mine, mine...

I'm not some feral animal sweeping through the forest, looking for a mate.

I'm a human being. Dominant by nature in the bedroom. Dominant in the boardroom as well.

Jesus Christ...

It's what I want, isn't it?

I want to be dominant twenty-four seven. I want a twenty-four seven submissive.

I want it to be Mariah Sandusky.

Blossom.

Other Doms have touched Blossom.

No one else will again.

Only me.

I send a text.

Me: *Where are you?*

Mary: *Is that any of your business?*

Damned right it is.

But I don't hit send.

Perhaps I need to take a step back.

This isn't who I am.

I don't demand that my submissive meet me at her place.

I will demand that she meet me at the club sometimes when I know we're both available.

That's part of being a Dominant.

But this...this is not.

Damn.

The woman is killing me.

Slowly and painfully...

It makes no sense at all.

All those years with Keira in Glasgow, and never once did I take her along when I returned to the States to see Mémé in New Orleans.

But what did I do, having known Mary for all of forty-eight hours?

I took her there.

I took her to my childhood home, introduced her to Mémé.

Hell, I'd introduce her to my parents tomorrow. All I'd have to do is get her on a flight to Glasgow.

So not me.

Or is it?

Could Mémé be right?

Maybe it's time.

Maybe I do want more.

Yes, I want her as a full-time submissive, but perhaps...

Maybe I'm thinking about a family, children.

All those things I never thought I'd have the time or desire for.

One way to find out. It's doubtful that Mary's at the club. It's Sunday night, and she has work in the morning. After she's been off for a week.

So I'll go to the club.

Maybe I'll meet someone there. Maybe I need a scene. A

scene with someone other than Mary. I ultimately chose not to play with Aurora at the club in Las Vegas, and perhaps that was my mistake.

Scenes remind me of what my life is truly about.

I'm not dressed in club gear, but I don't care. Jeans and a button-down are good enough for tonight. I've never had any trouble attracting submissives, and I don't expect to now.

I shove my phone back in my pocket, return to the car waiting at the curb, and ask Phillipe to take me to Black Rose Underground.

• • •

I head straight to a stool at the bar and order a scotch from tonight's topless waitress.

Once I'm sipping, I look around. No Mary, but I do see her friend, Brenda—Lotus—sitting at a table with a nice-looking man.

I take my drink, rise, walk toward them.

"Good evening."

Brenda widens her eyes at my voice. "Oh! Ronan, hi. This is my fiancé, Dalton."

The young man rises, holds out his hand. "Nice to meet you."

"You as well. Do you mind if I join you two?"

"Not at all." Dalton gestures to a seat next to Brenda.

I take the seat. "I've been trying to find Mary."

Brenda picks up her cosmopolitan and takes a drink. "Oh?"

"You mean Blossom?" Dalton asks.

"Yes, of course. Blossom."

"Oh, she's here," Dalton says.

Brenda sends her fiancé a panicked and glaring look.

"I didn't see her when I came in," I say.

Brenda is staring down Dalton.

He says nothing.

"What aren't you telling me?"

"Blossom's location is none of your business," Brenda says distinctly.

Technically, she's right. And I'm here at the club, so I need to act accordingly.

My hackles rise, though. I feel like an animal. I get up, and I'm ready to run into the back and pound on all of the private room doors, demanding that Mary show herself.

I'll be kicked out of the club, but who cares? There are other clubs in the city.

I spent so much time researching, though, and this was the best fit for me. The best underground BDSM club in Manhattan.

But I don't care.

Right now, all I care about is Mary.

I stalk toward the door leading to the back.

"Ronan!" Brenda's voice.

I turn.

"You'll be kicked out of the club, man." This from Dalton.

What does that matter? I have to move to Vegas in a couple weeks anyway. I'll join a new club.

I nod in acknowledgment, so he knows I heard him and I know the consequences, and then I return to business.

CHAPTER THIRTY-SIX

Mary

Boone is a Dominant I've played with more than once, but not since the scene with Jack.

Indeed, I haven't played at all until Ronan came around.

When I ended up at the club tonight, and he asked if I would be up for a scene, I said yes.

He's good-looking, of course. Tall with dark hair and dark eyes. I don't know much about him outside of the club except that he's an attorney. He doesn't say where he works or for whom. Only that it's a fairly well known New York firm.

I'm bound, naked, to the bed in a private room.

I'm not blindfolded, but he's instructed me to close my eyes.

Sounds rustle on the other side of the room. Drawers open and shut. He's choosing toys, and all I can think about...

All I can think about is how I don't want to be here.

Why did I come? Why did I acquiesce when he asked if I would play?

Am I trying to prove something to myself? That I'm finally back to "normal Blossom?" That I don't need Ronan, who apparently wants to control my whole life? That I'm over the botched scene with Jack?

Truth be told, I've been over the botched scene with Jack for a while now.

Darius was right. I'm at the tipping point. As much as I wanted to keep my emotions at bay, I'm growing, maturing, and that's not who I am anymore.

I want more.

I want...love.

And I'm going to have to assume the risks that come with it.

I don't want to continue this scene. I *can't* continue this scene. My head's not in it, and that was the whole problem with Jack. I won't do that to another person.

"Boone?"

"You have been instructed to stay quiet." His voice is harsh.

"Then Tesla," I say.

He comes to me quickly, unbinds my feet and hands, and pulls me into a sitting position. "Are you all right, Blossom?"

"I need to apologize," I say. "I don't want to do this."

"You disappoint me." He's using a stony voice.

I cock my head, widen my eyes a bit.

His gaze darkens. "What if I refuse to let you out of this room?"

"Boone, I used my safe word. You need to get out of character now."

He shakes his head. "Yes, of course. Forgive me."

I rise from the bed quickly, grab my clothes—black club dress, lace underwear, and platform sandals—and get into them as quickly as I can.

When I reach for the doorknob to the private suite, Boone's body covers mine from the back. "I'm sorry," he whispers in my ear.

His cock is still hard, brushing against the small of my back.

"I'm sorry too," I say. "I should have never agreed to this." I open the door, and I don't watch to see if he follows me out.

I don't want to go right back out to the table with Dalton and Brenda. For all I know they're already doing a scene in their own private room.

So, though I'm not a voyeur, I walk into one of the exhibition rooms.

It's the bondage room.

The art of bondage has always fascinated me.

Shibari is what I like best. I especially like the techniques that make a woman's nipples protrude. I walk through the room, looking at the scenes displayed for my viewing pleasure.

I'm drawn to a scene involving three women. One is clearly the Dominant, and two are submissive. Both of the subs are bound around their breasts, with nipples protruding, standing, their hands bound behind their backs, and the Dominant, dressed in a leather corset and thigh-high boots, teases them with a long feather on their nipples.

Though it's tempting, and I like what I'm watching, I don't get aroused.

I am intrigued, though. I would like to try something like that.

I've been a member of this club for five years, and for some reason, I've never attracted a Dominant skilled in rope bondage. I'm usually bound with leather or handcuffs. I continue to watch as the Dominant teases her two subs. She kneels in front of one of them, slides her tongue over her pussy.

The sub doesn't move, doesn't acknowledge it.

Clearly, she's been instructed not to.

Then hot breath on my back.

"See something you like?"

I turn, my nipples hard and achy.

Ronan stands there, and he's not dressed in club gear. He's dressed in jeans and a button-down, much like the clothes he wore when we were in New Orleans.

He's going to punish me. He's going to punish me for ignoring his text, for not being at my apartment when he demanded I be.

At the moment, as I look into his fiery blue eyes, for the life of me I can't remember why I did.

I say nothing.

"You defied me."

"I...I'm not your full-time submissive, Ronan," I say, willing myself to stop stammering.

He won't raise his voice.

He can't. In an exhibition room at the club, security is high, and there are rules.

A growl from him vibrates into me.

Then, "Come with me."

I turn, feeling even more defiant. "No," I say softly. "I want to stay here."

"Perhaps you didn't hear me the first time." His blue eyes nearly glow in the dim lighting. "I said *come with me*."

I stare into his eyes—that blue of the cerulean sky that fires and blazes.

And I put my hand in his, allow him to lead me out of the exhibition room.

"There are no suites available right now," he says, his voice low, deep, almost menacing.

"I didn't ask if there were."

"You want to be with me."

His words are a statement. A statement that he sees as fact.

He's right.

I *do* want to be with him.

It scares me how much I want it.

All those feelings long ago that I had for Lucas—the feelings I've suppressed for so long—have come bubbling back to the surface. And they're hundreds of times stronger.

That's not who this man is.

This man is a Dominant. He is the Yin to my Yang—rather, the Yang I was…until I met *him*.

"You do know, don't you, that I'm going to have to punish you?"

"Punish me for what?" I cross my arms. "I've said it before. I'm not yours. I'm not a full-time sub. You can't just order me around outside a scene."

"I can," he says through clenched teeth. "And I will."

A sliver of fear surges into me, but before I even recognize it for what it is, it has morphed into an arousal so profound I'm not sure I can stand it. I can almost feel my pussy swelling in anticipation, secreting my juices. My clit throbbing so much so that with every step I take, it brushes against my panties, threatening to send me further into a tailspin.

"What do you suggest?" I ask.

"My hotel suite."

All thoughts flee me. All complaints, arguments flee as well.

I barely look at Brenda and Dalton, still sitting at a table, as Ronan leads me out of the club.

After he gets his phone back from Claude, he taps on it. "My driver will meet us outside."

Sure enough, a shiny black limousine is waiting. I stop myself from gasping.

The chauffeur opens the door, and Ronan gestures for me to climb in.

He says nothing more as we drive the few blocks to his hotel.

"I have a suite on the top floor," he says. "You'll be spending the night."

"Ronan, I have to go to work in the morning. I've been gone a whole week. Remember?"

"You'll be spending the night," he says again.

"I can't. I absolutely cannot."

"What time does your shop open?"

"It opens at ten, but I have to be there at eight. I'm gunning for a manager job, Ronan. Remember?"

"You'll be well-rested. You'll be able to make it to work on time. Have you forgotten that I work as well? I have a Zoom meeting at seven a.m. with associates in the UK. This won't be a problem."

I open my mouth to argue, but nothing comes out. Indeed, I've nothing to say. Because I want to go to his suite. I want to let him do whatever he wants to me. If he feels I deserve punishment, I will take it. I'll take it because...

Damn.

How did I let this happen?

How did I fall in love with the most domineering Dom I've ever met? The one man who can*not* give me what I desire?

When I expressed my feelings to Lucas, he unceremoniously dumped me. While I was in the middle of the heartbreak over that, my father passed away, killed by a drunk driver. As much as I hated losing my father, having to leave school turned out to be a blessing in disguise. It got me away from Lucas. I was forced to find a way to fend for myself, and I got the job at Treasure's Chest. I learned about Black Rose Underground, and I became a member. I became a submissive and was open to scenes with anyone as long as the chemistry was right.

I was happy, damn it. When Brenda graduated two years later, I'm the one who introduced her to the scene. Showed her what was possible as a submissive. She and I frequented the club together, and then she met Dalton a year ago.

She found a Dominant who fell in love with her. Their timing was impeccable.

But my timing?

My timing has always been shit.

The limousine stops, and the chauffeur opens the door. Ronan gets out and takes my hand to help me exit.

A Dominant and a gentleman.

He holds my hand as we walk into the hotel and head toward the elevators.

He doesn't speak.

I don't speak.

We enter the elevator, he hovers his key card over the reading device, and the elevator ascends.

The doors open with the ding of the bell, and I walk at his side to his door, which he unlocks and opens.

Once the door is closed, he grips my shoulders, slams me up against the wall, his blue gaze searing into mine.

"We're going to get one thing straight now, Mary. When I say—"

But his words are interrupted by a voice. A female voice.

And it's not mine.

"Thank God you're here, Ronan. I'm back."

CHAPTER THIRTY-SEVEN

Ronan

I jerk my head over my shoulder.

You've got to be kidding me. How the hell did she get into my suite *again*? Heads are going to fucking roll.

"What the hell are you doing back here?"

"I never got on that flight, Ronan. I couldn't. I booked a hotel, and I've been waiting for the right time..." Keira glares at Mary. "Who the hell is this?"

"Who the hell are *you*?" Mary answers her.

"She's Keira," I say. "And she's leaving."

Keira narrows her gaze. "I'm afraid I can't leave, Ronan."

"I assure you that you can."

Keira slowly walks toward me. "There's something I didn't tell you before. I thought about not telling you. But honestly, I must."

"I think that's my cue to leave," Mary says.

I trail my finger over her cheek. "You stay. She's leaving."

"Ronan, I—"

"Damn it, Blossom. She's leaving."

"Not until I've talked to you," Keira says.

"Fine. Whatever. Maybe you've forgotten who's the Dominant here, Keira?"

"I'll never forget that."

"Oh my God." Mary shakes her head and rushes out the door before I can stop her.

I run after her, but Keira yanks me back. "We need to talk."

"I assure you, we do not." I leave the room, chase after Mary, who's already made it to the elevators and pushed the button.

"Don't go."

Her pretty face twists, and she turns away from me. "Seems you already have a companion for the evening."

"I don't. You're my companion for the evening. Haven't I made myself clear?"

"I'm not sure what to think, Ronan. I just don't—" The elevator door opens. She gets in. "There's something else I should talk to you about anyway, before we do another scene together. Call me tomorrow. Maybe we can figure this thing out."

Something else?

Instead of demanding she explain herself, I let her go.

It's against my nature, but I let her go.

Because I have to deal with Keira, and it's probably best if Mary isn't here to witness it.

Kiera and I were in a Dominant and submissive relationship for five years. That's all we were. We weren't in love. At least *I* wasn't. And when she broached the subject of something more, I broke it off. A month later, when the opportunity with Black, Inc. came, I chose to relocate to New York.

A clean break.

A new start.

And a new submissive.

Who knew I would find her my very first night at the club?

But I'm baffled by these feelings I'm having. All those years with Keira, and I never wanted anything more.

But with Mary…

What is it about her?

I go back to my suite. I have to deal with Keira once and for all.

"Where are you?" I open the door and slam it.

"Bedroom."

Probably naked in my bed again.

I walk in and…

Sure enough.

"I think I've made myself clear," I say. "You and I are over."

She spreads her legs, showing me her pussy. At one time, her actions would have had me hard and ready. No longer.

"I'm afraid we're not," she says.

I look away. "I'm afraid we are. And if we weren't, you'd be headed for a nasty-ass punishment for defying me like that."

In my peripheral vision, I see her get onto all fours, crawl on the bed, stick her ass in the air.

"Punish me, Ronan. Please. I need it. I need you."

"I ought to turn you over my knee and spank that ass until it bleeds."

She bites her lip, fingering one nipple. "Yes… Please."

"No."

I'm not into that, never have been. I don't make women bleed. And the fact that she looks so turned on freaks me out. I only said it as a last-ditch attempt to make her leave willingly. But now, I'll have to force her out.

"You're going to go, Keira. Or I will have you removed."

"Removed by whom?"

"Hotel security. Or if they fail, the NYPD. Right now you're trespassing."

"How do you think I got into this room?"

"The same way you got in the first time. I figured you were on a plane, so I didn't bother telling hotel security about you. But I'll be telling them now, for sure."

She reaches toward me. "Ronan, you don't understand."

"I'm afraid I do."

"No you don't," she insists. "I'm pregnant. I'm going to have your baby."

CHAPTER THIRTY-EIGHT

Mary

At first I tell the cabbie to take me back to the building where the club is located, but halfway there, I change my mind and tell him to take me home.

I walk into my apartment, take a shower, put on some jammies.

The woman in Ronan's suite was gorgeous—blond hair, blue eyes, and thin like a supermodel. Ronan's ex? How have we never talked about that? How didn't I know?

Easy. I haven't known Ronan for very long. Why would he bring up an ex? I haven't, either.

The ex said she needed to talk to Ronan. What about? She probably wants to get back together. I mean, who *wouldn't* want to be with him?

I should have talked to him sooner about what I'm feeling. Now, it's too late.

I'm heartbroken. Or am I? I've experienced heartbreak before, but this...

This is so much worse.

I feel...empty.

An empty shell.

I go to bed.

Back to work tomorrow.

Part of me is looking forward to it. I enjoy my work. I'm a good salesperson, and a new class on submission starts this week. I'll be teaching a few nights.

I pad to my bed, get under the covers, and wrap myself up like a cocoon.

As I close my eyes, a tear slides down my cheek.

. . .

I wake before my alarm in the morning, which is surprising. That almost never happens.

It's five thirty, and try as I might, I cannot get back to sleep, so I decide to get up.

I make a pot of coffee, and because I showered last night, I only need to do a quick wet-down of my hair and then blow it dry.

I dress in my black leather skinny pants and an orange-and-black corset that brings out the color of my hair. Then I sit, because I don't have to be at work for another two hours.

Maybe I'll get to the store early. I have a key, so I can open up. Maybe do some inventory.

Getting on the subway in a corset is never a good idea, so I put a cardigan over my shoulders and button it to hide my cleavage.

After my subway ride, I walk toward the store, but then I make a U-turn and enter a coffee shop instead.

Another cup of coffee will do me good, and sitting down with my thoughts? Maybe it will help as well.

I take a seat by the window once I order my coffee, and—

"Hands up!"

My heart drops to my stomach as fear slices through me.

Two men wearing masks and brandishing guns have entered the coffee shop.

In the morning?

Of course in the morning. When all the rich businessmen are getting their coffee.

Why the hell did I have to get coffee this morning at this damned place?

One of the masked men turns to the dining area. "No one fucking move."

My heart thunders in my chest.

The other one has his gun trained on the cashier. "Open it up. I want all the cash, now. If you even think of triggering some silent alarm, your brains are going to be splattered all over that cappuccino machine behind you."

Oh God oh God oh God...

I gulp for air, nearly hyperventilating. I can't breathe.

How is this even happening? All I wanted to do was go to work early. Get a cup of coffee. Think about things. About Ronan...

My God, Ronan...

I'm in love with him. I am. Nothing like seeing your life flash before your eyes to show you the truth.

I have to tell him. Even if he's with that other woman now. I just have to let him know. I can't live with myself if I never tell him.

But damn...

What if...

The unthinkable happens...

And I can never tell him?

My coffee. No, I don't have my coffee yet. No hot beverage to throw in anyone's face.

Of course, a bullet could penetrate my skull before I even threw the beverage.

No, fighting back isn't the answer. That will just decrease my chances of surviving this.

I dart my gaze around the room without moving my head.

Most of the women are crying, some of the men as well.

Under the table in the far corner is a young mother with two small children.

Oh God…

Please, no…

I glance outside the window where I'm sitting, hoping to see a cop walking by.

Nothing, of course.

I close my eyes.

God, this can't be the end.

But even if it is…please spare those children.

The little boy and girl are crying, holding onto their mother.

"Shut those brats up!" the man with the gun trained on us yells.

The mother hugs them, and I see her desperation. She's trying to be strong for them.

In that moment, all I can think about is my own life.

My own life. I'm young. Lucas be damned. If I get out of this alive, I will finish my business degree. I'll find another school. I'll get it done. I'll do it online but only if I have to. Part of me wants the classroom experience.

And Ronan…

I have to tell Ronan.

I have to tell him I'm in love with him. That if he wants a fulltime sub, I can do it. I won't even have to make myself do it—I *want* to, I realize now. Anything to be with him. To be with the man I love.

But my God… It's probably too late for that.

Because my life might end today.

My life…

There's more to me than being a salesperson at a lingerie and toy store. There's more to me than being a submissive who plays with different Doms and never lets her emotions get involved.

There's so much more to me…

And as I see that young mother, attempting to comfort her crying children, showing them all the love and the strength in the—

My God…

I want kids.

I want a life.

I want a life with Ronan, and I want to have his children.

If that's not what he wants…

Then I have to move on.

I have to find someone who wants what I want long-term, not just right now.

And I never knew…

Never knew, until just now, how much I want a lifelong partner and children to love.

I'll always be a submissive. My partner will most likely be a Dominant.

But we will raise our children with happiness and love.

And oh my God…

I may never have it.

What will I do if I can't have it?

I sniffle back tears.

Crying won't do me any good. I'm frozen in place, unable to move.

All I want…my *only* want…is to get out of here alive.

I'll do anything.

Absolutely any—

"Your wallet, bitch."

The man with the gun stands over me. I hastily take my wallet out of my purse, hand it to him. He takes my phone as well.

"That ring on your right hand. I'm taking that."

I hastily pull it off my finger. The ruby ring from my father. He gave it to me for my high school graduation. It's all I have left of him. He wasn't the greatest father, and he was a lousy husband to my mom, but this ring is my link to him. It means so much to me.

With a gun in my face, I don't think twice. I take it off and hand it away.

He moves on to the next table.

I heave a sigh of relief, but it's not over.

The mother and her small children, the last table in the corner...

Fear slices through me, but I wonder...

I wish I could do something. Protect those two children. I'm so scared.

The masked man makes his way around the place.

When he gets to her, "Your wallet, bitch."

Are those the only words this derelict knows?

I stare out the window again, wondering if the passersby can see the distress on my face.

No cops, no one even looking my way. Classic New York.

The little girl and boy—they can't be more than two or three years old—cling to their mother as she fumbles in her purse, her hands shaking.

A third gunman has entered the coffee shop. Standing at the door. None of us can get out.

More fear whips through me.

My bowels are churning. I have to go to the bathroom.

Pissing and shitting my pants isn't a good look, but at this point, I don't care. I don't care about any humiliation.

All I want is to live.

I want those two little children to live.

My God, this must be hell for them. They're so scared.

I've lived in New York a long time. I know how to handle muggers. You throw your purse and run the other way. Most likely they'll go for the money. Not that I've ever had to try it out, but I have friends who have, and it's worked.

This...

Masked gunmen holding up a coffee shop? No escape?

This I'm not prepared for.

And of course he took my phone.

Why didn't I think to call 911 before he took it?

Why didn't I think of everything?

Why?

I heave another sigh of relief as the masked man leaves the young mother, her children unharmed. Physically, that is. They're going to suffer emotional trauma. We all are.

Nausea claws at my throat, but all I had was a little coffee at home, so there's nothing in my belly.

But still, the fear will keep me from puking.

The masked man who took everything from me has now stolen from everyone here. The three businessmen sitting here are now without their Rolexes, their credit cards, and all of their cash. They even took one guy's cufflinks.

I don't care.

I don't care about any more *things*.

I just want them to leave. I want them to leave without firing a shot.

Why didn't I stay at Ronan's last night? He said I could stay, and he wanted the other woman to leave. I was too caught up in my own head to think clearly.

If I'd stayed, this wouldn't be happening.

I would've gone straight to work from his place.

Or I would've had to go back to my place to change, but then straight to work.

Either way...

I wouldn't have woken up early, taken the subway early, stopped to have coffee at this godforsaken place.

Why? Why? Why?

Except...what if he's still with the other woman? What if he's done with me because I left him with her after he asked me to stay?

The thought slices right through my heart.

I shouldn't have left him. I love him.

And I'll never be able to tell him.

CHAPTER THIRTY-NINE

Ronan

In the morning, I don't let Keira out of my sight. After making a few phone calls and rearranging some things on my schedule, I take her to the nearest pharmacy to pick up a pregnancy test. Then we come back to my suite. I open the test and pull out the stick.

"Here it is. Pee on it."

She stares at the test and scowls. "I can't believe you're making me do this."

"Look, Keira. If you're truly pregnant, and if I am the father, I will take care of my child. You have my word on that."

"A child needs a mother *and* a father, Ronan."

"If the child is mine, he will have his father."

She grabs my arm. "You don't understand. A child needs a mother and father who are married."

I clench my jaw, remove her hand from my arm. She's trying to manipulate me. I can't lash out, though. I need to tread carefully until I know the full truth of what's happening here.

"That is the best circumstance, I agree, but plenty of children grow up in different circumstances and they're fine.

Regardless, I am not ready to be your husband, Keira. That is why I ended our relationship in the first place. You and I both know that. Part of our agreement together was that you stay on birth control. We both know birth control can fail. If that is what happened here, I will stand by my child. I will support my child financially and emotionally. I will be a good father. Now the stick."

"Fine." She huffs. Then she moves to close the door.

I stop the door with my foot.

"Ronan…"

"I'm sorry, Keira. I'm going to have to watch you."

"What, do you think I have pregnancy hormones in my purse?"

I wouldn't put it past her.

She has feelings that I don't share, and honestly? I don't know much about her personally. Perhaps she *is* the kind of person who would try to trap a man. She showed up here—twice—without invitation and lied to get into my room.

So yes, I'm going to watch her pee on the fucking stick.

"Take the test, Kiera. I'm not moving."

"Really, Ronan. I just can't—"

"Then we'll go to a doctor. I will watch them as they draw blood. That's a more accurate test anyway."

"Please…"

I look her straight in the eye. "Are you lying to me?"

She bites her lower lip. And that's my answer. I know her body language.

"As I suspected." I blow out a frustrated sigh. "You're better than this, Keira. You don't need to trap a man."

"But you know my feelings for you."

"I do. And I respect them. However, I don't share them. We've been through this before, too many times. I don't like hurting you. It was never my intention to do anything like that. But you and I had an agreement, and I thought you understood the terms."

"I can't help it if I fell in love with you," she says.

"No one is blaming you for that. If I shared your feelings, I would tell you. But I don't, Keira. I'm so sorry, but I don't."

She throws the pregnancy test in the trash can.

"Oh no…" I point to the bin. "You're going to take the test. I need to know for sure that you're telling me the truth. I don't need you coming back seven months from now with a child."

She huffs. "Fine." She pulls the stick out of the wastebasket. "If I leave my purse outside the bathroom, can I at least pee in peace?"

I nod. I don't think there's any pregnancy hormone—or pregnant woman pee—in my bathroom.

I shut the door, giving her some privacy.

"How long does it take to see results?" I ask through the door.

"You insisted on buying the most expensive test. We should be able to see results in one minute."

Good.

I set the timer on my watch.

I'll give her two minutes. Time to pee on the stick and then time for the result.

When a hundred and twenty seconds have passed. I knock on the door.

She opens it, hands me the stick. It's negative.

Thank fuck.

My shoulders drop. My whole body nearly drops with relief, but I hold myself up.

"I'm going to take you to the airport. This time you *will* get on a plane. When you get back to Glasgow, I want you to get on with your life. It's going to be a life without me. You can find another Dominant. One that's open to something more. Or you can leave the lifestyle altogether and find a man who's looking for a relationship and children."

"All right." She sighs. Then her lip quivers as she says, "I tried. I tried, Ronan, because I love you."

"I'm trying to understand that," I say. "But faking a pregnancy was not the way to gain my sympathy. Don't come after me again. My feelings on this matter aren't going to change."

Tears well in her eyes.

I take her hand. "I never wanted to hurt you."

"I know you didn't." She sniffles. "It's my own fault. I didn't want to fall in love with you. It just happened."

"It's not your fault. I don't want you blaming yourself for this. You didn't do anything wrong—other than fake a pregnancy and lie to get into my hotel room. But I mean about us. Falling for someone isn't a crime. We *did* have an agreement, though, and my feelings aren't the same as yours."

She hiccups, gulping, and nods.

I hate the look of sadness on her face. I hate hurting her. But my sympathy has waned a little by the fact that she came here trying to trap me.

Did she think I wouldn't ask for proof?

And then I look at her again. She's utterly devastated.

This isn't who she is. She was simply feeling desperate.

I hope I've gotten through to her this time.

"Let's get you to the airport. I will personally fly you back to Glasgow, first class. I'll call my driver and have him take us to the airport now."

"You don't have to do that. I don't deserve it after what I've done."

"I don't mind doing this for you." I pull up a booking app on my phone. "All I want is for you to be happy. Find a good man who can give you what you want. Because it's not me."

She nods then, and by the look of resignation on her face, I believe I've finally gotten through to her this time.

I text Phillipe, and within ten minutes, Keira is all packed up and ready to go.

We walk down to the elevators, descend, and then meet Phillipe outside the hotel.

"LaGuardia," I tell him. "She's booked on a flight tonight. I booked a coach ticket for you as well so you can personally see her to the gate and make sure she gets on the plane."

I'm not taking any chances this time.

Philippe nods and begins driving through the midmorning traffic.

My cell phone rings, and I check the ID. My eyes widen. It's my grandmother.

She almost never calls me. She uses email instead.

"Mémé?" I say, my nerves up and on edge. "Everything okay?"

"I'm fine, Ronan." Her voice is frantic. "But I had a premonition."

I resist rolling my eyes. Not that she can see me anyway. But I like to take Mémé seriously. She puts a lot of stock in her religion.

"Yes?"

"It's your lady. Mary. She's in trouble, Ronan. You have to go to her. You have to go to her now."

CHAPTER FORTY

Mary

W hy aren't they leaving?
They have all our wallets, our phones, all the money the cashier could give them. The third person, who came in later, watches out the door.

He has moved the sign on the door from open to closed.

The people who walk by the building can see that there are people inside sitting.

No one's going to believe it's closed.

Still, people walk on by.

Passersby, passing by. No one cares. No one bothers to ascertain what's going on. No one bothers to see the situation for what it truly is.

Now I get why the gunmen haven't left yet. They're waiting. They're waiting so they can make a getaway. They're watching, waiting for crowds to settle down.

But the streets of Manhattan are never vacant. They will be waiting a long time.

Why did they choose a coffeehouse anyway?

A few buildings down is a jewelry shop. Rolexes and

diamonds in the window. Of course, shops like that have extra security.

No one thinks security is necessary in a coffee shop, and coffee shops always have lots of cash on hand and a lot of businesspeople wearing expensive watches and jewelry.

The perfect crime.

I have to go to the bathroom so badly. I know it's just nerves, but the last thing I want to do is soil myself.

On the other hand, what will it matter if I do, if I'm dead?

These people aren't killers, though. If they were, they'd have been shooting by now.

Or maybe not. I don't see silencers on any of the guns. If they shoot, people will come. Sure, the crowds on the street will run the other way, but the NYPD will get wind of what's happening.

I almost want one of their guns to go off—as long as a bullet doesn't fly into anyone here.

"I have to go to the potty, Mama," the little girl, the older of the two children, says.

The little boy is probably still in diapers. But the little girl is three or four, probably recently potty trained, and when she has to go, she has to go.

"Not now, honey," the mother shushes her.

"I have to go now!" she yells.

"You keep that brat quiet," the man who took our money says.

"Shush, honey. Please. You have to be quiet. Do what Mommy says."

I don't dare turn my head to look out the window again. Three men with guns are in here. If I turn my head for a minute, one of them could be trained on me.

Ronan, where are you?

Except I don't want him here. He would come in here unarmed, and any surprise could mean the worst thing possible.

Take any one of these gunmen by surprise, he may shoot.

And I can't have Ronan hurt.

As much as I wish he were here, saving me, comforting me, I'm glad he's not.

If I don't get through this alive, I at least want *him* to live. I love him that much.

"Oh, honey, it's all right," the mother says.

I look over at the little girl.

She's had an accident. There's a puddle on the floor.

"For Christ's sake," a gunman says. "Get some napkins and clean up that mess."

The woman nods, grabbing napkins from the napkin holder on her table and wiping her daughter's accident from the floor.

My God, these people are horrible. Of course they are. Nice people don't hold up coffee shops. Don't scare little children.

Finally, I can't take it anymore. I ball my hands into fists. "They're just children," I say, pleading. "Let them go. You've got the rest of us. Let the children go. Please."

"Yes, please!" The mother looks at me, gratitude in her eyes. "Just let my children go. I'll stay here. Let my babies go, *please*!"

"No one's going anywhere." The gunman puts the gun to the mother's head. "And you won't say another fucking word."

My God, what's going on? They got all the money. The cashiers and the baristas are huddled behind the counter. At least they have that bit of a shield. The rest of us? We have nothing.

I melt into my chair, wishing so much I could disappear. I wish magic were real and I could make myself invisible, slink out the door.

I'm one woman. I'm not close enough to anyone else to talk to them and formulate a plan.

There's nothing I can do.

Nothing—

"No!"

The mother yells and races after her toddler son, who has escaped her embrace and is running toward the door.

Then a shot. A fucking gunshot.

CHAPTER FORTY-ONE

Ronan

Mémé's premonitions have been wrong before, but where Mary's concerned, I cannot take a chance. Besides... on a few occasions, her premonitions have been right.

"Pull over, Phillipe," I say.

I get out of the limousine. "You'll have to do this without me."

"Sir?"

"Please. Stay with her. Make sure she gets on the flight. I have somewhere I have to be."

Once I'm out of the car, I call Mary.

It rings once, twice, three times, and on the fourth I get her voicemail.

I don't bother leaving a message. If she doesn't have her phone or can't answer, she won't get the message anyway. But if she does have her phone, she'll see that I called.

What time is it? Almost ten. Mary was supposed to be at work by now.

Is she still at home?

Where do I check first?

I don't know I don't know I don't know.

Most likely she tried to go to work. She made a big deal about having to get back to work today.

I head to Treasure's Chest.

The store isn't open yet, but I knock on the window.

A woman comes bustling toward me. "We're closed," she says.

"I need to see Mary. It's important."

She widens her eyes and then unlocks the door. "I've been trying to get hold of her. She should've been here to help open the store."

My heart races. "Something's gone wrong. Do you know where she could be?"

"She still has a landline at her place, and she's not answering that, either."

"She's not there. Or she can't get to the phone."

"Are you sure something's wrong?"

I shake my head. "I'm not sure of anything right now."

Except for one thing. I fell in love.

It hits me like a lightning bolt to my heart. I'll find a way to make this work. I'll be the Dominant she needs. If I have to go to Las Vegas and she refuses to leave New York, we'll make it work somehow.

We have to.

What I couldn't give to Keira, I want to give to Mary.

Damn.

"She sometimes stops for coffee at the coffee house a couple buildings down. It's called Bean There Done That."

"All right. I'll check there quickly only because it's on the way. Then I'm hightailing it to her place."

"Keep me in the loop," she says. "My name's Trish. You can call me here at the store."

"Right. Sure."

I'm sure Trish means well and she's concerned about Mary, but at the moment the last thing on my mind is keeping her in the loop about anything. Not until I know Mary's okay.

Coffee shop, coffee shop, coffee shop.

There it is. I walk toward it, noting the sign says it's closed. Odd that it would be closed in the middle of the morning, the busiest part of their day.

Thankfully I'm not wearing a kilt today. I'm dressed in a suit for my meetings later, and I blend in nicely with all the passersby walking down this Manhattan street.

I walk by as nonchalantly as I can. Is the door locked?

I see...

I see her...

She's in there... Mary...

Sitting at a table by the window.

I'm going in.

I go closer, and I notice men. Wearing masks. And they're armed.

My heart drops. God, *fear*. But nothing compared to the urge—a raw, animal urge—to protect the woman I love.

Now I wish I were in my kilt. I'd have my knife—even though it's ornamental—stuffed in my hose.

Ornamental it may be, but I can still do some damage with it.

Right now, though? I've got nothing. Nothing but my muscles and my fists. Which I will use.

Mary... I must get to Mary...

I walk closer, trying to look nonchalant. One of the men is watching out the doorway.

Is the door locked? If there were any way for them to lock it, it most likely would be.

But I can't tell.

I pull out my phone, call 911.

Thank you for calling 911.

Seriously? Voicemail for 911? Nine fucking one fucking one?

Jesus Christ. I dart my gaze around, looking for a beat cop or anyone else. A constable. Fucking Scotland Yard. I don't care.

Anyone. Anyone who can help.

No one.

People walk by. Minding their own business. I haven't been in New York long, but this seems typical.

I walk slowly now, take a look inside the door.

Out of the blue, the man standing guard turns around, and I take my chance. At the door, a small boy comes running across the floor, and then, one of the gunmen notices me.

In slow motion his arm rises, his gun pointed at me.

A shot. The sound rings in my ears, vibrates through my body. A sharp rock—maybe a shard of glass—hits me.

Shrieks. Screams.

And time. Slow motion.

Down. Blood. Searing pain in my shoulder. Then my stomach.

Searing fucking pain.

Is the little boy okay? Mary?

"Ronan!"

Mary's voice. Except it's garbled. Coming through water.

Blood. The scent of blood. Iron. Red. Smells fucking red. Smells like veins, guts.

And then...

I love you, Mary...

Everything goes dark.

CHAPTER FORTY-TWO

Mary

"Ronan!" I shout. My heart is beating rapidly, and my skin is on fire.

The little boy runs back to his mother.

Two of the men closest to the door make their escape.

God, one of them find a cop. Please!

"Stay away, bitch," the first man says.

"But... He's..." I gulp.

"Christ," another one says. "What did you shoot him for?"

"He came in. Then the little boy..." He throws his hands in the air, waving the gun around. "What the fuck was I supposed to do?"

The second guy looks out the door where a small crowd is forming. "Cops are going be here soon. We need to get the fuck out of here."

"Come on. Get everything. Let's fucking go."

They shove their guns into the back of their pants, covered by their shirts. Then they remove the masks and leave, trying to look nonchalant.

I don't bother looking at their faces. Someone should, and

I hope someone else did. But all I can think about is Ronan.

Ronan, who's bleeding out on the floor.

I run to him then. "Someone help me. *Please*."

No one comes to my aid except the young mother.

The young mother whose only thought has been her children this entire time.

She's the one who comes.

"No. You make sure your children are okay."

"They're fine. Thank you. Thank you for trying to help me."

"Please, just see to them." I dart my gaze around. "The rest of you? Why won't one of you help me?"

Most of them go running out the door.

"He took all our phones."

"There must be a landline in here." The young mother turns to the counter. But all of the employees have fled as well.

"I'll find one," she says, darting behind the counter.

I look up at her two children sitting at the table, their eyes wide.

"It's okay. Your mom is a hero."

I cover Ronan's stomach wound with my hands, applying pressure, desperately trying to stop the bleeding.

"Don't you die on me, Ronan. Don't you fucking die!"

"I found a phone!" the young mother yells.

"Thank God. Call 911, please!"

Two cops enter the shop then, guns drawn. "What's going on here?"

I don't look away from Ronan's pale face. "We were robbed. Three men. They all got away. But I need help here. Please."

"Yes, ma'am. We've already called it in. An ambulance is on the way."

An ambulance. In New York traffic. *Please*, I beg silently.

Please save him.

Please save the man I love.

• • •

I'm drenched in Ronan's blood by the time the ambulance comes.

Paramedics enter with a stretcher. They say words, hook Ronan up to machines, but it's all a garbled mess in my brain.

"I need to ride with him," I finally say.

I'm surprised they allow it. I'm not family, but perhaps they think I am.

Let them think that.

Somehow we get to Mount Sinai, and Ronan is still alive, thank God.

Doctors meet the ambulance, dressed in scrubs.

"Male, thirties, gunshot wound to the shoulder and the abdomen. BP ninety over forty. Pulse weak."

I run with them as they enter the hospital, Ronan on a stretcher. My heart has been racing this whole time, but I don't care. I don't care if it pops right out of my chest. All I care about is Ronan.

"I love you, Ronan," I finally say. "Please. Be strong. Get through this."

He came for me.

He came to the coffee shop to find *me*.

He *can't* die for me.

"Ma'am, you can't come any farther," a doctor says. "Have a seat in the waiting area. You're going to need to fill out his paperwork."

Paperwork.

I don't know anything about him, other than his name. I'm not even sure how old he is. All I know is that I love him.

I can't lose him.

I'll be whatever kind of submissive he needs, if only he'll live.

People are staring at me, at my blood-soaked clothes.

I should be at work now. I remove my white—now *red*—cardigan, and underneath I'm wearing the orange and black corset.

More stares, but I don't care.

Everyone in this waiting room is waiting for someone, but I'm betting I'm the only one waiting for someone who's been shot twice.

My God, so much blood on me.

So much blood on me that's supposed to be inside of Ronan, keeping him alive.

But we're at the hospital now. They have blood here. Blood banks. I don't even know what his blood type is. I don't even know...

"Ma'am?"

I look up as a woman in light blue scrubs hands me a clipboard.

"Is that your husband in there?"

I shake my head.

"Brother, boyfriend?"

Boyfriend?

Maybe it'll get me somewhere to say he is.

"Yes. My boyfriend."

"Good. I'm going to need you to fill this out for him."

"I don't know anything about his insurance, or..." I shake my head. "I don't know anything. Don't know anything."

"Start with his name and birthdate. That's all we need."

Birthdate. I don't know his birthdate.

Last name. O'Connor.

First name. Ronan.

I hand it back to her. "I'm sorry, I just…"

"It's okay. Do you know his place of employment?"

"He's a real estate developer, just moved here from Glasgow. I know he's got a deal with Black, Inc. I'm sorry. I just can't think." Did he tell me? Did he? I rack my brain. "O'Connor, Inc. No. O'Connor Enterprise."

"That's fine. We'll figure the rest out. Is there anything we can get you? A glass of water? A cup of coffee?"

"I should go home and change."

"That's fine. We probably won't know anything for a while."

"I can't leave him. He doesn't have any family here. His mother and father are in Scotland, and his grandmother's in New Orleans."

"All right, ma'am. Have a seat. If you need anything, let me know."

I gulp. Sit down. Only one magazine sits on the table next to me. *Field and Stream.*

I pick it up, open it, stare at the glossy pages.

But I see nothing.

I see only the blood. Ronan's blood. His pallid face.

And I wonder how I will get through this.

• • •

Half an hour later—or could be five minutes, for all I know— someone comes out to see me. "Ronan O'Connor?"

I rise, nearly losing my footing. "That's me."

"Are you family?" she asks.

"His girlfriend. He doesn't have any family in the area."

"All right. I'm Dr. Ludwig. We're taking Mr. O'Connor back for surgery. He has internal bleeding, which we have to stop and then repair any damage to his organs."

"And the shoulder?"

"The bullet passed through his shoulder, ma'am. That will heal, although he may need some physical therapy to gain back range of motion."

"All right." I'm numb. So numb.

"The major issue is the gunshot wound to his abdomen. He's lost a lot of blood, but his vitals are hanging in there. That's all I can tell you at this point. We're going to do everything we can."

I gulp, nodding. I say nothing.

Because there's nothing to say.

I could beg them to save him. But I already know they're going to do whatever they can.

Besides, that would require me to form words.

"The surgery may take several hours. I'll send out updates from the OR."

I nod again.

"We'll do everything we can, ma'am." She smiles, sort of, and walks back through the doors.

I have no idea how to get in touch with his family.

And then it dawns on me.

I remember the name of Yvette's restaurant. Chez Yvette.

But do I call her? She'll be able to get in touch with Ronan's parents.

Maybe she has a voodoo prayer she can say.

Maybe...

I don't have my phone, though.

I hurry to the front desk. "A gunman took my phone. I need to make a call. I need you to find a number for me."

"Of course. What's the name?"

"Chez Yvette. It's a Creole restaurant in New Orleans."

She clicks on her keyboard, and then she shows me the screen, motioning to the landline.

I dial the number.

"Chez Yvette," someone says.

"I need to talk to Yvette, please."

"She's busy in the kitchen. May I take a message?"

"No, it's an emergency. Her grandson, Ronan. He's..." I gulp back the bile threatening to erupt in my throat. "He's been shot."

"Oh my God. Just a minute. Who is this?"

"Mary. Mary Sandusky. Yvette knows me."

A moment passes.

Then, "Mary? What's wrong?" Yvette's voice is high-pitched and full of worry.

I soften. All this time I haven't been able to cry, but now, at the moment when I need to communicate this news to Yvette, I cry.

"He was shot. A coffeehouse got held up. He... He's in surgery... Can you come? Can you call his parents? I don't even know how old he is, Yvette. I don't know his birthdate."

"Don't you worry about a thing. Go to the front desk, and you give the phone to whoever's in charge of records. I'm going to give them all the information they need. And then I'm getting on a plane."

I gulp. Thank God for this woman.

"All right."

I hand the phone to the desk clerk. "I've got Ronan O'Connor's grandmother on the phone. She can give you the information you need."

"Perfect. Thank you."

I listen as she taps on the computer.

"Thank you very much, ma'am." The nurse hands the phone back to me.

"Yvette?"

"Yes, chérie. I need to call my daughter and her husband. Then I will be there. Ronan is a strong man. He has so much to live for. But he needs your strength now, Mary. Yours and mine. And we're not going to let him down."

CHAPTER FORTY-THREE

Ronan

I am lying on an operating table, but I am not in my body. I am hovering above, watching as the surgeons prepare to operate. The bright lights overhead are blinding, but I am not bothered by them. I see everything clearly.

The surgeons are dressed in their green scrubs, masks covering their faces. They move with a sense of purpose, their hands steady and precise as they prepare to make the first incision. I watch in awe as they work, amazed at how effortless they make it look.

One of the nurses notices me floating above and gasps, but the surgeons don't seem to notice. They are focused on their task, their attention unwavering.

As they begin to cut into my flesh, I feel a strange sensation. It is not painful, but I can feel something pulling at me, like I am being tugged away from my body. It is a bizarre awareness, but I am not afraid. I feel calm, almost serene, as I watch the surgeons work.

Peace. I feel utter peace, and I know without a doubt that whatever happens, everything will be fine.

The surgery continues, and I watch as they repair my damaged organs with skill and precision. I am amazed at how they seem to know exactly what to do, as though they have done this a thousand times before.

As the surgery comes to an end, I feel a strange stir again. This time, it is different. I can feel myself being drawn back into my body, like a magnet pulling me toward it.

Mémé.

I see Mémé, her brown eyes pleading with me, and I feel her love—I feel her comfort as I did when I was a little boy and she held me in her arms.

She's there, in the OR, telling me to come back. It's not my time yet. It's not my...

Not yet, chéri. You have so much to live for. Someone special who's waiting for you...

The sensation is overwhelming, and suddenly, I am back inside myself with a crash.

Pain. I remember the pain...

A knife is lodged inside my gut, throbbing, stinging, pinching.

Unbearable.

I long for the serenity of Mémé once more, for her arms around me, for—

I open my eyes and look up at the surgeons, except they're not surgeons. They're nurses. They smile at me and tell me that everything went well. I smile back, but I know that they do not understand what I have just experienced. For me, it was a journey unlike any other—a journey I will never forget.

CHAPTER FORTY-FOUR

Mary

I don't hear from Yvette again, and I don't have the number for Ronan's parents.

They won't be able to get here for at least twenty-four hours, being overseas and all.

But perhaps Yvette can make it by this afternoon or evening.

Normally I love wearing corsets, but it's become binding and uncomfortable. I long to take it off, to breathe.

But I can't leave.

Can't leave until I know he's okay.

Time passes in a warp.

People walk in slow motion, and then quickly as if I'm above them, on a different point in time.

My imagination has taken over, and my eyes aren't working properly.

Hours.

The clock on the wall says noon.

And then one.

I should call Trish. I may lose my job, but I don't care right now.

I can't talk to anyone. I can't give her the reason why I'm not at work.

That will make it too real.

"Ronan O'Connor?"

Dr. Ludwig stands near the doorway.

Oh God...

No.

Please *no*.

I stand.

Walk toward her.

She removes her surgical mask. "The surgery went well, Miss..."

"Sandusky." I heave a sigh of relief.

"We were able to repair the damage to his organs. But we did find an anomaly."

My jaw drops.

"We found a small tumor on the edge of his pancreas, Ms. Sandusky."

"A tumor?" I gulp.

He's alive. Everything was supposed to be okay as long as he lived.

Everything is *not* okay.

"Yes. We have to send it to pathology, but at first glance, it looks like it is probably cancerous."

I gulp. *No. No, no, no.*

"But this is good news, Ms. Sandusky."

Her words hover around me, echoing. Good news. Good news? *Cancer?*

"Good news? How is cancer good news?"

"We were able to excise the entire tumor. If it is cancer, and we got clean edges, that gunshot wound to the abdomen just saved Mr. O'Connor's life."

"What?"

My mind goes blank.

"Pancreatic cancer is almost impossible to diagnose until it's in its advanced stages. Almost no one survives. But this tumor is small. Mr. O'Connor wouldn't have begun to show symptoms until two or more years down the road. And then it would've been too late. Now, he can be monitored. Yearly CAT scans of his pancreas to make sure the tumor doesn't return. And if it does, we'll get it early. He's going to live, Ms. Sandusky. Your boyfriend is going to *live*."

I stand there, my mouth dropped open.

I know I must look like a halfwit, but how do I process this?

How do I process that those horrible armed robbers, who permanently scarred those two children and the rest of us, may have saved the life of the man I love?

Yvette's words ring in my mind.

I see something when he looks at you. I see something I've never seen in him before. I believe you're the one. You were placed in his path and he in yours.

"He's in the ICU right now, and I can't allow you to see him until after the anesthesia has worn off. That will be a couple hours. But he's okay, Ms. Sandusky. Go home. Take a shower and change your clothes. He'll still be here when you get back."

"He will?"

"I can't make any guarantees, but he's strong. He's had a blood transfusion. His vitals are looking good. He's a survivor. It's a miracle that we found the tumor."

I'm still trying to process her words.

"You can't see him for a while anyway. So go take care of yourself."

"His grandmother's on her way. His parents are out of the country. They won't be here until tomorrow."

"Good."

I'm babbling. I know I'm babbling. I'm still trying to process everything this nice doctor has told me.

"Please. Go home and take care of yourself. He's going to need your strength when he wakes up."

I can't take the subway. I had to throw away my white cardigan. And there's still blood on my arms and my corset.

I grab a cab, go home, throw the corset in the trash, and take a deep breath.

Then I figure it's time to call my boss and tell her why I'm not there.

Once I deal with that, I turn on my shower. I let the warm water pelt me, washing the last of Ronan's blood down the drain.

And then I sob.

I fucking sob, giant racking loud sobs.

Until I slide down the wall into a sitting position, and I sob some more.

All the sobs I couldn't get out while I was waiting. Scared, scared my life was ending.

And then even more scared when I feared Ronan's life was ending.

It's too late now, but the sobs are coming.

God, I'm going to need some serious therapy after this. The water becomes lukewarm, and then borders on cold. I turn it off.

I leave the shower, dry off, put on clean clothes. Comfortable clothes. Leggings and an oversize tee. I dry my hair quickly, put it in a ponytail at the back of my neck.

I glance at my makeup.

And I don't care. I apply some lip balm to my parched lips. The rest?

Take me as I fucking am.

Because none of it matters anymore.

I could've lost my life today.

Ronan nearly did lose his.

And I'm done.

I'm done settling for scenes at the club.

I'm done settling for scenes at my place.

I want *more*.

I want a relationship. Children. I want to finish college. Maybe open my own shop.

I want…a future.

A future with Ronan, but if he doesn't want that? I'll survive.

One thing I found today.

I'm a survivor.

And so is he.

I'm going to do everything I can to be with the man I love. But if he doesn't return my feelings, I will survive.

I will *fucking survive*.

Back at the hospital, I check on Ronan.

He's come out of the anesthesia, but he's still asleep.

They allow me to go into the ICU and see him for a moment.

I kiss his cheek. "Thank God you're going to be okay, Ronan."

The machines beep. I watch his heartbeat on the screen. His pulse-ox is ninety-two, which the nurse told me is absolutely fine for having just had surgery.

"You're going to have to leave now, Ms. Sandusky."

"All right." I nod, walk back out to the waiting area.

And Yvette is here. Despite her short stature, she appears like a giantess to me. I take in her strength. God, how I need it.

"Mary!" She grabs me in a hug.

"He's okay. I just saw him. He's asleep, but the nurses promised me his vitals are good."

"Thank God."

I hold onto her hands. "I don't know much, Yvette, but it looks like this gunshot wound to his abdomen may have saved his life."

I expect her to look surprised, but she doesn't.

"Don't you want to know how?"

"Of course."

I relay the story to her about the possible pancreatic cancer.

"The lab hasn't come back yet, but the surgeon was almost sure it was cancer. And if they got good margins...he's going to be fine."

"The universe works in mysterious ways," is all she says.

Then she closes her eyes, clasps her hands together, looks up to the ceiling.

She's praying or spellcasting.

And I have so much respect for her in this moment.

"You can probably go in and see him for a minute if you want," I say a few moments later, when she opens her eyes.

"Yes, I'll see if that's possible. His parents are on their way. They should be here tomorrow."

"I should probably go."

"Nonsense."

"I'm not family," I say. "They've only been giving me information because there's no one else here."

"I feel very strongly, Mary, that you will *be* family."

Her words give me a sliver of hope.

"I would like that. But I'm just glad he's okay. I'll walk away if I have to." I turn.

Yvette grabs my arm, and when I turn back, the look on her face is stern, and despite her four feet ten inches of height, she is a force in this room. "You will not. You *fight* for him."

"Oh, absolutely. I didn't mean to sound like I wouldn't. But if, in the end, I'm not what he wants, I will walk away. Because what I want more than anything, Yvette, is his happiness."

"And that's why you're the one for him, Mary." She reaches up and cups both my cheeks. "Don't you see? That's what true love is."

"How can I be in love with him? Don't get me wrong, I *am* in love with him. But we've known each other for only a week."

"Sometimes it takes a while. Sometimes not so much. Love can't be defined, chérie."

I open my mouth to speak, but she gestures me not to.

"I felt very strongly when I first saw the two of you together that you were meant to be. I'm not usually wrong."

"But he…"

"I know." She smiles. "He's a businessman, first and foremost. He doesn't concern himself with emotion." Her monotone makes me chuckle. "That can lead to a very lonely life, Mary. When you get to a certain age, you realize your life is built on straw."

"Straw?"

"You need a foundation. You can have all the money in the world, all the *things* in the world, but if you don't have someone to share it with…will you ever truly be happy?"

"I've turned off my emotions for so long," I tell her. "I was hurt once."

"You're young."

"Yes, but is that an excuse?"

"Not an excuse. A reason. Young people make mistakes. It's how they grow. But you can't let one bad experience turn you off relationships forever."

"Is that what you think Ronan has done?"

"In a way, yes," she says. "But I'm not sure he's ever been hurt, Mary. Not in the way you were."

"Who could hurt him? I mean…look at him."

"Oh yes, he's very strong, my Ronan. But he's been hurt in other ways. He didn't have the love of his mother and father. I basically raised him."

"He mentioned as much."

"Declan was always running back and forth to the UK on business, and Simone would go with him sometimes. She loves Ronan. But she also loved being the wife of a jet-setting multimillionaire. The little boy… Well, he got in the way of that."

My heart breaks a little then.

Breaks for that big, strong man lying in a hospital bed, recovering from surgery, breaks for the little boy he was. A freckle-faced little redheaded boy who only wanted his parents. Their presence. Their love.

"I'm sure you gave him all the love he needed, Yvette."

"I certainly did my best, but I was running a restaurant as well. Ronan grew up there."

A nurse comes out. "Ronan O'Connor?"

Yvette and I both stand.

"He's awake. He's asking for someone named Mary?"

My skin warms. "I'm Mary, but this is his grandmother, Yvette Thibodeaux. She should see him first."

Yvette smiles at me, squeezes my hand. "Nonsense. He's asking for you, and I want him to have what he needs. What he yearns for."

"If you're sure."

She leans toward me and whispers, "Did you use the love spell?"

"It wasn't a spell, Yvette. But you already know that."

Yvette shakes her head and smiles warmly. "It was a note written from a grandmother's love. My love poured through the ink in that pen and onto the parchment. So yes, it was a spell. I knew you were special when I first laid eyes on you, Mary. I believe you're what my grandson needs. Could I be wrong? Of course. Nothing is ever set in stone. But if he's asking for you, my dear, you must go to him."

I nod then, squeeze her hand back, and follow the nurse to the ICU recovery room.

CHAPTER FORTY-FIVE

Ronan

A warm hand grasps my own.
I recognize the feel of her soft flesh.

Mary. My Mary.

I turn my head. It's a struggle. But she's there. Beautiful Mary.

I widen my eyes as much as I can. I don't feel a lot of pain. They've probably got me dosed up with drugs.

But I remember.

Remember seeing Mary in the window of the coffee house. Opening the door, the little boy running, and then the gunshot.

Another shot.

Then suspension of time, of pain, and Mémé's face.

That's all I remember until a few moments ago.

"Mary," I say softly.

"Yes, Ronan. I'm here."

"The little boy?"

"Who?"

"The little boy from the coffee house, who ran toward me. Is he all right?"

Mary bursts into tears then. Seriously starts sobbing. "Ronan, yes, he's fine. Thank God. What a wonderful man you are. Everything you've been through and the first thing you ask about is that innocent little boy."

I saw myself in the little boy. He didn't look anything like me as a kid, but his demeanor reminded me. After the shot was fired, he ran back. Back toward his mother. Back to the woman who was his safety net.

How many times did I go running toward my mother when she came home from one of her many trips with my father? She always grabbed me, hugged me, peppered my face with kisses. Told me how much she missed me.

Only to leave again, too soon.

My true safety net was Mémé. It still is, but I have another now. Another in this lovely young woman before me—if she'll have me.

I have to leave New York. But somehow I'll convince her to go with me. Or if she won't, I'll find a way to make it work.

"Don't try to talk, Ronan," Mary says. "You need your rest."

"Seems I'm a lucky man."

"Did the doctors talk to you? Tell you what they found?"

"They tried to. My mind was still kind of a mush. But something about a tumor?"

"Yes. A small tumor in your pancreas. Most likely cancer, and caught very early, Ronan. You're going to be okay. Pancreatic cancer is almost never caught this early. It's almost always a death sentence, but not for you."

"Because I went looking for you, Mary."

"Is that why you were there?"

"Yes. I'll always come for you, Mary."

My eyes close then.

Sleep overtakes me.

CHAPTER FORTY-SIX

Mary

In the waiting area, after Yvette has gone in to see Ronan and come back, she takes my hand.

"Do you see what I mean, Mary? The two of you were meant to be."

"I've fallen in love with him."

"You don't have to tell me that, chérie. The look on your face tells all."

I nod, suddenly exhausted. "Do you have a place to stay here in town?"

"Yes. I booked a room at the hotel where Ronan is staying. I also booked a room for my daughter and son-in-law. I just got a text. Their flight from Glasgow leaves in an hour."

"Good. Okay. That's good."

"I want to stay here for another hour or so," Yvette says. "But Mary, love, you need to go. Go home and get some sleep."

"I can't leave him."

"He's in the best hands here. And if anything goes wrong, there's nothing you can do anyway."

"Nothing's going to go wrong," I say adamantly.

"I agree." Yvette places a hand over her heart. "I feel very strongly that everything's going to be fine. But that doesn't mean we shouldn't be praying. Sending our energy into the universe, wishing for the best outcome for Ronan."

"Believe me. I've been doing only that since this happened."

"I know you have, my dear. Now go. Rest that weary body."

I nod, and then I stare into Yvette's dark eyes. This woman is an icon. She's young yet, but she won't live forever. Her knowledge and wisdom can't be lost.

"Yvette?"

"Yes, chérie?"

"You said your daughter wasn't interested in learning Voodoo."

"No, she wasn't."

"Teach me," I say. "I may not be your daughter, but I felt such a connection to the culture when I visited New Orleans. Please. Teach me what you know."

Yvette closes her eyes a moment, a smile spreading across her pretty face. "I had a feeling about you from the moment I saw you," she says, opening her eyes. "You're the real thing, Mary. So genuine. You've been searching for something, haven't you?"

This time I close my eyes. "Yes. Though I'm not sure I knew it at first."

"Open your eyes, love."

I obey.

She takes my hands. "Have you found what you're searching for?"

Something surges through me as her small fingers entwine with my own. "I think I have."

She raises her eyebrows.

"I *know* I have," I say. "I know it as sure as I know the sun will rise tomorrow."

• • •

At home, I talk to Trish again and tell her about Ronan. Then I get a call from the NYPD on my landline. After answering their questions, I get off the phone and realize I haven't eaten anything all day.

I'm not hungry, but Ronan needs me strong. I fix myself a sandwich quickly, and then I eat it, although it tastes like sawdust.

Time for bed.

I don't think I'll be able to sleep, worrying about Ronan, but surprisingly...

Sleep comes quite quickly.

• • •

I'm back at the hospital by eight the next morning. Yvette arrives a few minutes afterward.

The doctor brings the lab results. "It is indeed pancreatic cancer," she says, "but we got amazing margins, and now that we know he has a propensity for pancreatic cancer, he'll come in for CAT scans every six months, and we'll be able to find it in plenty of time if it pops back up. But it's most likely gone forever."

I breathe a sigh of relief. "Thank God."

"Yes, the universe does work in mysterious ways." Yvette smiles as she echoes her sentiment from yesterday, shaking the doctor's hand with both of hers. "Bless you, Doctor. Bless you for being such an amazing healer."

The doctor's cheeks redden a bit, but she nods. "Bless you, too, ma'am."

Yvette and I take turns sitting with Ronan. He's asleep, but his vitals are good.

It will be a while before he's released.

Whatever he needs, I will give him. If he wants me to be his part-time submissive? That is what I'll be.

On the off chance that he wants more, as Yvette feels he does?

I will give him more.

Because I'm in love with him. I will take all of him, or part of him. Whatever I can get.

Around eleven, after I leave Ronan's side to get Yvette, I find her talking to two people.

Clear as day, I know who they are. The man is tall and broad, like his son, his auburn hair streaked with silver. And the woman is taller than Yvette, but with the same eyes and nose, slightly lighter brown skin.

Ronan's parents.

"Mary, chérie," Yvette says. "This is my daughter, Simone, and her husband, Declan."

"It's very nice to meet you." I shake Ronan's mother's hand first. "I'm a friend of Ronan's."

"Sounds like you may be more than a friend," Simone says.

My cheeks warm. "I suppose we'll see. Ronan's asleep. But he's doing well."

"Yes, we just talked to his nurse. I've got a call into the doctor," Declan says.

"You go see him, chérie," Yvette says to her daughter.

The nurse takes Yvette and Simone back, and Declan, wearing a three-piece suit and carrying a briefcase, looks me over. "Very nice to meet you."

"Nice to meet you, too, sir."

"Declan." Then he takes a seat, pulls his phone out of his briefcase, and begins tapping on it.

Always business, just as Yvette said.

Same as Ronan.

The apple doesn't fall far from the tree.

We'll see.

If this is the life Ronan wants, I will be part of it. I'll find a way for us both to have what we desire. If he wants a full-time sub, I'll make it work while I finish my degree and learn Voodoo from Yvette. I'll make sure he gives all he can to his business if that's his dream, and I'll be in his bed every night, obeying all his commands.

That's how much I love him.

About fifteen minutes later, Simone returns. Declan stands.

Simone shakes her head at him. "He's awake now. He wants to see Mary."

"Oh, that's all right," I say. "Go ahead and see him." I nod to Declan.

Yvette takes my hand. "If it's Mary he wants, it's Mary he shall have." She looks at me. "You go ahead back, dear."

I bite my lip, but I nod, heading back to Ronan's room.

I crack the door softly. "Ronan?" I enter.

His eyes are open, and their blueness is so bright.

"Hey, baby," he says, his voice hoarse.

"Hey yourself. How are you feeling today?"

"I can feel the pain today. The drugs are great, but they're not infallible."

"You should be sleeping."

"I opened my eyes, expecting to see you. Instead I saw my mother."

"Yes. She and your father came all the way from Glasgow to make sure you're okay."

"It reminds me of something. When I broke my leg when I was twelve years old. Bike accident. They had to come home from a business trip in the UK. My father was angry."

"He's not angry now."

"It doesn't matter if he is. I love my parents, but they weren't there for me when I was a kid, so why should I care if they're here now?"

"Because they're your parents, Ronan. I'd give anything to have my father back." I absently look down at my right hand. The ruby ring he gave me is gone. But the memory isn't. I treasured the ring, but it was only a thing. He wasn't the perfect father, and he was a terrible husband, but part of him lives in me. It always will. I don't need an object for that.

"I'm sorry. I didn't mean to sound callous." He looks at my hand. "Your ring."

I nod. "The gunmen took it during the robbery."

"Tell me about your father," he says. "Please."

"You should rest."

"You telling me something about your past won't tax my body or mind, Mary. Please."

I sigh. "It's not anything terrible. He was there for me—until he died, that is. But he was a rotten husband. He kept a secret apartment—the one I now live in, actually—and had affairs all during their marriage. When my mother found out, they divorced. He wasn't perfect, but he paid for my college. I had to leave when he passed away because my mother didn't have the money for my tuition, and his estate got eaten up by debt."

"Yet he meant something to you, even though he treated your mother so badly."

"He did. I don't expect you to understand. I hate what he did to my mother—and part of the reason I was turned off of marriage was because of what he put her through—but he was family, Ronan. I got some of my good qualities from him."

I stroke his arm gently. "Your parents may not be perfect,

but they are your parents. Enjoy them while you have them. However you can."

He swallows, coughs a bit. "My throat is still sore from the tube they had in it during surgery."

"Let me get you some water."

I pour some from the pitcher on his table and bring it to his lips. He takes a few sips.

"You've taught me so much, Mary."

"I have?"

"I should tell you about Keira."

"Another time, Ronan. You're exhausted."

"No." He breathes in. "I want to. I once told you that the deal with Braden Black wasn't the only reason I left Scotland. That there was another reason it was a good time to leave the UK. Keira and I were together for five years in an exclusive relationship as Dominant and submissive. Then recently she came to me. She wanted more. More than I could give."

My heart drops. No. He's going to tell me he can't give me a permanent relationship. No family. No children.

I steel myself. I can deal with this. He's alive, and I'm alive, and I have a lot to be grateful for. I love him, and I will mold myself into what he wants. That's how much I need him in my life.

"Go on," I say simply.

"She fell in love with me, but I didn't return her feelings. You see, Mary, I didn't know how to love."

I swallow the lump in my throat. I don't know what to say.

"So when the opportunity to come here on business arose, the timing was perfect. I took it."

I nod. I can't talk. If I try, I might burst into tears.

"But you, my beautiful Mary. You taught me something I wasn't sure I'd ever learn."

Warmth surges through me. "What's that?"

"You taught me how to love."

I open my mouth, but he gestures with one hand for me to stop.

"Please, let me say this. I have to say it. I'm lucky to be alive, and I can't wait to say this one moment longer. I'm in love with you, Mary Sandusky. I fell for you, and I fell hard. I didn't mean to. I didn't think I could. But I did. And if you don't return my feelings, I won't force it. But I'm alive, Mary, and I had to let you know."

Tears well in the bottoms of my eyes. "Oh my God, Ronan. Do you? Do you truly love me?"

He nods. "I do."

I lean over him, press my lips against his. "I love you, too, Ronan. I was so afraid... So afraid you wouldn't want that. I never thought it was what I wanted,. The only other time I let myself love someone—my first Dominant—he broke my heart."

"He's an asshole, then," Ronan says.

"He wasn't right for me. I see that now. But I was afraid of love after that. That's why I played only at the club. But then I met you, and..." I shake my head. "It seems so silly, us only knowing each other for a little more than a week."

"When you know, you know," he says. "That's what Mémé says."

I think about the talisman still in my purse. "She's a wise woman."

"She always has been. Wise and loving. She hasn't had the easiest life, but she's always made the best of it. And I..." He trails off, choking a bit.

"That's enough. No more talking for you."

He nods.

"I love you," I say, more and more weight lifting off me. "I love you so much. Go to sleep. I'll send your father in. I know he wants to see you."

Ronan nods again, closing his eyes.

And I walk out of the room, floating on a cloud.

CHAPTER FORTY-SEVEN

Mary

Six months later...

Ronan had his first CAT scan, which came out clean—no more pancreatic cancer—and Brenda and Dalton are headed toward their honeymoon in Jamaica.

Ronan ended up only spending two months in Las Vegas. Two months was too long being away from me, he decided—even though he flew home every weekend—and he found someone who would put up with his long-distance micromanaging to finish the yearlong project.

I gave my notice to Trish a month ago.

Next week, Ronan and I are moving to New Orleans. New Orleans, where I gave an offering to Madame Laveau along with a wish.

I wished for guidance, to find where I'm supposed to be. My place in this world.

I've found it.

Ronan and I aren't engaged yet, but we've committed to each other. He'll continue to head up O'Connor Enterprises, which will soon be headquartered in the Big Easy.

I'll begin my new part-time position at Odette's Botanica while I take classes at the local university.

More importantly, I'll begin to learn the practice of Voodoo from Mémé, as I now call her.

Ronan and I stop at Black Rose Underground for the last time after Brenda and Dalton's wedding reception.

We head straight to a private suite that he reserved.

"Kneel," he says, once I'm naked.

I kneel before him, my gaze pointed toward the ground.

"I'm going to bind your wrists."

"Yes, sir."

He binds my wrists, this time with fur-lined handcuffs.

Then he pulls me to my feet, gazes deeply into my eyes.

"I love you, Mary. I'm going to give you a new name. Because you're no longer a Blossom. You're a full-fledged flower. A rose. That's what your name will be from now on here at the club. Rose."

I love it. A thrill of excitement courses through me. "Yes, sir."

Suddenly, he drops down on one knee.

I widen my eyes. Have we traded places?

Then he pulls the velvet box out of his jacket pocket. He opens it.

I gasp. A ring? Is he...doing what I think he's doing?

"I love you, Mary Sandusky, my Rose. You've blossomed under me, you've effloresced, and I want to be with you always. I want to have children with you, live a life with you. I once thought I wanted a submissive in every way, but I no longer want that. I want you, Mary, exactly as you are. I want this to be permanent between us. I'm your Dominant, and you're my submissive during play. But in the rest of our life, we're equals, with equal responsibility to love and care for each other and our future children."

My heart pounds, and my chest heaves. I've never felt so powerful and so fragile all at once.

He takes the ring out of the box, pulls my handcuffed hands upward, and places the ring—a beautiful, sparkling diamond solitaire surrounded by rubies—onto the ring finger of my left hand.

"You have a safe word." He smiles. "But I sure hope you won't use it for this."

I shake my head. "Never. I will marry you, Ronan. I love you. I love you so much."

"Then lie on the bed, my wife-to-be, mo leannan. And I will take what's mine."

ACKNOWLEDGMENTS

With *Blossom*, the Black Rose Series comes to an end. I hope you've all enjoyed the adventure!

Huge thanks to my brilliant editorial team, Liz Pelletier, Lydia Sharp, and Rae Swain. You all helped *Blossom* shine. Thanks also to my proofreaders, Claire Andress and Rebecca Paulin, for your excellent catches. And of course Bree Archer and Elizabeth Turner Stokes, who design the most beautiful covers. *Blossom* is so gorgeous! Thanks to everyone else at Entangled whose tireless efforts always amaze me—Jessica, Meredith, Curtis, Heather, Katie, and copy editor Jessica Meigs.

Thanks also to the women and men of my reader group, Hardt and Soul. Your endless and unwavering support keeps me going.

To my family and friends, thank you for your encouragement. Special shout-out to Dean—aka Mr. Hardt—and to our amazing sons, Eric and Grant. Special thanks to Eric for helping with preliminary work on this book before I turned it in to Entangled.

Blossom is a steamy, sensual thrill ride that will leave you begging for more. However, the story includes elements that might not be suitable for all readers. A hostage situation including gunfire and gunshot wounds is shown on the page. Readers who may be sensitive to these elements, please take note.

I thought a weekend away would be the perfect escape. Until I woke up married and trapped...by the king of the Dark Fae.

the
dark
king
GINA L.
NEW YORK TIMES BESTSELLING AUTHOR
MAXWELL

For Bryn Meara, a free trip to the exclusive and ultra-luxe Nightfall hotel and casino in Vegas should've been the perfect way to escape the debris of her crumbling career. But waking up from a martini-and-lust-fueled night to find herself married to Caiden Verran, the reclusive billionaire who owns the hotel and most of the city, isn't the jackpot one would think. It seems her dark and sexy new husband is actual royalty—the fae king of the Night Court—and there's an entire world beneath the veil of Vegas.

Whether light or shadow, the fae are a far cry from fairy tales, and now they've made Bryn a pawn in their dark games for power. And Caiden is the most dangerous of all—an intoxicating cocktail of sin and raw, insatiable hunger. She should run. But every night of passion pulls Bryn deeper into his strange and sinister world, until she's no longer certain she wants to leave...even if she could.

The fantasy gift every woman deserves.

aphrodite
in bloom

a n o n y m o u s

Don't miss this extraordinary collection of twelve inventive and sophisticated stories guaranteed to awaken the forbidden desires of a new generation. From the sweetly romantic to the sublimely taboo, each provocative novella offers an opportunity to explore your most secret fantasies.

A virgin receives an especially satisfying gift at a masked ball...

A duke offers to settle a man's debt for one night with his wife...

As an introduction to a secret club, a viscount's heir is made over into a woman—and discovers her true self...

Plus nine more sensual stories of libidinous lust, catering to the tastes of varying sexual appetites. Whatever your fancy, *Aphrodite in Bloom* is ready and willing to serve...

Newly edited, and for the first time in print, discover the smash-hit series.

FILTHY RICH VAMPIRE

GENEVA LEE
NEW YORK TIMES & INTERNATIONALLY BESTSELLING AUTHOR

Julian Rousseaux has a problem. He's single, and for the world's wealthiest vampires, the social season is about to begin. Julian would rather stake himself than participate in the marriage market. But as the eldest eligible Rousseaux, he's expected to find a wife before the season ends—whether he likes it or not.

When cellist Thea literally stumbles into his life at a gala, he knows she's the last person he could ever fall in love with. She's too innocent, too kind, and way too human. But now that she knows about his world, she's also a walking target. She needs protection. He needs a fake girlfriend to discourage overzealous vampire matchmaking.

So, Julian makes Thea an irresistible offer: pretend to be his lover and he'll change her life. For one year, they'll attend the season's social events together in exchange for his protection and a way out of her mother's crippling medical debt.

She can't say no. But the vampire world is impossibly decadent and darker than Thea ever imagined, and Julian's filthy rich vampire family wants her out of the way. But with each moment they share, new dangers emerge: a desire as forbidden as their stolen touches, an awakening of a long-dead heart, and secrets that could tear them both apart.

Sensual, dangerous, provocative — step into a daring new world of dark magic, primal attraction, and breathtaking romance.